THE RUSSIAN ASSASSIN

A MAX AUSTIN THRILLER - BOOK ONE OF THE
RUSSIAN ASSASSIN SERIES

JACK ARBOR

HIGH CALIBER BOOKS

THE RUSSIAN ASSASSIN
(A MAX AUSTIN THRILLER - BOOK ONE)

This book is a work of fiction. The characters, incidents, and dialogue are drawn from the author's imagination and are not to be construed as real. Any resemblance to actual events or persons, living or dead, is fictionalized or coincidental.

ISBN-13: 978-1-947696-00-6
ISBN-10: 1-947696-00-9

Requests to publish work from this book should be sent to:
jack@jackarbor.com

Edition 1.1

Published by High Caliber Books

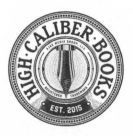

Cover art by: www.damonza.com
Bio photo credit: John Lilley Photography

For Jill, the love of my life and my biggest fan

"Many are stubborn in pursuit of the path they have chosen, few in pursuit of the goal."

~Friedrich Nietzsche

ONE

Brussels, Belgium

Max toyed with the garrote in his jacket pocket while he waited in the dark alleyway. As the small hand on the city's clock tower swung past one a.m., fog settled over him. A gentle drizzle started, causing the cobblestone streets to glisten in the sparse light. Max snapped the top button closed on his leather jacket, and wished he had on a more rain-appropriate coat. He tugged the brim of his hat down tighter on his head with a gloved hand. Not a soul stirred in the alleyway, and if he didn't know better, he'd think he was in London in the late 1800s, about the time Jack the Ripper stalked his prey.

The garrote was handcrafted from piano wire and two thick, wooden dowels. For jobs of this nature, where silence was of the utmost importance, Max preferred this kind of weapon. It was clean and quick, and left little mess. An expertly yanked garrote would instantly sever the windpipe, making outcry impossible. It also left very little forensic evidence to identify the make and model of the weapon. This particular one was called *la loupe*, a two-strand garrote made with a double coil of wire. Even if the victim managed to get their hand in between their neck and one of the coils, they'd only succeed in making the other coil tighter. For backup, Max carried a silenced SIG Sauer P224, his favored subcompact, in a shoulder holster.

Even Brussels, the city at the epicenter of modern Western Europe, had a red light district. The area was small compared to the famous De Wallen in Amsterdam, and started just outside the Gare du Nord train station along the Rue d'Aerschot. Windows lit with red and blue lights lined the dirty street, their lithe fare advertising themselves in a silent, un-choreographed ballet. Well-heeled tourists, business travelers, and diplomats strolled through, lured by temptresses from exotic locales. The street was well known worldwide for the quality of its offerings, its safe environment, and its reasonable prices.

Just around the corner, in an alley off Rue d'Aerschot, those with discerning tastes and fat wallets shopped for the highest-quality treats. This area was known as *Chique*, the Dutch word for *posh*. There were only six brothels lining the alleyway, but these were the crème de la crème. In Chique, there were no windows displaying scantily clad seductresses. Instead, the entrance to each was guarded by a formidable iron door. There, one needed to be on a list to gain entrance. If one made it through the iron door, they were led to a small foyer where large men with expert hands searched for weapons and established bona fides. No credit cards were accepted; Chique accepted only pre-established credit lines. This was where the world's elite came to enjoy pleasures of the choicest flesh, free from the prying eyes of the world.

It was also a place unpatrolled by the city's *Politie*. This was partly to avoid the awkward sighting of a high-ranking diplomat, and partly because there had been no violence or reports of any crime in the one hundred years of Chique's existence. Max knew this, of course. This was the reason he'd chosen this spot to assassinate the lawyer.

While he waited, Max's mind performed a series of calculations. This was a high-value target, which would move him closer to his retirement goal. He checked the burner phone in his pocket. It was silent; no text messages. If this bloke didn't finish with the girl soon, Max would delay the job for another time. *Patience, my boy*, his father's voice echoed in his head. *It will keep you alive.*

His mind turned to the target. The man currently in the throes of ecstasy with one of Brussels' Albanian beauties was a well-known lawyer who spent most of his time negotiating corporate mergers and acquisitions for large transportation conglomerates. Unbeknownst to everyone except Max's client, the lawyer used his shipping connections to support the Islamic State by moving weapons in and out of Turkey, Syria, Jordan, and Iraq. Max didn't know why the man did it; perhaps for the money, maybe for the thrill, perhaps an idealistic devotion to some higher calling. Frankly, he didn't care. Max had spent considerable time on research to confirm his client's assertions before he'd agreed to the job. After weeks of painstaking preparation, the moment had arrived.

The burner phone in his pocket buzzed. Max removed it and glanced at the screen.

Done.

Max confirmed that no one had entered the alleyway, then positioned himself next to the exit. The door would swing out, blocking him from the target's view. He also knew from exhaustive surveillance that the man always turned right, away from Max's position, and toward the Gare du Nord train terminal. There, the lawyer would catch a train out of the city, back to his wife and children in the tony neighborhood of Woluwe-Saint-Lambert. He wouldn't make it tonight, Max knew. And Chique would have its first homicide in its one hundred-year history. He removed the garrote from his pocket. The double loop of wire glinted in the sparse moonlight.

The rain picked up in intensity, splattering off the cobblestones and Max's black leather boots. He could not have orchestrated the weather any better. The heavy rain would keep people off the street, and the white noise of the rain on the cobblestones would hide the sound of his footsteps. Max waited, breathing, staying aware of his heart rate. It remained even and slow, just as he'd trained himself.

The door finally opened on silent hinges, then swung closed. Without a backward glance, a short, stout man pulled a hat on a mostly bald head and started toward the Gare du Nord. Max wondered for an instant if the man was busy concocting some tale to tell his wife.

Two strides on his long legs and Max caught up to the lawyer, resizing the garrote's loop to account for the man's hat. He slipped the fine piano wire around the man's neck, then jerked with a controlled and practiced force. The wire cut into the target's neck like a cheese slicer. The lawyer emitted a quiet gurgle as his windpipe was severed, then he stumbled forward, clutching at his throat. His hat fell off and came to rest on the wet cobblestones. Max gave another yank and the man's head jerked back, before he fell face first to the ground. Max bent as the lawyer fell, and straddled his prone body. He tugged on the garrote again, and held on through the man's spasms, finally letting go when the obese man stopped moving.

Max dropped the garrote, shoved his hands into his pockets, and made his way slowly out of the alley. He let the adrenaline run its course as he walked the Rue d'Aerschot, waiting for the inevitable fatigue to come. He paused at a public trash can to light a cigarette, noting with satisfaction that his hands were not shaking. Then he dropped the burner phone into the trash receptacle. He continued his stroll, letting the pulsing red neon lights wash over him, pausing often to pretend to gaze at a half-naked woman, all the while watching intently for any sign of a tail or police activity. He saw none, and knew that the body would not be reported until the following morning. No one leaving Chique would want their name on record.

As Max walked, the rain gradually let up and steam began to roll off the cobblestone streets. He left the red light district behind and walked south on Boulevard Emile Jacqmain until he reached L'Archiduc, a hole-in-the-wall bar Max knew was owned by a Russian expatriate. He pulled the door open and walked into a cloud of smoke.

Max settled on a barstool and spoke in Russian, asking the old man behind the bar for a short glass of chilled vodka. When the bartender set it down on the scratched oak bar, Max gulped it back and asked for another. By the fourth glass, he felt a warmth in his chest. By the sixth, the warmth had spread to his head. By the tenth, Max was finally able to forget for a moment that he'd just killed a man. The television over his head showed a football match between two local clubs. He asked for a cold lager and sipped it as he watched the game.

Eventually, he pulled out his Blackphone and turned it on. The phone had cost him several thousand euros, but it had security that prevented it from being tracked. When the phone had warmed up, he accessed a secure email program and typed a quick note to his client. *It is done. Remit final payment.* He moved to shut the phone down, but an email in his inbox caught his attention. The sender was Arina Asimov, his sister. He gazed at the email header, and his stomach dropped as he noted the subject line. It read, *Mother*.

It had been over a year since Max had corresponded with his sister. Back then, the emails had been about his mother's cancer: how they were fighting it, and how good the prognosis was. Max touched the phone's screen, exposing the body of the email. It was short, but an unexpected wave of emotion hit him.

The message was only one line. It read, *She has two weeks to live.*

TWO

Minsk, Belarus

Max drew in one last, luxurious drag on his cigarette, then flicked the butt into the terminal's pickup area with a shower of sparks. He shook his wrist and a watch appeared from under his sleeve. His sister was late. To Max, the trains ran on time or they didn't run at all. Another one of the many influences of his father, he supposed, cursing the agitation he felt in his gut. Then he realized the later she was, the longer it put off the inevitable confrontation.

He stood on the curb at Minsk National Airport and watched the taxis, shuttles, and cars jockey for position in a cacophony of blaring horns. Nine p.m. was a popular time for the arrival of international flights, and the pickup zone was thronged with activity. Dread settled in Max's stomach as he contemplated seeing his father. It had been over five years, and that's how Max preferred it.

He scuffed at a blotch of dried gum on the curb with a shiny black shoe. He'd chosen his attire on purpose. He had on a well-tailored black sport coat, faded jeans, and black shirt open at the collar. His leather jacket was in his bag. He wanted to convey a persona of easy affluence. To deal with his father, he needed to feel confident when he walked through the door.

He didn't know if the dread he felt was at the prospect of seeing his father, or because of the news his sister had shared with him the previous day. The guilt he carried from not visiting his ailing mother was pervasive and, for an instant, he considered simply returning to Paris.

He patted his jacket pocket, feeling the reassuring lump of the pack of cigarettes. Among the many things he appreciated about his adopted home of Paris was the excellent smokes he could get for cheap. He fought the urge to light up again, not wanting to suffer his sister's glances. Instead, he looked at his watch again.

He cursed Arina's tardiness, and considered grabbing a cab. For some reason, she had insisted on picking him up. He suspected she had something to tell him away from their parents. He glanced at the taxi line filled with men with briefcases and women in severe suits. A woman's long, bare legs caught his eye, and he let his gaze linger. She was tall, with the giraffe-like body and angular features of a Russian model. Perhaps she was from Moscow, in Minsk for a shopping excursion, or maybe a photo shoot in Gorky Park. Or maybe she was in town just long enough to pull an all-nighter at one of Minsk's famous clubs. The woman shifted and turned her head, catching Max's eye. She flashed him a shy smile, then looked away.

Max turned away and fished in his pocket for a pack of gum. He knew he was attractive to women. It was his height, he knew, and his rugged jaw. Some women appreciated his shaved head, while others were turned off by it. He got a lot of compliments on his eyes, and most women seemed enamored with his large, muscular hands. He glanced over and caught the woman's eye again. Just then, Max was jerked from the moment by the loud honk of a horn.

He looked over and saw a blue minivan pulling to the curb. He could see his sister's profile in the driver's seat. The expression on her pretty face looked grim and she waved an indifferent hand at the van's sliding door. A young boy sat in the front passenger seat. His brown hair was tousled, his wide eyes taking in the frantic scene around him.

With a sigh, Max grabbed his bag and pulled the door open. Whatever his sister wanted to tell him, he was about to find out. He tossed his bag onto the bench seat and levered himself in. As soon as he yanked the door shut, the van shot away from the curb, pushing Max back into the seat. He felt around for a seatbelt, and found none.

"Alex, do you remember your Uncle Max?" Arina said to the boy in the front passenger seat. No greeting. No, *How was the flight?* The boy craned his neck around, straining to look at Max while strapped in by his seatbelt. The last time Max had seen Alex, the boy had been about four years old.

"No, Mom, I don't."

"Well, that's because he never comes home to visit, Alex."

Fuck you, Max thought to himself. It was starting already, and now she was even turning the boy against him. It was shaping up to be an annoying couple of days. He felt like telling his sister to let him out so he could grab a cab.

"Nice to see you too, Sis," he said instead.

"How long's it been, Max?" she asked, guiding the van at a brisk pace through the curved airport exit and onto the expressway. She drove with both hands on the wheel, as if holding on for dear life.

"Don't remember, Arina. How about we drop that and talk about Mom?"

"Try five years, Max," she said. "You want to talk about Mom? How about we talk about you not ever coming home to see her after her diagnosis?" He saw her eyes flash in the rearview mirror.

Max avoided her gaze and watched the road. He'd thought that by agreeing to the pickup, he'd have an opportunity to find some common ground with his sister before he arrived home. Perhaps he'd be able to develop an ally; someone on his side he could confide in. It looked like he'd been wrong.

"How's she doing?" he asked.

"She's dying, Max, how do you think she's doing?"

"Fuck, Arina, how about giving me a break? Or let me out and I'll get a cab."

"Max! Watch your language in front of the boy."

"It's okay, Mom," Alex assured her. "I hear that word at school all the time. I know it's a bad word. I would never say it. Only bad people say that word."

Great, Max thought. *Now even the boy hates me.* He watched Arina look at her son, and saw the love in her eyes. Or maybe it was pride.

"What's the official diagnosis?" Max asked.

"Breast cancer. Spread to her lungs. Terminal. Two weeks to two months, depending. Nothing can be done. She's decided to stop fighting it. Wants to be home, comfortable, among her friends." She glanced in the rearview mirror and caught his eyes. "And family."

This time he held her glance. Finally, she looked away. The reality was that he'd never been close to his mother. He remembered her as cold and distant, uninvolved in his child-hood, often judgmental and harsh. Instead, he'd spent almost all his time with his father. At sixteen, Max had left Minsk to attend military school in Moscow. From there he'd disappeared into the Russian Army, then the KGB. During the infrequent visits home, all his time had been spent with his father.

His sister kept the speedometer pegged at 140 KPH, and they sped past slower cars. Max shot a couple of glances out the rear window, and confirmed they had no followers. Noticing one of his glances, his sister said, "Don't worry. I'm watching. No tail." Max sighed. Such was the life of the children of one of Moscow's most celebrated spies. While the other kids were playing stickball, Max and Arina had been learning tradecraft from their father.

Arina guided the van down an exit ramp and onto the quiet streets of downtown Minsk. Max felt a jolt in his stomach – the same jolt he always felt when visiting home after being away for a long stretch. Arina interrupted his thoughts.

"I wanted to pick you up to tell you that Mom asked for you specifically," she said. "She pulled me aside yesterday morning, and asked me to get you here without Dad know-ing. She said she had something to tell you, but didn't want Dad to know." His sister let that hang in the air.

Max was surprised. Since he'd left home as a teenager, he couldn't remember his mother ever asking about him. He watched the houses roll by, lit by the yellow haze of the street lamps. The view turned from city streets to suburban boulevards, with large homes spread out on wide tracts of land covered by endless grass. Wrought iron fences started appearing and the lots turned into estates with gated drives. The knot in his stomach grew as the van wound its way up a street lined with leafy trees. His parents had lived in this home his entire life. Max and Arina had grown up here. The house would now experience the full cycle of life, from his sister's and his birth to their mother's death.

"Did you hear me?" Arina asked, jolting him to the present.

"Yes," he said absently. "Do you know what she wants to tell me?"

"No, she wouldn't tell me. She said it was for you only."

Arina turned into the drive and stopped the car at the closed gate. Later, Max would go over this moment in his head dozens of times, looking for clues, and finding none. In the moment, though, he only knew what his gut was telling him.

Something was wrong.

The next few minutes unfolded in slow motion. Max saw his sister press the button on the opener that caused the large wrought iron gate to roll back. Out of habit, Max glanced behind them and saw a van parked on the road behind them, its windows dark and silent. A telephone company logo was plastered to its side. Max turned back and Arina drove on, through the gate and down the winding drive. The gate rolled closed behind them. Well-manicured shrubs lined the long drive. Arina steered the van around the last curve, and the house came into view. Max saw the large rental truck parked next to the house, and several things clicked into place in his mind.

"Stop the van, Arina," Max said. Then he yelled, "STOP THE VAN!" Her foot jerked to the brake and the van shuddered to a stop.

"What the—?"

Arina never finished her question. The night sky lit up with a bright explosion directly in front of them. The white burst of light sent flashing stars through Max's vision, then blinded him into blackness. The booming crack of the explosion was followed by a loud *whoomp*, and Max felt a searing popping in his ears, before all sound ceased. The windows of the van imploded, sending a shower of razor-like glass shards through the vehicle's interior, lacerating the skin on his face and arms. Max felt himself being lifted, then thrust backward. He came out of the seat as the van tipped on its side, smacking his head against the metal sliding door. His last thought before blacking out was the hope that his nephew had still been wearing his seatbelt.

THREE

Minsk, Belarus

The Stranger was hustling now, prioritizing information over discretion. As he moved faster, his limp became more pronounced. Once, he'd feared the limp would relegate him to a desk for the rest of his career. Over time, though, he'd proven it wasn't a hindrance, and took solace in the fact that he'd eventually die in the field.

The gate had been wedged open and rescue vehicles and other authorities were still speeding toward the house. The main fire had been extinguished, but smoke still hung in the air, creating a nighttime haze that reminded him of the air in Mexico City. Firefighters used handheld extinguishers to put out smoldering patches in the forested area around the house. He flashed a badge at the policeman stationed along the drive and was waved along.

The badge was fake, of course, but it would hold up under scrutiny. It identified him as a high-ranking member of the Russian Federal Security Service, also known as the

FSB. The FSB was created in 1991 in the wake of the disso-lution of the KGB, and focused on counter-terrorism, border security, and counterintelligence in Russia. Confus-ingly, some of the former satellite states of the Soviet Union preserved the KGB moniker. Because the bombing happened at the home of the Assistant Director of the Belarusian KGB, the presence of an FSB official from Moscow would not be questioned.

His heart was pounding as he hurried up the drive. Years of work by him and others was at risk of being flushed down the drain because of one bomb. A light spring rain had started, making the firefighters' jobs easier, but making life miserable for the rubberneckers and emergency work-ers. His overcoat kept him dry, but at this point he didn't care. He needed information, and needed it fast.

In his pocket were two items. The first was a bulky satellite phone, its thick, stubby antenna poking his thigh as he half walked, half ran up the drive. The second item was a box the size of a pack of cigarettes. A screen covered one side, and if someone was to look closely, they'd see a map on that screen, similar to a Google map, and a blinking green dot winking at him at the location of the house. The fact that the green dot was still blinking was a good sign.

The Stranger adjusted his fedora, pulling the brim down over his eyes. He rounded the last corner of the drive and emerged into a scene straight out of a movie. Two fire trucks had come to a halt on the front lawn at angles to where the house had once been, and were spraying columns of water and chemicals into a smoldering crater. The only remaining structure of the main house was a corner of the brick foundation. He could see an outbuilding, perhaps a small barn, still standing a distance behind the crater. At an angle to the crater was the scorched remains of a blue minivan.

The Stranger blended into a group of civilians, and found himself standing next to a man in his late fifties wearing a jacket over a grey T-shirt. White tufts of hair stuck out around his head.

"Do you know if anyone was in the house?" the Stranger asked the man.

"I heard the whole family was," the man said, wide-eyed. "Such a shame. They were such nice people. Is it true the husband was a KGB agent?"

"Doubtful," the Stranger said, as he craned his neck and looked over the crowd. He elbowed his way to the front of the pack to get a better view. An ambulance was parked on the front lawn, close to one of the fire trucks. Its back doors were open and a paramedic was tending to a man sitting on the back bumper wearing a tattered black sport coat. The paramedic was dabbing at the back of the man's skull with a cloth. In front of the patient stood a woman in jeans and a pink shirt, her back to the Stranger. Next to the man on the bumper sat a young boy. Another paramedic was dabbing at the boy's face.

The Stranger strained his eyes in the dim light, willing his eyes to be right. The man sitting on the back bumper resembled the man named Mikhail Asimov, nicknamed Max, but the Stranger had to be sure. Staying behind a group of well-wishing neighbors, he got closer to the ambulance. He saw the man's bald head, his square jaw and intense eyes. The man ran his hands over his pate and down to the back of his head, perhaps to show the attendant the location of a wound. Then the man looked up and seemed to peer directly into the Stranger's eyes. His heart leapt with relief.

He used his smartphone to snap several photos of the group at the back of the ambulance, then backed away from the crowd. The lack of light might make identification difficult, but he knew his people had the technology to brighten the image and make it larger. He strode purposefully down the drive with his hat pulled low. When he reached the gate, he made a hard left, then plucked the satellite phone from his pocket.

After acquiring a connection, the man hit a speed-dial button. A moment later, a woman's voice came on the other end.

"Tell me," she said.

"Still alive," the Stranger said. "I have a picture for confirmation that I'll send momentarily."

An audible sigh of relief came through the handset. "Any other survivors?"

"Looks like the sister and nephew are also alive," he said. "That's all I can confirm."

"Good. Stay on him."

"Roger that," the Stranger said, but the connection had already been terminated.

FOUR

Minsk, Belarus

The pain and ringing in his head were overshadowed only by the immense sadness in his heart. Every time the paramedic dabbed at the back of his head, it felt as if a nail were being driven into his skull. His sister stood in front of him, her rain-soaked shirt bloodied from the nicks and scratches in her face and arms. Tears mixed with the blood on her face created a horror effect in the bright lights from the fire trucks. A first responder tried to wrap an emergency blanket around her shoulders and lead her to another ambulance, but she refused.

Alex sat perched next to Max, letting an attendant wipe his face and apply ointment. The boy was stunned to silence, likely still unable to make sense of what had just happened. On instinct, Max put his arm around Alex's shoulder, and felt the boy lean in.

He looked over at the crater where his childhood home once stood. He was having a difficult time processing the event himself. Despite having purposefully stayed away from this place over the years, he couldn't fathom that both of his parents were suddenly dead. He thought about his mother, a tall, handsome woman who had aged gracefully. His father had always said she was the true brains of the family. She'd raised two children, then filled her time running a not-for-profit raising money to fight children's cancer. Her own cancer diagnosis was a bitter irony, juxtaposed against all the good her foundation had done to fight the horrors of the disease. Max knew his sister had been devastated by her diagnosis, unable to cope with the brevity of human existence and the imminent loss. Arina had confided during one of their infrequent phone conversations that she couldn't bear to think about living in a world without her mother. Max didn't have the same reaction, but couldn't let go of the guilt he felt for not visiting. It felt terrible to think, but Max wasn't sure he'd miss his mother.

The loss of his father was a different thing entirely. Max couldn't place his feelings. To his own chagrin, he admitted that he felt some relief at being released from the lifelong hold his father seemed to have over him. The man's influence even extended as far west as Paris, where Max had been stationed years earlier by a newly formed and confused Moscow Foreign Intelligence Service. Still, the sense of freedom that washed over him was quickly replaced by feelings of loss. The fact was, his father had an enormous impact on his childhood and career direction. Now, when on a job, he felt the presence of his father at every turn. Max knew that despite their differences, he was going to miss his father terribly.

His sister wedged herself in between him and the ambulance door, propping her behind on the bumper. Max put his other arm around her, and she dropped her head on his shoulder. Odd, he thought, how tragedy could bring people together.

Max had been told that he'd been knocked unconscious after hitting his head on the metal sliding door of the minivan. When he'd come to, he was laid out on his back on the ground, surrounded by emergency workers and his sister and nephew. The first thing he'd seen when he opened his eyes was Alex's face, hovering over his own. The first sound he'd heard was Alex's hushed voice pleading with him to wake up. *Wake up, Uncle Max, pleeeease?*

When he'd opened his eyes, Alex had given him a big hug, hanging on until Arina pulled the boy away. Now they sat in dazed silence, unable or unwilling to talk about what had just happened.

Through his dulled senses, Max heard the bellow of a loud voice booming over the din of the emergency workers. "Where is he? Where is he, goddamnit? Get outta my way!"

Max looked up to see the large form of Anatoly Burov making his way through the crowd toward the ambulance. Anatoly's massive round face was flushed red with exertion and his bald spot glistened with raindrops. The wisps of white hair that had once been combed over his bald head flew behind him like streamers. Anatoly's overcoat billowed out behind him, revealing a badge affixed to his belt and a gun strapped to a bulging waistline. He arrived in front of them with a huff, and knelt down in front of Alex.

"Are you alright, my boy?"

Alex looked at him dumbly and nodded. Then Arina got up and hugged Anatoly. Max tried to stand, but felt a wave of nausea wash over him and sat back down. He shook Anatoly's hand from the safety of the ambulance bumper.

Anatoly seemed to have aged by dog years since Max had last seen him. His nose was red and veined from a lifetime of hard drinking, and his cheeks had loosened into jowls. His shirt was grease-stained and one tail was untucked. For years, Anatoly had been his father's friend, confidant, and drinking partner. They'd been in the Red Army together, then had joined the KGB. While Max's father had risen to prominence, earning awards and rank for his prowess both in the field and behind a desk, Anatoly had languished in the basement, never finding his way. For some reason, it hadn't affected their friendship. Max knew his father had idolized his friend Anatoly, although for the life of him, Max couldn't figure out why. The man was, however, considered family.

"We'll get these people," Anatoly said, his voice hushed. He was looking directly at Arina. "Don't you worry, honey. We'll find these fuckers and we'll hang them from their pricks using twine, then we'll flay them and decapitate them with sabers."

"Anatoly! The boy," Arina admonished.

"Sorry, forget you heard that, Alex," Anatoly said, looking chagrined.

"I'm with you, Anatoly," Alex said, his voice low. Arina shushed him.

"Who has jurisdiction, Anatoly?" Max asked.

"Officially, Minsk City Police do since we're within the city limits. But the KGB will take over, given your father's position. This is a matter of national security now. In about ten minutes this place will be sealed up tighter than a drum."

"What do you know so far?" Max asked.

"It's still early," Anatoly said. "But it looks like it was a simple RDX bomb, similar in size and configuration to the ones used in the Moscow apartment bombings back in '99."

"The rental truck parked by the side of the house," Max said.

"Exactly. How it got there and why it was there are still a mystery," Anatoly said.

"It wasn't there when I left to pick up Max," Arina said.

"There was a van out on the street with the insignia of a utility company," Max said, and he described the logo. Anatoly pursed his lips, then pulled out a notebook and jotted something down.

"I'm sorry I have to ask this," Anatoly said, "but can you tell me exactly who was in the house at the time of the blast?"

Max looked at Arina. She burst into tears and Anatoly put one arm around her.

Max said, "I think just father and mother, right? Anyone else, sis?"

Arina nodded her head, and the sobs grew louder. "My husband was in there too," she managed to say.

"Oh, Christ," Anatoly said. Max just looked at her. Arina's husband was a mid-ranking administrative member of the KGB, working under their father. Within the KGB, family ran deep.

Arina wailed a long, mournful sob. "What am I going to do now? Who will help me raise Alex?"

The boy inched closer to her mother and put his arm around her waist.

"We'll figure something out, Arina, don't you worry," Anatoly said. "The KGB takes care of its own. Don't you worry."

Max's stomach turned in anguish as he suddenly felt his sister's predicament. It was hard enough to raise a child with two parents, he thought. Sure, there would be some money from inheritance and insurance, and the wives of other KGB members would help out where they could. But eventually, Alex and Arina would have to get by on their own. Suddenly he got angry. He pushed away from the bumper and, ignoring his swimming head, pulled Anatoly aside.

"Anatoly, who did this? Who hated my father enough to take him out this way, with so much collateral damage?"

Anatoly just shook his large head side to side. "We don't know, Mikhail," he said, using Max's given name. "Everyone is just shaking their heads. It could be a terror group like the Chechens, or it could be a foreign government. I mean, you know your father. He had just as many enemies as he had friends. This investigation will take a while, but we'll figure it out. We always do."

Max stared Anatoly directly in the eyes. "When you do, I want to be there. I want to know who these people are, and I want to know exactly where they are. Are you reading me?"

"Max, you know I can't involve you—"

Max grabbed Anatoly by the lapels of his overcoat. "You know what I'm asking, Anatoly. You can't say no to me on this." The dull roar in his head had been replaced with an anger that cut through every other emotion. As he stood there with Anatoly's lapels in his fists, staring into the man's startled eyes, Max vowed to himself to find whoever had done this. No one, including the powerful KGB, better stand in his way.

FIVE

Undisclosed Location

Nathan Abrams strode into the airplane hangar and walked directly toward the activity in the center of the massive space. Footsteps from his ostrich cap toes echoed in the chamber with sharp cracks, each like a shot from a pistol. As he walked, the group in front of him gradually grew quiet and turned to face him.

The hangar was large enough to fit one of the new 787 Dreamliners. The building was part of a complex of airplane hangars Nathan's firm owned, all arranged around a defunct airstrip. During the Cold War, the strip had been part of the Soviet military machine. In 1994, the base had been decommissioned, and Nathan's company had purchased it for a song. He hadn't known what he'd do with it at the time, but the price was so cheap he'd proceeded with the deal anyway. Since then, the place had come in handy for operations just like this one.

Before he got close to the others, he could smell the fear. It radiated from the man at the center of the group like a pungent odor from a rotting piece of fruit. The man was naked and on his knees. His entire body was covered in sweat, even though it was a cold night. His arms were tied behind his back, and his head lolled forward. Blood dripped onto the concrete from open wounds on his face and torso.

To the group's left was a makeshift command center, with two rows of tables covered in computer monitors, laptops, routers, and other gear. Aeron desk chairs were spread out among the tables, and several of his staff were in the midst of tearing down the machinery and stowing the equipment in large Pelican cases for transport. A man with a flattop, dressed in suit pants and shirtsleeves, had been directing the disassembly before Nathan interrupted.

"Gunny!" Nathan said to the man, ignoring the captive and extending a hand to the man with the flattop. "Great job with this operation. Can't thank you enough."

Gunny turned and took his hand. "Thank you, sir." He pumped Nathan's hand once, then let go. Gunny had just completed an operation to rescue the kidnapped daughter of oil baron Sheik Mohammed Al Amoudi. It seemed the princess had dodged her bodyguards and disappeared during an all-night rave on Ibiza, the Spanish party island in the Mediterranean. No ransom had been demanded. A midnight raid by Gunny's team on the girl's Spanish boyfriend's compound had yielded a stoned princess naked in a hot tub. The sheik had been generously thankful, and a payment arranged by the princess herself had guaranteed her privacy. A win-win all the way around.

"I trust the princess is recuperating with her family?"

"Of course, sir."

Nathan turned his attention to the prisoner. Long ago, Nathan had reconciled himself to the violence his job required. He didn't believe himself psychopathic, although he'd considered it with an open mind during long stints of therapy. Instead, he thought of himself as a man who believed the ends justified the means. His life was devoted to his agency, and if he was to honor that devotion, there were consequences he had to accept. Accept, and not judge, he reminded himself. That was how he slept at night.

"Wing," Nathan said in greeting to the small dark-skinned woman in the banker's suit who stood behind the prisoner. "Thank you for meeting me here. I trust Ivan here didn't cause you any trouble."

"No, sir," she said. Wing, his most trusted lieutenant, held a pistol to the back of the captive's head. The two men towering behind her wore suit pants, shirts with loosened ties, and sidearms in shoulder holsters. They both had their hands clasped in front of them, and remained passive. Nathan knew that, if needed, each of the men could instantly kill the prisoner with a single strike, or draw their pistols in a split second to protect their boss. But Nathan wasn't worried. The warehouse complex was secured by a larger team. There was only one way out for this prisoner.

Nathan removed his suit jacket, folded it lengthwise, then draped it on a folding metal chair. Conscious of his audience, he rolled up his sleeves and regarded the prisoner. The man's face was puffy from wounds, his swollen eyes almost sealed shut by caked blood. At one time, the man in front of Nathan had been a strong, barrel-chested warrior, a veteran of many battles and a survivor of many wounds. But not tonight. Tonight he was on his knees, a broken man, ready to accept his fate.

"Ivan, my friend," Nathan said, his voice soft. He

squatted down in front of the prisoner. One of the guards grabbed Ivan by the hair and forced his head up so he was facing Nathan. "Ivan, can you hear me? Nod your head if you can hear me."

Ivan's jaw had been broken and his mouth was a bloody mess. Had Ivan been able to open his mouth, Nathan knew, most of his teeth would be missing. The man nodded his head once, slowly.

"Ivan, do you know why you're here?" Nathan asked, using his most friendly tone.

Ivan nodded his head once again. Nathan realized his team had done a remarkable job of breaking the man down without outright killing him. There was a time when Nathan would have done that work himself. Now, he could rely on trusted lieutenants to carry out the job for him.

"You fucked up, didn't you, Ivan? You let me down. You let us down. You let us all down."

Ivan nodded again, once. A drop of blood slid off his nose and fell to the floor.

"We had a deal, Ivan. You and me. You knew the price of failure, yet you still didn't complete the mission." Nathan's performance was for the benefit of his team. He wanted them to witness the implication of Ivan's failure. "I know what you're thinking, Ivan. You're thinking that you managed to kill three of the six targets. But fifty percent is not good enough. And now we have a problem that Wing has to clean up."

This time, Ivan didn't seem to have the energy to respond. Nathan regarded his former operative with sadness. Once, this had been one of his most trusted lieutenants. But lately, there had been whispers of Ivan's desire to retire. Nathan knew the man had been making preparations to disappear with a new identity. Something about a beach in Croatia where he planned to live out his days drinking the local beer and running a beachside bar. Then had come the latest stumble: Ivan had screwed up an assignment that had embarrassed Nathan and put him in a compromising position with a key client. Nathan had finally agreed it was time for his old colleague to disappear. It just wouldn't be the way Ivan had envisioned it.

"Your son will be taken care of, Ivan. I've arranged a trust fund to pay for his education and living expenses until he's twenty-five. Whatever you may think, you can't accuse us of being ungrateful for your many years of service."

Ivan slumped at that news, and the two guards had to work hard to keep him upright. Nathan meant what he said about the boy – he was a man of his word, and Ivan knew that. The knowledge his son would be provided for, Nathan suspected, would put Ivan at ease.

Nathan reached behind him and removed a pistol from the small of his back. For a moment, he savored its heft and the feel of the rosewood double-diamond grip. The gun was an American-made Kimber Gold Match 1911 .45 ACP, and it was Nathan's pride and joy. He'd put well over 1,000 rounds through it on the range behind his house, and the pistol was finely tuned and well cared for. The pistol had also dispatched its fair share of men. The gun had been a gift from an especially pleased client, and Nathan prized it like a trophy. He moved his finger to the trigger and pointed the gun point-blank at Ivan's forehead. Wing let her own pistol drop and moved three paces to her left.

"Goodbye, Ivan," Nathan said.

He pulled the trigger. The room was filled with a deafening pop, like an M80 firecracker had gone off under their feet. The hollow-point bullet tore through Ivan's head, then exited, taking with it most of the back of his skull and spraying blood and brain matter onto the concrete. The two guards let Ivan fall to the floor.

Without ceremony, Nathan returned the pistol to his waistband, grabbed his jacket and slung it over his shoulder. He turned and walked out of the hangar, leaving his staff to clean up the mess as a reminder of the cost of failing him.

SIX

Minsk, Belarus

In ten minutes, this place will be sealed up tighter than a drum. Anatoly's words were ringing in Max's ears as he stepped away from the group.

"Be right back," he said, and Arina nodded, a blank look on her face.

The expansive grounds were filling up with emergency personnel as Max made his way toward the back of the property. In the distance, he could hear the distinctive sound of a chopper approaching from the east. He guessed that would be his father's boss, the director of the KGB in Belarus. Even though Belarus had become independent in 1990 as part of the fall of the Soviet Union, the Belarusian president still maintained close political and economic ties with Moscow. The intelligence community was also still shared between the two countries. Some called Belarus the last European dictatorship, and the president ran a subtly brutal authoritarian regime. Until about an hour ago, Max's father had been the heir apparent to the directorship. No doubt this place would soon be crawling with KGB personnel. Max's free time on the property would be short-lived.

Max gave the crater a wide berth, avoiding the firefighters still dowsing the embers from the fire. Powerful halogen lights were being set up on tall tripods around the perimeter, and men in bright yellow suits had started to sift through the wreckage. He was walking fast now, ignoring the chaos around him.

Behind the main house, set back a hundred meters, was a barn his father had built many years ago. On Max's last trip home, his father had taken Max out to the building and given him a brief tour of some improvements he'd made. As Max made his way through the darkness toward the building, he could still hear his father's voice. The words had been almost prophetic.

Mikhail, my boy, someday they'll get me, and when they do, I want you to do something for me. They had been standing in front of the building's massive barn-like sliding doors. His father was talking in his usual baritone voice, raspy from a lifetime of cigarettes and hard liquor. *When no one is looking, I want you to come out here and clean this up for me.* With a flourish, he'd yanked open the massive doors and led Max into the barn.

Now, Max pulled the large barn doors open and slid inside, pulling them closed behind him. He paused to let his eyes adjust to the gloom. There were several ATVs and a pickup truck parked in the main area of the barn. Hunting equipment lined one of the walls. Another wall held rows of bridles and horse tackle. Max knew the far door led to several horse stalls. He ignored this room and found the set of stairs on the left leading down. He took them two at a time until he came to a door with a keypad instead of a handle. Max paused, searching his memory.

Every man needs a sanctuary, Mikhail. Yes, I've got my study back at the house. But down here I can really get away from everything and think. His father had been tapping at the keypad while he was talking to Max. Then his father had turned and reeled off a seven-digit number. *Memorize that number, Mikhail,* his father had said. *Someday, you may need it.*

Now, Max searched his memory, hoping his father hadn't changed the code in the last five years. Blessed with a memory like a vault, Max punched in the seven-digit code and pushed. The big door heaved open, letting out a *swoosh* of air.

When they get me, my boy, I want you to come down here and clean everything out before anyone can find this room. Your sister and your mother are the only others who know this room exists and know the password. Not much of it will make sense to you, just find a shredder and get rid of the papers.

"What's down here?" Max had asked.

"Nothing too sinister," his father had said. "Just some family papers and some files that I'd prefer not get into the wrong hands." He had pointed to a small file cabinet next to a desk.

Now, Max stepped through the door, found the light switch, and flicked it on. He sucked in his breath. The room was in complete chaos, like a mini tornado had just gone through. The desk was upside down and looked like someone had gone after it with a sledgehammer. The cushions of the leather couch had been cut open, stuffing pulled out and strewn around the room. The file cabinet's drawers hung open. Max walked over to it. A quick inspection showed the cabinet as empty. The leather desk chair was similarly destroyed. The room seemed as if someone had been looking for something. His father had been character-istically opaque, and Max had not questioned him. Now, of course, Max wished he knew what had been in the filing cabinets.

Behind the desk was a large gun cabinet, its doors hanging open. Weapons lay in a jumble at the foot of the cabinet. *That's odd*, thought Max. *If you're going to ransack a room, wouldn't you take the weapons?* Obviously, that hadn't been the thief's objective. Max found a SIG Sauer P226 among the pile, and racked the slide to ensure the chamber was empty. Then he dry-fired three times. He rummaged through the pile again and came up with two loaded magazines that matched the SIG. He slammed one magazine into the handle and racked the slide again, cham-bering a bullet. Then he slipped the gun into his waistband at the small of his back and put the extra magazine in his back pocket. Things were getting weird around here fast, and he felt naked without a weapon. The bulk of the pistol against his back felt reassuring.

He took one last look around the small office, then made his exit, pulling the door closed behind him. The state of the room had him concerned. Had it been ransacked before or after the bomb had gone off? If only three people knew about the room's existence and the door code, then who had done the ransacking? His sister? She hadn't had time unless she'd done it before departing for the airport. But that didn't seem like his sister. Max thought it likely that his father had confided in someone else. But who? One name jumped out at him as the most likely.

Max took the stairs up two at a time, then turned and

yanked open the barn doors. A bright light flashed in his eyes, temporarily blinding him. He heard the unmistakable sound of several weapons being raised, and someone shouted "Freeze!" in Russian. Max slowly lifted his arms above his head.

SEVEN

Minsk, Belarus

"Mikhail Asimov, it's been a long time," a sharp voice rang out. "You can put down your weapons, boys. This is Andrei Asimov's son, come back to visit us from the land of the frogs." Laughter rang out from the group. "Usually the French run away from their problems," the speaker continued. "Maybe Mikhail hasn't quite gone native after all." More laughter from the men. The lights dipped and Max blinked until his eyes adjusted to the darkness. He was standing eye to forehead with none other than Victor Dedov, the director of the Belarusian KGB.

Despite his diminutive stature, Max knew Dedov commanded great respect from both his peers and his team. He ran the KGB in Minsk with a ruthless efficiency, earning himself the nickname behind his back of The General. It was rumored he put risers in his shoes to give himself another inch of height. Impeccably put together in a black tie and overcoat, he looked as if he'd just left the symphony.

"Hello, Victor," Max said. Dedov regarded him with a stern look, and Max immediately felt uncomfortable, like he was doing something wrong. Six soldiers in paramilitary garb were arrayed behind Dedov. Four of them held tactical shotguns and two held pistols. Max recognized them as members of an elite tactical team assembled by Dedov and charged with his personal security.

"I'm sorry to hear about your parents," Dedov said. "Rest assured, the KGB will do everything in its power to find the perpetrators of this horrible terrorist act."

"What makes you think it's terrorism?" Max asked.

"Isn't it obvious?" Dedov's face was impassive. "Who else would use such a crude device to engineer such catastrophic destruction? Using a large RDX bomb is a signature of several terrorist groups in Georgia and Chechnya, just as we saw in the gruesome apartment bombings in Moscow back in '99."

"I think we both know those apartment bombings were staged by the KGB to allow the continuation of military action in Chechnya and to drive support for the election of the Russian president," Max said, looking Dedov straight in the face.

Dedov's eyes narrowed. "That is dangerous speculation, Mikhail," he said, his voice a low growl. "If I were you, I'd keep my opinions to myself." Then his face lightened, and he craned his neck to look around Max. "Just what were you doing back here? I'll have you know this is now a crime scene under my jurisdiction."

"Just checking to make sure nothing had been damaged," Max said. He didn't like the way Dedov was looking at him. He'd known the man for many years, but technically didn't work under him. Max worked directly for the Foreign Intelligence Service in Moscow. This had been a source of great contention between Max and his father, who had fought hard to keep Max on the Belarusian side. He decided to test Dedov a little. "Where is my father's security team? He was assigned four men on a rotational basis. Why were they not here? Certainly they never would have let an unknown truck that close to the house."

Dedov squinted at Max for a moment. "Budget cuts, Mikhail. They'd been reassigned."

Max was incredulous. "That sounds like bullshit, Victor." He knew he was on thin ice talking this informally to the director of the KGB, even if Dedov wasn't Max's superior. He pressed on anyway. "What's the real story?"

Dedov bristled. "I'd urge you to watch your mouth, Mikhail. Do not forget your position here. I'll let it go in light of the tragedy that you just suffered. Now, please join the group at the front of the house. Anatoly will escort you back." Dedov stood aside so Max could pass.

Max let his temper calm as he walked past the group of soldiers. Now was not the time to antagonize people who might be able to help him. He spotted Anatoly standing quietly, looking at something on the ground. Max moved around Dedov and joined his father's old friend.

"Sorry, Mikhail, but he asked where you were. We guessed you'd be here."

"Its fine, don't worry about it. I was on my way back." Max started walking toward the front of the house. "Something isn't right about this, Anatoly." Anatoly trailed next to him, remaining silent. Max turned so he was standing in front of the other man. "Did my father confide in you about anything before his death?" Max asked.

Anatoly didn't answer right away. The older man's face

was illuminated by one of the spotlights, and Max watched his eyes. He'd been trained extensively in techniques of interrogation, including how to tell if someone was lying. Lie detection, he knew, was an art, as was the act of lying itself. He also knew Anatoly had been trained in both, as well. They were in a standoff. If Anatoly asked a question, or paused too long, Max knew he'd be stalling for time to manufacture a plausible answer. If he answered right away, his eyes may shift in a tell, giving the lie away. Other tells included a sudden shift of the head, shuffling of the feet, excessive pointing, a change in breathing, or even staring too much. Max watched the older man closely.

"I don't think so," Anatoly said. "Like what?"

The delay tactic, Max thought. Anatoly was staring right at him, just as he'd no doubt been trained to do.

"Did he ask you to do anything for him if he were killed? Like clean out a file or hide something?" Max watched the older man's eyes.

Anatoly rubbed his hand over his mouth. "No, not at all, Mikhail. Nothing like that. Why do you ask?" Anatoly's tell had been subtle, but it was enough to give him away.

Max turned and continued walking back to the front of the house. Anatoly scrambled to catch up. Max let him fall behind as he hastened to find his sister. Anatoly was clearly lying. The question was why?

EIGHT

Minsk, Belarus

Max awoke the next morning with a dull pain in his neck from sleeping on Arina's couch and a thudding ache in his head from the collision with the rear of the minivan. At midnight, he'd finally dragged Arina away from the scene and to her home, where he'd convinced her to take a mild sedative. Then he'd managed to get Alex into his pajamas and into bed. The moment Max turned out the lights, Alex cried out. Not knowing what else to do, Max sat at the boy's bedside until he'd finally fallen asleep. While he watched Alex's breathing turn from hyperventilated worry to slow, raspy slumber, Max thought about his relationship with his own father, and wondered what Alex's life would be like growing up without one.

Max's self-induced estrangement from his father was a relatively recent occurrence. During his entire childhood, they'd been inseparable, the elder Asimov taking Max under his wing and teaching him tradecraft at an early age.

At eight, Max had fired his first gun. By nine, he could clean and reassemble just about any pistol or rifle. While the other boys were playing stickball and ice hockey, Max and his father were practicing surveillance and counter-surveillance in the streets around their home.

During his last visit, Arina had told Max she wanted to keep Alex away from the realities of his uncle's and grandfather's professions. She hoped to create a better life for the ten-year-old. Alex was a budding star forward on his school's ice hockey team, got good marks in school, and was picking up English at a rapid pace. Arina was going to have her hands full on her own.

Now, Max padded shirtless over to Arina's kitchen and started the kettle. He found some instant coffee and stirred a heaping spoonful into a mug, added hot water, then took a sip. He grimaced, then took another sip. Paris had taught him to appreciate fine espresso, but this would have to do. He rummaged in his suitcase and shrugged on a black T-shirt, then put on his leather cafe-style motorcycle jacket. He pulled the SIG from under the pillow on the couch and tucked it into his waistband at the small of his back.

When he stood and turned, he found his sister staring at him from the hallway. Her eyes were red and puffy, and she held a wad of tissues in one hand. The other hand played with a strand of her blonde hair. Tall and broad-shouldered, his sister was a handsome woman, even in grief. She leaned against the doorjamb and wiped away a tear with the wad of tissues.

"Where are you going?" she sniffled.

"Back to the house. I want to look around, and talk with the investigators."

"Was that a gun I just saw you with?"

"Yes," he replied. No sense lying about it. He knew she'd seen him put it there.

"I don't want that gun in my house, Mikhail." When she used his given name instead of his nickname, Max knew she was serious.

"Arina, in case you forgot, someone just killed our parents and your husband. We might be in—"

"How dare you!" Her voice was low, her words measured. "You don't need to remind me that my parents and my husband were just killed. I'll not have guns in my house and that's final."

"Arina, we might not be safe," Max said as gently as he could. He opted not to tell her about the four Minsk city police officers Anatoly had arranged to stand guard on the street.

"You don't know what it's like, Mikhail, to raise a son. You just live your life of a playboy over there in Paris, without being burdened with children or responsibilities. When is the last time you actually cared for anyone? What do you do over there, anyway? Go to clubs? Late dinners? Travel around Europe with no cares in the world? You don't even come home when Mom is diagnosed with cancer. What kind of son are you?" Her hands were working over the tissues, folding and re-folding them into small squares.

Here we go, Max thought. All of his sister's anger at him was going to come pouring out. He moved toward the window with his cup. Best to just let her get it all out. He supposed he deserved it. It was all true. He enjoyed a life of minimal responsibilities in Paris. But there were reasons he stayed away. Reasons his sister would never understand.

"You never call, Mikhail. Father hadn't seen you in five years. Did you know he'd had a scare with prostate cancer?

Do you even remember when their birthdays are? You don't even know what grade your nephew is in."

Max struggled to control his own temper. "Have you forgotten, Arina? Have you forgotten how mother treated me growing up? Are you conveniently ignoring how cold that woman was to me all those years ago?"

"That was over twenty years ago, Mikhail," she said. She continued working at the tissues, shredding them into tiny tufts and letting them drift to the carpet. "Why couldn't you just forgive her, and be her goddamn son?"

"I don't expect you to understand, Arina. You never did. You always took her side."

"Oh, so it's my fault."

"I didn't say that. I'm just saying that I wish you'd see my side of it for once."

Arina looked down at her hands. "I guess you'll just go back to Paris now," she said finally.

"I'm not leaving," Max said, his voice quiet. The guilt from his estranged relationship with his mother was something he'd lived with for the past twenty years. Now he would never have a chance to fix it. The least he could do was try to find out the real reason his parents had been killed.

"But for how long, Mikhail? Now that you're relieved of the burden of our parents, you'll probably just get on the first plane back to France and we'll never see you again. Well, just go, goddamn it. Just leave." She turned and went into the kitchen, and Max could hear the sobs coming hard and loud.

Max had to admit to himself this was foreign territory. The guilt was now coming in waves. He barely remembered the last time he'd seen his parents, and now they were dead, vaporized by a truckload of RDX. He'd never get to see them again, not even resting in a coffin. The anger started to burn alongside the guilt.

He wasn't used to dealing with his own emotions, let alone those of a loved one. In fact, he'd been raised by his father to avoid emotion. His current job required him to separate action from emotions. He suspected that was why he avoided personal relationships with both women and friends. He lived the life of a loner by nature and by necessity. He walked toward the kitchen and saw Arina leaning against the counter with her arms wrapped around herself, her body wracked with sobs. He said the only thing that seemed logical.

"I'm not leaving until I find whoever did this and I kill them with my own bare hands. I promise you, Arina, I'll make this right."

Arina's face tipped up to the ceiling and she let out a loud wail. Then she turned and threw the remainder of the tissues at him. They fluttered to the floor like confetti. "Just get out of my house," she howled. "Get the fuck out of my house and don't come back!"

Confused and unable to think of anything else to say, Max turned, snatched his bag off the floor, and walked out.

NINE

Minsk, Belarus

The neighborhood surrounding his parents' estate was abuzz with activity when Max drove up to the gate. He parked his rental car on the street behind a wide, black Mercedes sedan with tinted windows, and walked up the drive.

The sky was overcast and threatening. It felt like November. Max could swear fall was right around the corner but for the flowering buds in the trees and the perennials that were threatening to bloom. The grass was wet, like it might have rained overnight. He was surprised at the number of onlookers still permitted on the property. The local police had a section of the front yard cordoned off well away from the blast area, and it was filled with several news reporting teams and a few civilians. The crater where the house had been was surrounded by a small fleet of police and forensics personnel. A half dozen other men in suits, who Max assumed were KGB, milled about. By the corner of the crater, where a few charred bricks of foundation still stood, he saw Anatoly talking to Dedov. Their heads were close together, and they seemed to be talking in hushed tones. They both looked like they'd been there all night. Anatoly's hair was flying in all directions and Dedov's bow tie was undone.

Max walked toward them. They saw him as he approached, and stopped their conversation. Dedov regarded him with a passive stare, his hands clasped behind his back.

"Mikhail, I'm afraid this is a crime scene now. We can't have you wandering all over the place," Dedov said with a frown.

Max ignored him. Instead, he turned to Anatoly. "Can I have a word?"

Anatoly shrugged, and guided Max toward the corral of onlookers. "You shouldn't antagonize him," Anatoly said when they'd moved far enough away where Dedov couldn't overhear. "He can make your life difficult, you know."

Max looked at Anatoly. The man looked tired, stooped, forlorn. Almost wistful. Max thought he might be carrying a heavy weight around with him, a burden that he couldn't drop. "How could my life be any more difficult, Anatoly? My parents are fucking dead and my nephew is without a father."

"Well, if you're anything like your father, and everyone says that you are, you're going to start looking under rocks for your parents' killer. Rocks that are perhaps better left unturned. If you piss off Dedov, you're going to make an enemy of him very quickly."

Max didn't give a damn about Dedov. He knew the man would stonewall him every step of the way – it was his job, and Max almost forgave him for that. Instead, he focused on something else Anatoly had said.

"What rocks are better left unturned, Anatoly?" he asked. Max could feel irritation creeping into his throat at Anatoly's reticence.

"This is the KGB, Max. Nothing has changed since independence, except now the KGB's mission is to protect capitalism instead of protecting communism. It's the same tactics, just the outcomes that are different. The KGB doesn't want anyone poking their noses where they don't belong. If the KGB says this is a Chechen terrorist bomb, then that's where you should leave it."

"You know I can't do that," Max said. The irritation was slowly turning into anger. "You just said it yourself. This is family we're talking about."

"What I know and what my counsel is to you are two separate things," Anatoly said. "I knew your father well. He was a stubborn bull of a man, who wouldn't rest until things were right in the world. Since he raised you to be just like him, I'm going to guess you won't let things lie."

"If I were killed and my father were still alive, what do you think he'd do, Anatoly?"

"He'd scour the ends of the earth until he found your killer, then he'd make that person pay a hundred times over with pain and suffering."

"Exactly," Max said. The anger was at full boil now. His eyes bore into Anatoly's. "I will not rest, Anatoly, until I find answers. Then when I find answers, I will not rest until whoever did this to my family," he paused and swept his arm around the grounds, "pays a hundredfold."

Anatoly was silent, staring back at Max. "Then I guess you won't listen to me, will you?"

"No. Save your fucking breath."

Anatoly spread his arms out wide, then let them fall back to his sides. "Just don't say I didn't warn you."

Max lost control of his anger. It rose up from his gut, propelled by his own frustration, and blinded him. An image of his father flashed in his mind, holding Anatoly in an awkward hug while Anatoly sobbed at the death of his teenage daughter. Then an image of Alex flashed in his mind, alone and fatherless, unable to experience the strong hand of guidance as Max had been able to. *What was Anatoly hiding?*

Max grabbed the lapels of Anatoly's jacket and shook the older man so hard that Max could hear his teeth rattle. "You're lying to me! Tell me what you know, goddamn it," he said through gritted teeth. "Tell me who did this, Anatoly, or by God I'll kill you myself with my bare hands." Max was shaking the man so hard he tore Anatoly's coat.

The commotion attracted the attention of two members of the city police, who came running. Before they could reach the pair, Max cocked a fist and swung it, hitting Anatoly's jaw. "Tell me what you know," Max hissed. He held onto Anatoly's coat as the KGB man stumbled backward, his hands going to his face. Max pulled back his arm for a second punch, but four strong hands grabbed onto his forearm and held tight. Max struggled to free his arm, but the policemen were young, strong boys trained well in hand-to-hand combat. They held on until a third policeman arrived and forced Max to the ground, his face pressed into the wet grass.

The fight went out of him. He heard Dedov's voice above him. "Put him on his knees." Max was jerked upright, then felt a kick to the back of his legs. He stumbled forward, held by a police officer at each arm. The third policeman put a night stick across Max's trachea from behind. Max gasped for breath, trying to force gulps of air. He could see Anatoly on his hands and knees, spitting blood onto the ground.

Dedov bent down, and put his face an inch from Max's. Max could smell a faint odor of sardines, and maybe alcohol. Or maybe it was the man's aftershave.

"I'm only going to say this once, Asimov. Stay away from this case. The KGB will do everything in its vast power to find and punish the parties responsible for killing your parents. Let us do our job. If I find out you've been as much as pissing distance from anything related to this case, I will have you sent away to the furthest gulag in Siberia and you will do hard labor in a rock quarry using only a garden trowel. Am I clear?"

Max stared hard at the man. For a moment, he envisioned snapping Dedov's tiny neck with his bare hands. Then he rasped, "Go fuck yourself, Dedov."

Dedov stared at Max for a long moment, and Max braced himself for some kind of blow. But Dedov remained passive. He said, "You've been warned, Asimov. Don't try my patience." To the policemen holding Max, he said, "Get him off this property and out of my sight." With that, Director Dedov turned on a heel and strode back toward the crater in the ground.

Max was jerked onto his feet and half dragged, half bum-rushed, down the drive and into the street. The largest policeman pushed Max hard in the back and sent him stumbling onto the pavement, where he came to rest on his hands and knees. By the time he rose and dusted himself off, the three policemen had turned and were walking back up the drive.

Max wasn't a self-conscious man, but he wasn't used to making himself the center of attention. Several of the neighbors had stopped to watch the altercation, and Max turned to glare at them. They quickly looked away. But there was one man who turned away just a little too slowly. Max caught his eye, then immediately memorized his face. Many of the neighbors wore housecoats or casual clothing, having perhaps ventured out at first light to witness the commotion. The man who caught Max's eye wore a full-length, dark grey Macintosh, pulled tight at the waist. On his head, he wore a brimmed hat. A pair of sunglasses covered his eyes, which Max thought odd given the overcast skies. He caught a glimpse of a weak jaw, a full mustache, and tufts of white hair escaping from underneath the hat. Max started toward the man, who instantly turned and started walking away. Max noticed he moved with a slight limp. After a moment, Max realized something was familiar about the man.

"Hey, you," Max called. "Hey, you there. Stop. I want to talk with you."

The man in the grey overcoat started moving down the sidewalk faster than Max thought possible, given the limp. Max ran after him, shouting.

Then, the man simply disappeared. One moment he was there, hustling along the sidewalk; a second later, he'd vanished. Max wove through the smattering of people, looking for a man in an overcoat with a limp. After a few minutes of searching, he gave up and started back toward his car. What was it about that man, Max wondered as he pulled away from the curb. Then it hit him. The man had been in the crowd the night of the explosion. Max remembered because the man's hat was just like one his father used to wear: a short-brimmed, grey fedora with a black band. What alarmed Max was the fact that the man had been using a smartphone to take pictures of the scene.

TEN

Minsk, Belarus

The cheap door lock opened with a metallic *snick*, and Max pocketed his lock picks and drew the SIG. He pushed the door open and paused, listening for activity in the room beyond. At five a.m., the morning light was murky, so he used his ears and his nose, a skill drilled into his head by his father. *Don't rely just on your eyes, my boy*, he'd said hundreds of times. *What do you smell? What do you hear?* They'd performed drill after drill in which Max had been blindfolded, then required to find his way out of a room or down a city block. At the time, the drills had been maddening. Since, the skills he'd learned had saved his life on more than one occasion.

This morning, his senses told him the house was silent, its occupants still sleeping. There was no smell of brewing coffee, no sizzle of bacon in a skillet, just the strong odor of something rotting. He stepped through the door and into a small kitchen, pausing to let his eyes grow accustomed to the dim light.

The room around him was in dire need of cleaning. Dishes encrusted with food were piled high in the sink. Pots and pans with food remaining in them sat on the stove. The counters were covered with disposable takeout containers and empty frozen-food boxes.

Max grimaced as he walked through the kitchen, his soft-soled boots silent on the cracked linoleum. A doorway led to a small living area, equally messy with dirty dishes, discarded clothing, and empty beer cans. A half-full bottle of vodka sat on the coffee table among overflowing ash trays and crumpled pornographic magazines. Opposite a leather recliner sat a new-looking, large, flat-paneled television.

Five years ago, Max recalled, when he'd last been here, the house had been abuzz with life. The rooms had been a mess from two teenage girls and a demanding wife. Instead of the beer cans and empty food containers, the living area had been awash in girls' soccer clothing and gymnastics paraphernalia. The walls had held framed pictures of the girls holding trophies from their exploits on the field and in the gymnasium. All of that was gone now, replaced by the filth of a bachelor who didn't care.

Max stole up a set of carpeted steps and into a hallway. He heard wet snoring coming from down the hall. Quick glances told him the two bedrooms previously belonging to the girls were empty. He walked to the end of the hallway, stepping carefully to avoid any creaking floorboards. He peeked into the master bedroom and saw a single figure sprawled on his back on a king-sized bed. The large form was dressed only in stained boxer shorts. His massive gut heaved with each ragged breath. Max saw the butt of a pistol next to an overflowing ashtray. He crept into the room and placed the gun in his pocket. Then he retreated from the room and went back downstairs.

Max felt both disgusted and sorry for his father's old friend. Clearly, the years had not been good to Anatoly. He searched the rest of the house and found more of the same. He made his way back to the kitchen, found the kettle, and made room for it on the stove. A half-used container of instant coffee was on the counter. He found a relatively clean mug and made himself a cup. He was really starting to miss the espresso machine in his flat in Paris, and the readily available cafes on every corner. He went back into the living room, positioned the leather recliner so he could see the stairs, then sat down to wait. He put the SIG on his lap.

Remarkably, Anatoly was an early riser. At half past six, Max heard footsteps and the sound of water in a basin. A few minutes later, he saw bare ankles emerge in the stair-well. A few seconds later, Anatoly stood in front of him staring incredulously into the barrel of Max's gun.

"Good morning, Anatoly."

"What the fuck are you doing?" Anatoly asked. He absently scratched his balls through his yellowed boxers. He glanced around, then looked back up the stairs.

"Looking for this?" Max took the Makarov pistol from his pocket with his left hand. Max saw Anatoly's face fall just a fraction. It was enough to suggest it was the only gun on the premises.

"Max, why are you here? Why are you pointing that gun at me?"

"We need to have a little talk, Anatoly, and I need you focused on that little talk." Max waved his gun at the couch. "Have a seat."

"Can I at least put some clothes on?" Anatoly looked up the stairs again.

"No. Sit down." Max indicated the couch again with the barrel of the SIG. Anatoly pushed aside a jacket and some old newspapers and sat, the cushion sighing under his weight. He crossed his arms over his naked chest and stared at Max.

"Where is Stasya?" Max asked.

Anatoly glared at him. "She left me, what do you think? After Sofie died. Took Sveta and moved to St Petersburg. Sveta is taking college classes, I heard." For a moment, wistful pride crossed his face, then sadness. "I don't see them much."

"Sorry, Anatoly," Max said. The last time he'd seen Anatoly's living daughter, she'd been a star forward on her high school's soccer team.

"Fuck it," Anatoly said. "What do you want? Ask your questions, then get the fuck out of my house."

Max brought his mind back to the present. "Why is the KGB covering up my parents' death with a false story about terrorists from Chechnya?"

Anatoly groaned, and Max's guess was confirmed. "Why do you think they're covering it up, Max?"

"Either because they don't know who did it and are trying to sweep it under the rug, or they do know and they don't want anyone else to find out. Which is it?"

Anatoly groaned again. "If I knew, I would tell you." Max watched closely as Anatoly rubbed his face. The same tell he'd used yesterday. Anatoly knew more than he was sharing.

"Why should I believe you, Anatoly?"

"Because I loved your father like a brother, Max. Because I'm as pissed off as you are about the whole thing."

"I seriously doubt that. What did my father keep in his secret office?"

With an exasperated sound, Anatoly put his hands in the air. "I told you, Max. I don't know. I didn't even know the office existed." Then, as if he was measuring his words, Anatoly continued. "Your father and I had grown apart in recent years, Max. We weren't working on the same things. I had a feeling that your father was pulling strings to get me assigned away from Minsk. I've been on the road a lot lately."

Max got the sense Anatoly was telling the truth about this part, but he was still clearly hiding something. He knew more about Max's parents' death than he was letting on.

"How long have you been back in Minsk?"

"Five days. I'm due to head to Turkey next week."

Max contemplated that for a moment. If Anatoly'd had anything to do with Max's parents' death, he would have had ample opportunity. Max wasn't sure he suspected the man of the actual deed, but something wasn't adding up.

As if reading his mind, Anatoly said, "I know what you're thinking, Max. I had nothing to do with that bomb. Your father was still my best friend."

"You're lying to me," Max said, growing exasperated.

"I'm not lying, Mikhail. I swear I'm not."

"If that's true, then help me. I'm going to find out who was behind the bombing and make them pay. So, come clean. Give me some information I can use. Tell me something. Anything."

Anatoly stared at Max for a long time. Finally he said, "There is one thing I can think of."

"Tell me," Max said.

"He kept a go-box buried in a hidden location."

The notion that his father kept a go-box wasn't a surprise to Max. A go-box was a hidden cache of items that may become useful to an agent if forced to run or disappear for a while. It usually contained false identification paperwork, cash, and perhaps a weapon. Max kept several himself: two in bank safe-deposit boxes in London and Zurich, and one in a storage locker near the airport in Paris.

Anatoly continued. "It's buried in the basement of a butcher shop in Minsk. I think you know the one. The one your mother used to shop at?"

He did indeed know the butcher shop. "What's in this go-box?"

"I don't know," Anatoly replied. "But your father took great pains to keep it safe. A few years ago, he bought the building. He told me it was to keep the hiding place secure."

Max considered this for a moment. Then he stood. "Get your act together, Anatoly. There are plenty of fish out there, but no woman wants to be with a man who lives like this."

"Fuck you, Max."

The words were ringing in Max's ears as he disappeared out the back, leaving his half-drunk cup of tepid instant coffee on the counter.

———

Anatoly sat on the couch for several long minutes after Max had left, listening to the silence. Then, somewhere outside a dog barked. A truck went by. His anger at the unwelcome intrusion was quickly replaced by shame. A deep sense of humiliation set in, stemming from his failure as a father, as a husband. He felt contempt for himself as he regarded the filth surrounding him. The house felt empty. His life felt empty.

Finally, he got up from the couch and walked into the kitchen. He rummaged through an overflowing junk drawer and came up with a plain, white business card showing only a number. With a shaky hand, he dialed the number on his mobile phone. When the other party answered, he said simply, "I know where Mikhail Asimov will be."

He listened to a question from the other party, then he supplied an address. When the line went dead, he tossed the phone onto the messy counter, grabbed the bottle of vodka, and took a gulp. When he set the bottle down, his hands had stopped shaking, but a tear rolled down his cheek.

ELEVEN

Minsk, Belarus

After grabbing a quick plate of eggs, potato pancakes, and rye bread from a diner, Max did a drive-by of the butcher shop. This early in the morning, it was shuttered, with a closed sign hanging askew in the window. The front of the building was whitewashed and faded. A peeling sign advertising the name of the shop was painted on the front window. Next door was a small grocery. An alleyway ran along the other side of the building.

Just the sight of the old shop brought back a flood of memories of his mother. Every few days when Max was growing up, she'd walk down to this butcher shop pushing her wheeled grocery cart to stock up for the week. Prices were astronomical, but his father's position with the KGB had its perks. She'd return from her shopping with the cart stuffed with cuts of beef, mutton, and pork, and they'd eat like kings.

Then Max remembered his mother in the kitchen. Max

would come home from school, or hockey practice, or from outings with his father, and she'd be cooking up a storm. Max would try to grab food from the counter, but she'd shoo him off with barely a comment. At the dinner table, she'd serve the family, then eat silently while his father would carry on about politics or rage about the West. Then his mother would wordlessly clear the table and clean up the kitchen. As Max got older, he began to notice the obvious way in which his mother cared for Arina, helping her with homework and chiding her to do better in school. She never had a spare word for Max. Eventually, Max stopped caring and simply spent more time with his father.

Max drove a second circuit around the neighborhood, then parked two blocks away and did a walk-by. The sidewalks and roadway still glistened with moisture from last night's rain. Blue sky was trying to peek through clouds and the air was warming. A man in a coat was sweeping the sidewalk in front of the grocery. It was just an ordinary weekday morning on a commercial street in Minsk.

Max put his collar up and pulled his hat down, and ignored the man's greeting in front of the grocery. The butcher shop was dark. The hours of nine a.m. to five p.m. were painted on the glass door in white. He stopped, made a point of checking his watch, and glanced around looking for surveillance. He saw no one; the streets were quiet. Max turned down the alley and walked around the back. A service door led from the rear of the shop into the alley. He tried the door and found it locked. Although it would take him only a few seconds to pick the lock, he kept walking.

He tried to keep his mind focused, alert and aware of his surroundings, but his thoughts drifted to his father. More than once, his father had told Max that in their line of work, you could trust no one. Especially the KGB, the elder man had continuously warned, until it was stamped into Max's brain. The KGB, his father said, only cared about itself. Each employee was expendable, easily sacrificed for the greater good. In the KGB's case, his father reminded him, the greater good was the vitality and longevity of the organization itself. The fact that it had been created to protect the party had long ago been forgotten, replaced with the idea that the KGB existed to protect itself. Now, his father's warnings rang in his ears. The odds were good that his father's killer or killers were inside the KGB or, at a minimum, the KGB had sanctioned the hit and provided assistance. Max guessed that Anatoly was not part of the actual hit team, but was likely aware of who had been, and maybe even provided support. The thought made his stomach turn in disgust and anger.

Max doubled back, then strolled around the block, re-emerging on the main street just as a shower of rain started. Across the street from the butcher shop, Max saw a French-style cafe. Next to the cafe was a vacant storefront. Painter's tarpaulins covered the store's windows on the inside.

Happy to see a reminder of his adopted home, Max ducked into the cafe and sat down at a table by the front window. He ordered coffee and a croissant, then picked up a newspaper that had been left behind. The lead story's headline screamed, "Chechens Take Responsibility for KGB Head's Assassination." Max tossed the paper aside. The propaganda machine, it seemed, was in full motion.

Something about the speed with which the Chechens were blamed was too pat, too easy. First, there was the conspicuous absence of any security around his parents' house. Then there was the large truck that had been parked next to the house. Then, there was the almost-immediate appearance of the team from the KGB, including his father's boss. Finally, there was Anatoly, clearly hiding something. Alarm bells were ringing in Max's head, and he urged himself to be cautious.

Traffic started to pick up as more people braved the wet streets to make their way to work. He started memorizing the cars and pedestrians that passed the window. Just as his father had taught him, he played little games with himself to remember unique details about each passerby. A pretty woman with blonde hair and a floral print coat would become his girlfriend. *Flowers for my girlfriend*, he'd remember. A dilapidated lorry with a picture of a fish on the side would become a *fishy truck*. He sipped his coffee and glanced at his watch. Through the front window of the butcher shop, Max could see a thin, white-frocked man moving around behind the counter. The sign in the window had been flipped around to "Open."

One of the first things Max had learned from his father was that being a spy was mostly boring. *Hurry up and wait*, his father would often quip. A properly planned operation would involve weeks or months of planning, surveillance, and setup, followed by a short burst of activity that was often peppered with pure fear. The rest of the time was spent waiting and worrying. Max had come to terms with the reality of his chosen profession and developed certain mind tricks to help him cope. The memorization game was one such tactic.

By midmorning, a pattern emerged in the traffic. Two tall and capable-looking men had made repeated trips by the butcher shop. Two vehicles had also made multiple trips down the road. One was a beaten-down van, lacking hubcaps and wearing a large amount of rust around its wheel wells. The second vehicle was a dilapidated Volkswagen with a bent front fender that reminded him of the car his sister had driven when they were teens.

The presence of the vehicles made Max think through the various possibilities. Why would the butcher shop be under surveillance? Maybe the better question was, why was Max under surveillance? Did it mean Anatoly had called in Max's visit to someone? How deeply was his father's old friend involved? Where did Anatoly's allegiances lie? Max thought of the brand-new television in Anatoly's living room. On his way out, Max had peeked in the garage and seen a new Mercedes gleaming in the dusky light. Somewhere, Anatoly was getting money.

Max left some rubles on the table and ducked through the cafe's service door. He cut through the small kitchen, finding it empty. Next to the back door, a white baker's jacket and a wool cap hung on a peg. Max grabbed the jacket and put it on, then shoved the cap on his head, pulling it down over his ears before stepping out the back door. Outside, the rain had stopped, but the alley was slick with water. He turned out of the side street and made a pass in front of the cafe. As he walked by the vacant storefront he kept his head down, but noticed a camera lens poking from a gap in the tarpaulins that covered the window. He kept walking, found his car, then took a meandering route back to his hotel, looking for signs of additional surveillance. He saw none.

TWELVE

Minsk, Belarus

Cezar peered through the viewfinder of the digital camera fixed to the tripod in front of him. He could see the butcher shop's facade in high definition. The shopkeeper was waiting on a heavyset *babushka* with a dingy scarf covering her head. For a moment, Cezar imagined his target in disguise as a stooped babushka and chuckled to himself. He watched as the old woman stretched up to place bills on top of the display case. Then, Cezar's view was blurred as a figure walked in front of the camera. When the picture came back, the old woman was making her way down the front steps.

For the hundredth time, he checked his sidearm. It was a customized Walther P99 with an attached silencer. Cezar's orders were to shoot to kill on sight, and knowing this was a high-value target, he wanted to be in the right place at the right time.

He drained the dregs of his coffee. Black grounds

remained behind in the Styrofoam cup. Next to him, his partner Andre snored gently in a folding aluminum chair. Andre cradled a silenced Makarov pistol in his lap. Andre, Cezar knew, thought this was a dead-end gig, but he preferred to think positively. He guessed the target would appear that night, or perhaps the following night at the latest. He was patient – it was one of the secrets to his success.

Cezar got up and fussed with the coffeemaker until a stream of black liquid started filling the round glass pot. He slid the pot out from under the stream and replaced it with his Styrofoam cup, watched the cup slowly fill, then quickly moved the pot back under the stream. He added healthy doses of sugar and powdered creamer until it was the color of light mud. He sipped it, approved, then resumed watching through the viewfinder, patiently waiting to spring his trap.

———

Max heaved on the folding shovel and levered a chunk of dirt from the floor of the butcher shop's basement. Sweat dripped from his brow and he had to constantly readjust his headlamp. A thin, bright beam of light shone on his work area. The southeast corner of the butcher shop's basement had deep holes dug in a grid radiating from the corner. So far, Max had found nothing. Dust covered his face and clothes and dust particles hung in the beam of the headlamp.

He'd put the rest of the daylight to good use. Back at the hotel, he'd taken a long hot shower and eaten a full meal. He'd visited a camping store, then found the department of urban planning and used an old spy technique to get the blueprints of the butcher shop: he flirted shamelessly with the young, dark-haired clerk, telling her he planned to make an offer to buy the building, and wanted to confirm the square footage. Would she be a doll and fetch him the blueprints and a copy of the deed? She had smiled at him and returned a few minutes later with the documents.

His objective had been to make sure the building had a basement, as Anatoly indicated. If there was no basement, he would know Anatoly had sold him out. But what he found made him smile. Before he'd seen the blueprints, his options had been to return to the butcher shop days later and hope the surveillance had petered out, or take out the surveillance team. Neither option was appealing.

The blueprints, however, had offered him a third choice. Posing as a grocery store customer, he pretended he needed the bathroom, then ducked down the stairs to the basement of the grocery store. There, he found the double door that had been clearly marked on the blueprints. Oddly, the basement door between the grocery and the butcher shop was well maintained, with the hinges oiled and the lock in good working order. A few seconds with his lock picks had gotten him into the butcher-shop basement.

Now, he moved back to the corner of the basement and dug the spade into the first hole, making it larger and deeper. He worked quickly and steadily, perspiration dripping down his forehead from the post-rain humidity. His back was stiff and his hands were caked with dirt. He moved on to the second hole, expanding the width and depth, tossing the dirt far to his left. The pile was growing larger, and Max was starting to think he was on a wild goose chase. He'd give it another thirty minutes of searching before quitting. He moved to the third hole, and kept digging.

As he dug into the fourth hole, his spade hit something hard and unyielding. He began clearing dirt from the top of a large, wooden slab with the spade, then dug out a trough around the edges. A large box emerged from the dirt as he worked. Finally, he was able to pry the box loose.

It was about two feet long by a foot high and a foot deep, resembling the many wooden boxes of wine bottles stacked in his wine cellar at the club. There were handles on either end made from rope. He brushed away dirt, half expecting to see a coat of arms from a wine producer in the southern Rhone River Valley. Instead, he saw Russian letters indicating the box had once been used to carry hand grenades. He stepped back, stretched his back, then squatted down on his haunches. Something was making him hesitate, but he couldn't put his finger on it.

A small padlock hung from the box's latch. Ignoring his misgivings, Max removed a thin strip of metal from his wallet and opened the lock with a deft movement of his wrist. He pried at the lid with his tactical knife. Gradually it opened, and a musty smell wafted up from the darkened interior. He angled his headlamp to illuminate the inside of the box. The first thing he saw was a pistol. The dull grey metal glinted in the light from the headlamp. The pistol was an older-model Makarov. Max picked it up, checked the action, and found it oiled and in perfect condition. He slid out the magazine and saw it was loaded with eight hollow-point bullets. The gun had been sitting on top of stacks of papers and documents held together with rubber bands.

He pocketed the gun, then rifled through the rest of the box's contents. There were six packets of documents. Each packet was topped with a passport, and contained various credentials and credit cards. He thumbed one of the passports open. It showed a picture of his father as a younger

man, and was filled with stamps from travel around Eastern
Europe. The name on the passport read Nikolay Rostov.
Max thumbed through a few others, finding similar pictures
of his father, all with different names. Each document in the
packet matched the name in the passport. He tossed the
identifications aside and found stacks of cash in the bottom
of the box. There were piles of euros, straps of US dollars,
and stacks of Japanese yen. He fanned through them, esti-
mating there to be about 100,000 euros in total. He set the
stacks of currencies on the ground and peered into the box
with his headlamp. It was empty save for a single envelope,
yellowed from time, tucked into a corner. He plucked it
from the box. It was unadorned with any writing, stamps, or
address. The rear flap was unsealed.

He paused and looked at the envelope. So far, he'd only
found what he'd expected to find. For all of Max's childhood, his father had been like a god to him. The man had
seemed all-powerful, with a high position in the KGB,
worshiped by his staff, respected by his peers, and feared by
his enemies. Max grew up wanting to be just like him.
When Max had left Belarus to live in Paris, his father had
been supportive, encouraging him to experience *the enemy*,
as he'd put it. *Go, Mikhail, learn the enemy and then return
home and we'll put that knowledge to work,* he had said.
Now, by delving into the old man's past, Max realized he
was in danger of uncovering something that might tarnish
his love and admiration.

Then a thought occurred to him. If he didn't delve into
his father's past, he'd never know why his parents had been
killed. His sister and young Alex would never know the
truth, and perhaps they'd never be safe. Max realized that
whatever he was to uncover along the trail of his parent's
killer would be necessary to ensure their safety and protec-

tion. Max felt the outside of the envelope. It was faded from time and had started to turn brittle. Through the paper, he could feel the outline of something flat and square, but thick and pliable. He needed to put Alex and Arina's well-being ahead of his own emotional comfort. Whatever he was to discover would be worth the anguish if it helped save their lives.

Still he hesitated. Was this something he wanted to see?

THIRTEEN

Minsk, Belarus

The Stranger sat hunched behind the wheel of his rented white Hyundai. He'd chosen the nondescript vehicle to blend into his surroundings, but he detested the tinny whine of the small engine and the plastic interior. During moments of inaction, he found himself yearning for the thunderous V8 engine in the 1965 Pontiac GTO he kept under a dust cover in his garage. Other times, he wondered how his college-age children were doing, but that thought was rare.

The evening had given way to a murky darkness, and he could just barely make out the front of the butcher shop. He glanced to the left, seeing a flash of light emerge from behind the sheets that covered the vacant store window. It looked like the light from a match or a lighter. The satellite phone balanced on his knee buzzed with an incoming call. He pushed the receive button, then waited for the blinking red light to indicate a secure connection.

"Yes," he said once the red light shone steady.

"Status?" the female voice barked at him. The Stranger didn't mind the terse order. If there was anything his boss was good at, it was efficiency. No energy was ever wasted, no irrelevant words were used. The Stranger found it refreshing.

"He's still in the basement of the butcher shop," he said. "Not clear what he's doing, but he's got company. A team of four surveillance types. Two in a shop across the street and two in a van watching the back. Might be KGB, might not be. Not clear if they were here waiting for him, or if they were watching the butcher shop and he simply stumbled into their trap."

The line was quiet for a moment. Then, "What's he been doing all day?"

"He visited Burov early this morning. Then he scouted out the butcher shop. He spent the morning at a hotel, then visited the Office of Urban Planning this afternoon. Then he killed time at the hotel before returning here just as the grocery store was closing."

"So the butcher shop was definitely his destination?"

"Yes, the clerk at the urban planning office confirmed he was looking at the shop. He pretended to be interested in buying it. Those clerks must make almost no money. It only took a few rubles to get her to open up. According to the shop's blueprints, there is a door between the basement of the grocery and the butcher shop."

"Stay with him for now," her voice came back.

"I think we should bring him in," the Stranger said. "It looks like he's getting hot. If something goes down, I may not have the opportunity or resources to intervene."

There was silence on the other end. He knew his boss was calculating a hundred different permutations in her head, a skill he knew very few others possessed at her level. During these moments, he knew to keep quiet. Once, she had likened it to the sport of baseball, when the team's manager had to evaluate an endless array of odds and statistics to know when to replace the pitcher or insert a pinch runner or batter. His boss could easily manage in the majors.

Finally, she issued her decision. "No. Leave him in play for now. Let's watch his next move. But be ready."

The line went dead.

FOURTEEN

Minsk, Belarus

"Hold the gun with both hands," his father instructed, "like this." Andrei Asimov, perhaps Belarus' most famous spy, positioned Max's hands so that the thumb on his left hand rested along the side of the barrel, pointing forward, instead of over the thumb of his right hand. The metal of the gun felt cold and heavy in his eight-year-old hands. But it also felt comfortable. Max's hands were large for his age, and the small 9 mm Makarov fit them perfectly.

"That's so your left thumb isn't hurt from the gun's recoil," his father explained. "Now leave your finger off the trigger until you're ready to shoot." His father gently moved Max's right index finger so it rested alongside the barrel.

They were at an outdoor range, in a field behind a farmhouse owned by the Belarusian KGB. "When you move your finger to the trigger, do so intentionally," his father said. "Then put the tip of your finger on the trigger, like so." The elder Asimov guided Max's finger into the trigger guard, and positioned it with a slight bend, so the pad of Max's finger rested on the trigger. "When you pull the trigger, don't yank or squeeze. Simply pull backward. This will help prevent the gun from jerking to the side. Over time, you'll come to learn the recoil of the gun and begin to master it. But for now, just get the feel of it. Fire when ready."

Earlier that morning, Max's father had taken him out to the garage and handed him a box wrapped in silver paper. When Max had opened it, he was staring at the brand-new Makarov. The gun rested in a velvet case, the dark brown plastic grip surrounded by sinister black metal. He'd squealed in delight and hugged his father with as big a bear hug as he could manage around his father's barrel-sized chest.

Max's hands trembled, but he felt powerful. He didn't want to disappoint his father or feel shame by missing the target. He squeezed his left eye shut, lined up the muzzle sight with the rear sight and tried to aim at the target that was waving in the breeze about seven meters downfield.

"Just breathe easy," his father's baritone voice came from behind him. "When you breathe out, make your mind calm. Then pull the trigger."

Max did as instructed. He tried to let everything go from his mind, held his breath, and pulled the trigger. The loud pop surprised him and the gun jerked in his hand. On instinct, he forced the gun back down, breathed out, then fired another shot. He fired until the slide locked out, then he laid the gun on the table in front of him, just as he'd been taught. Max squinted down the range, trying to discern whether he'd even hit the target, but his father's broad back hid the piece of paper from view. When he returned, his father presented the target to Max with a wide, proud grin.

Two of the eight shots had gone through the center of the bullseye.

"You're a natural," his father said.

Max felt on top of the world.

Max shook his head to clear the memory. He was still squatting in the butcher shop's basement, holes in the earthen floor all around him, the go-box empty. Max looked at the envelope in his hand. No matter what he uncovered about his father, he decided, nothing would change the love and the pride he felt for the man. Nothing would take away the things his father had taught him, the values he'd imparted. Max thumbed the envelope open.

Inside was a single Polaroid photograph. He pulled the picture from the envelope, holding it gently between his thumb and forefinger. It was faded with time, with a natural patina of yellows and browns. The picture showed a woman wearing only a man's button-up shirt loose around her, sitting on a bed. The shirt was held closed with a single button down around her navel, revealing a deep décolletage. Her long bare legs were stretched out to one side and she leaned back on one arm. She had a coy grin on her face. Max peered closely at the woman's face. She was beautiful in a way commonly associated with Western models in the 1970s. High cheekbones, full lips, and almond-shaped eyes. Her smile displayed an even row of full, white teeth. Her hair was full and wavy, parted in the middle. The woman was beautiful, and was most definitely not his mother.

———

Max paused at the grocery store's rear exit. He'd been in the butcher shop's basement for over two hours. He had no way of knowing whether there was a greeting party waiting for him outside.

Behind him, the dark, cavernous room around him was piled high with pallets of grocery supplies. The photo was tucked into his pocket. In his left hand, he carried a small duffle bag containing the cash, his father's fake identifications, and the Makarov. It was the Makarov that had triggered the memory of the first weapons lesson from his father. From that auspicious start, Max had gone on to break every record in the KGB books for pistol target shooting. He could hit the center of a bullseye with a pistol from thirty meters with ease. Most of his pistol records at the academy, officially known as the Andropov Institute, were still unbroken.

In his right hand, he carried the SIG. It was un-silenced, and he hoped he wouldn't have to use it. The memory, combined with his parents' death, made him realize how little he actually knew about his father. Sure, his childhood had been spent learning tradecraft with the man, but during that time, Andrei Asimov had never revealed anything about himself to his son. His memories of those years, Max realized, were filled with a certain ideal of his father – a loving but forbidding hulk of a man who taught his son everything he knew about spycraft, but who was otherwise nonexistent. A workaholic, his father would disappear for months at a time, only to return with more lessons and discipline. Invariably, when kids at school heard his last name, they treated Max with a reverence reserved for those they feared. It wasn't until later that Max learned how important his father was in the KGB.

Max held the SIG close to his chest and pushed on the door. It swung open to his left on squeaky hinges. The spring rains had started again, and the pavement shone in the dim moonlight. He looked to his right and spotted the front of a dark blue van, half visible in the mouth of the alley. The van's wheel well was rusted out, matching the van Max had spotted earlier that day. Nothing moved in the alleyway.

He realized he had two choices: Leave the relative safety of the doorway and make a left, away from the van, trusting his abilities to shake his surveillance once he reached his vehicle, or exit the front of the grocery store and take his chances with surveillance there. He thought briefly of the roof, but realized he'd not scouted it. He didn't want to find himself in a dead end. Keeping the pistol alongside his leg, he stepped into the rain and turned left.

Before he'd gone five paces, he heard footsteps on the cobblestone behind him moving fast. Alarm in his throat, he calculated the distance between the grocery store and the van's location at the end of the alleyway at about fifty meters, beyond the scope of even Max's pistol skills. The sudden movement meant either the runners wanted him alive, or they were closing the distance to give themselves more accuracy.

Just ahead of him, looming in the darkness, was a large metal dumpster on wheels. The mouth of the alley was still another thirty meters past the dumpster. He stole a quick look behind him and saw two dark shadows sprinting toward him, each holding what looked like a gun in their outstretched hands. Max ducked behind the dumpster, and felt the air displace next to his cheek as a bullet sang by.

Max peeked out from behind the dumpster and brought the SIG up. He estimated the two men had closed to within twenty meters and were still moving fast. In a dry pistol range with good lighting, this would be an easy shot for

Max. In the field, aiming at moving targets with cold rain on his face, it would be more difficult. He braced his arm against the wet metal of the dumpster and squeezed off four rounds. The sound of the un-silenced pistol reverberated in the alley. One of the figures went down; the other kept coming. Shots plunked into the side of the trash dumpster. Max concentrated, let his mind relax and his breathing slow, then pulled the trigger twice more in rapid succession. He saw the second figure stagger and pitch forward.

Max left the safety of the dumpster and walked to the first body. He rolled him over and peered at the man's features. Caucasian with a flattop haircut, the dead man didn't look Russian or Belarusian. Max though maybe he looked Serbian or Croat, or some other southern Slavic ethnicity. Max searched him quickly, and found nothing in his pockets.

The second attacker's body was another ten meters down the alley. Knowing the shots would draw attention, Max abandoned the second body and took off at a trot down the alley, away from the location of the van. When he reached the street, he slowed to a quick walk and took a right, toward his car. He kept the SIG down along his leg and kept watch behind him while he moved, but he saw no additional pursuers.

As he pulled away from the curb, he found himself amazed at the brazen attack in public. The game had just changed. He was no longer simply being watched, he was being actively targeted. Maybe someone didn't want him rummaging through his father's life. Who was watching, and what were they afraid Max would find?

He took a circuitous route back to his hotel, simultaneously lost in thought and attuned to everything going on around him. For the last few years, his relationship with his father had grown distant and cold. He realized again just how little he knew. How ironic, Max thought, that perhaps the only way to discover his parents' killers would be to learn about his father in ways he'd never known him when he was alive.

He pulled the Polaroid of the woman from his pocket. It was his only lead. It was clearly an intimate moment, shared between the photographer and the woman. Had his father been the photographer? Was the woman his lover? Clearly, his father treasured the photo and wanted to keep it secret, otherwise why keep it hidden? Maybe the trail of his father's secrets started with this woman, whoever she was.

FIFTEEN

Undisclosed Location

Nathan Abrams' mobile phone buzzed in his pocket. Stepping back from the crowd of parents around him, he pulled out the phone and looked at the screen, then answered with his characteristic annoyance. "What is it?"

"He slipped through our fingers, sir." It was Wing, his second in command – a woman he loved like his own daughter. Seeing her name pop up on the screen was the only reason he'd answered the phone.

In that instant, a cheer erupted from the crowd and Nathan looked up to see his son peel away from the soccer goal, fists pumping in the air. The goaltender batted the ball from the net in frustration. Nathan threw his arms in the air, chiding himself for missing the goal. His son would ask him if he'd gotten it on video and Nathan would have to admit he hadn't. He flashed a thumbs-up at his son, who was looking over to the sidelines for his father while running back for the kickoff. Then Abrams turned away from the group of parents lining the pitch and put the phone back up to his ear. He was vaguely aware of his bodyguards behind him, but knew he wasn't the only father visiting the exclusive prep school who brought his own security.

"Who?" He was having difficulty making the transition from the soccer game back to work.

"Asimov," came the reply.

The job came rushing back to him. "Fuck," he said, rather too loudly. Several of the parents standing on the sidelines gave him a disapproving glance. He moved further away from the group. "Details," he barked.

"Based on Anatoly Burov's call, we had the butcher shop staked out with a team of four. Two covered the front entrance, two covered the rear."

"I know that part. Skip ahead," Nathan interrupted.

"At ten oh four p.m., the rear team saw a man step from the back of the butcher shop, and was able to identify the man as Asimov. He carried a duffle bag in one hand. He'd taken no steps to disguise himself. Asimov turned the opposite direction from our surveillance team. Both members of the rear team exited their van and pursued. Here is where the details break down. Cezar heard four shots, and found his two men dead in the alley. Asimov got the drop on them. Cezar elected to clean up the scene rather than give chase."

Nathan groaned, but grudgingly admitted Cezar had made the correct decision.

Wing continued with her debrief. "After securing the two dead men in the van, Cezar entered the butcher shop through the rear door by force and performed a search. In the basement, they found holes dug in the dirt floor, and a wooden box that looked like it had been unearthed from one of the holes. The box was empty. The assumption is that whatever Asimov found in the box had been transferred to the duffle bag, and is now in his possession."

"Fuck," Nathan said again. "Have we interrogated Burov yet?"

"A team is on the way to retrieve him," Wing said. "We need to find out why he sent Asimov to that butcher shop. We need to know what he was looking for."

"Precisely," Nathan said, knowing Wing would be way ahead of him on the next stages of the operation. There was a reason he considered her his best operative. "What next?"

"Whatever is in that box may help us find Asimov," she replied. "So we start there. I've also got the FSB watching airports, train stations, bus stations, and the like. If Asimov leaves town, we'll pick him up. FSB is monitoring police activity, as well. If he gets so much as a parking ticket, we'll know and be on him. We'll get him, sir."

"Fucking find him. You have forty-eight hours. I need this mess cleaned up. It's getting uncomfortable."

"I understand, sir. We're on it."

He hung up the phone, and turned back to the game. He saw his son substituting out, and cursed. The only thing he hated more than failure was when the job took him away from being with his son.

SIXTEEN

Minsk, Belarus

Max sat in his rental car and tapped on the keys of a small laptop computer. On the passenger seat next to him was a grey box about two inches high and six inches square, connected to the laptop via a USB cable. The box was called a Software Defined Radio, or SDR for short, an expensive piece of gear he'd picked up earlier that evening from a storage locker he'd left behind when he moved to Paris. He was parked across the street from Anatoly's house. From his vantage point, Max could see the blue metallic sticker of a home security company stuck to the front window. The sticker hadn't been there the last time Max had visited. It was one a.m., and the light in Burov's bedroom had gone out two hours ago.

A few more taps on the keyboard, and Max had what he needed. The SDR was designed to pick up and transmit radio signals. Home security systems sent and received radio signals from various contact points around the home like windows and doors. If a signal was broken, the contact point would send a signal to the transceiver, which would then notify the homeowner and the security firm. What most homeowners didn't know was that the signals were often not encrypted. Max had just programmed the SDR to send fake signals to Anatoly's transceiver, so when he picked the door lock and pushed the door open, the alarm would be tricked and fail to trigger. He left the grey box on the passenger seat and walked across the street and around the house to the back door. Thirty seconds later, he was in Anatoly's kitchen, the alarm system silent.

Max stole up the stairs, taking each one slowly, peering closely at each step with the thin beam from a small Maglite. He didn't want to trip a wire connected to a grenade. That was an old KGB trick, but both the steps and hallway were devoid of traps. Finally, he stood in Anatoly's bedroom. The air stank of cigarette smoke and he could see a mostly empty bottle of vodka on the nightstand next to the overflowing ashtray. Anatoly was sleeping on his back, snoring loudly. The sheets had been kicked to the floor, revealing a pair of new-looking pajama bottoms. Max walked closer to the bed, removed the SIG from his pocket, and inserted the barrel into Anatoly's open mouth.

The older man's teeth clamped down on the metal and he awakened, sputtering. A panicked look came over his face.

"Good morning, Anatoly," Max said. "Show me your hands."

A dark anger crept over Anatoly's face, but he brought his hands up and held them next to his face.

"Where's the gun?"

The old man gestured with his left hand toward the pillow next to him.

"Toss it. Slowly."

Anatoly fished a shotgun from under the pillow and tossed it onto the floor. Max kicked it under the bed.

"Cheap alarm systems are useless." Max removed the gun from Anatoly's mouth.

"Fuck, Mikhail," Anatoly sputtered. "Can't you just ring the bell like a normal person?"

"There was surveillance on the butcher shop," Max said. He kept the pistol pointed directly at the older man's face.

"Don't know anything about that," Anatoly said. Max could tell he was seething inside.

"You're lying, Anatoly. You've been lying to me since the beginning."

"I didn't lie about the go-box. Did you find it?"

"No one except you knew I'd be there. I doubt the KGB would be staking out a random butcher shop for no reason. Is your house bugged, or are you lying to me?"

"Why do you think it was the KGB?" Anatoly asked.

"Who else would it be? Moscow Rules, right?" The Moscow Rules had been developed by Western spy agencies to contend with the fact that the KGB was particularly adept at surveillance. The number-one rule: Assume you are always being heard and watched. Max used to laugh about it, but now they seemed to apply to him.

Anatoly said nothing. Max knew he was at an impasse. If it were anyone else, he'd start breaking fingers until he got the truth. But Anatoly was an old friend. They shared history. They'd spent holidays together. Anatoly was family.

"They also took shots at me, Anatoly. Whoever it was tried to kill me." Max watched closely for any emotion. He saw none.

When Max was younger, his father and Anatoly had been inseparable. Anatoly had attended all of Max's childhood milestones, from baptism to his high school graduation. When Max had started smoking in grade school, it had been Anatoly who had provided the cigarettes. They'd shared many bottles of vodka over the years. Now Max was faced with the choice of hurting his father's oldest friend or giving Anatoly a pass, hoping the man would eventually confide in him.

"We go way back. Don't make me escalate this. You set me up to have me killed. Why?"

Then Max saw moisture in the old man's eyes. Anatoly stayed silent for a moment, then pleaded with Max. "I wouldn't do that, Mikhail. I wouldn't do that to my own godson."

At the reminder that he was Anatoly's godson, Max paused, resigned. He already felt some compassion for the old man. His wife and kids had left him. It made Max guess Anatoly was in some kind of compromised position.

"Fine. Don't tell me. But know this: I will find out with or without your help. I will find out what happened to my parents, and I'm going to find out who is trying to kill me. When I do, if I learn that you had anything to do with it, I'm going to come back and make you wish you'd helped me. This is your chance, Anatoly. Tell me what you know."

Anatoly said nothing. Then Max saw a tear roll down the man's face. In that moment, he knew Anatoly wouldn't, or perhaps couldn't, reveal anything.

Max pulled the picture of the woman from his pocket and pushed it close to Anatoly's face. There was enough moonlight coming in the open window to illuminate the image. "Who is this?"

Anatoly blinked at the picture, unable to hide his recognition. "Where did you get that?"

"It was in the go-box," Max said. "Who is she and why did my father have her picture hidden?"

Anatoly seemed surprised. "Really? In the go-box? Did you find anything else?"

"Just cash, some fake identification, and a pistol," Max said. "That's it. Did you expect anything else would be in there?"

Anatoly was silent for a moment. Then he said, "You never know."

Max looked at him. Anatoly was now perspiring freely, even in the chilly room. "You're a shitty liar."

"Fuck you, Max," Anatoly said. "You have no idea what you're dealing with. I'm nothing. Do what you want with me. I don't care anymore. But just know that you're treading on very thin ice. You get in too far, and I will not be able to help you."

"What do you mean?"

"I can't. I've already said too much. Get the fuck out of my house, and stop coming back here. The next time you try to break in, you're going to walk into a shotgun blast to your face."

Max considered that. Anatoly's confession had at least confirmed Max's suspicions. He didn't want to put the old man in more of a compromised position than he was already in. He decided to focus on the girl. "I'll leave as soon as you tell me who she is," he said, pushing the picture at Anatoly's face again.

Anatoly was silent, but his eyes shifted around like he was calculating odds, or maybe deciding how much to reveal. Max could see the gears turning fast. Finally he spoke. "Her name is Julia Meier. She's your father's – sorry, *was* your father's mistress."

The words hit Max like a freight train. His mind spun for a minute. "Mistress?" He unknowingly took a step backward. Anatoly shifted in the bed and Max quickly brought the gun up again. Anatoly stopped cold, up on his elbows.

"Max, put the fucking gun down, for God's sake," he said.

"She's German?" Max asked, lowering the gun but keeping it pointed at Anatoly's torso.

"Swiss, actually," Anatoly said.

"Jesus," Max said. He didn't know what was more shocking: the fact that his father had a mistress, or the fact that she was European. "How long was this going on?"

"A long time," Anatoly said. "On and off. Your father once said she was his one true love."

"Where is she now?" Max asked.

"I don't know," Anatoly said.

Max fixed him with a stare.

"I swear, Max. I don't know. Your father hadn't spoken of her in years. I had forgotten she even existed." Then Anatoly's face changed when he realized Max's angle. "Don't go looking for her, Max. She doesn't know anything about any of this. Just leave her out of it."

Max backed away from the bed, holding the gun on Anatoly. He knew he'd gotten everything he was going to get here. "Remember my warning," he said from the doorway. "If I find out you're involved in this, the next visit won't be so pleasant." Then he moved away from the door, into the hallway, and down the stairs.

In the distance, he could hear Anatoly yell, "Come back here again, Mikhail, and you'll get a face full of buckshot!"

SEVENTEEN

Minsk, Belarus

Max pulled away from the curb in the rented Skoda. In the trunk, he had the overnight bag he'd brought with him from Paris and the duffle containing his father's money, identification, and the pistol. He stowed the SIG on the passenger seat, under a hand towel from the hotel.

As he drove, he rolled down the window and lit a cigarette, in clear violation of the car's rental policy. He doubted Hertz would see the car any time soon anyway. Out of habit, he'd used a fake identification and an untraceable credit card to rent the car. He was on his way out of Minsk, and the only safe way was to drive. He assumed airports and train stations would all be watched, and he didn't want anyone knowing where he was headed. Once on the Beltway, he found Route P1 and pointed the car southwest, keeping to the speed limit. As he drove, he tried to sort everything out in his head.

His parents had been killed by a large but crude bomb made from the same materials as the Moscow apartment bombings back in 1999. RDX was an explosive similar to TNT that was widely available in Russia. In 1999, four apartment buildings had been destroyed with the same material, killing 293 people and injuring 651. Also similar to his parents' death, the apartment bombings had been blamed on the Chechens. Despite Dedov's denials, Max knew from conversations with his father that the bombings had been the work of the KGB to build support for a certain Russian presidential candidate. Not long after the bombings, Russia had attacked Chechnya, and the famously nationalistic Russian population had unanimously elected the candidate. There were too many parallels to his parents' death to ignore the connections. The FSB in Moscow, or else the KGB in Belarus, had to be involved. The question was whether they'd been the driving force, or just an accomplice.

Max flicked the cigarette butt out the window, then pulled into an all-night service station. He filled up with petrol and bought a large, black coffee in a Styrofoam cup and three packs of Belomorkanal cigarettes. Just the sight of the famous Russian brand brought a brief smile to his face. The legendary filter-less smokes were some of the strongest in the world. He dumped the packs on the passenger seat and sipped the coffee as he pulled back out onto the road.

Assuming the FSB's involvement was true, what had his father done to anger them? His father had practically bled Russian red, devoting his life to the protection of the Soviet empire. The list of his father's accomplishments on behalf of the KGB was legendary. As a young man, his father had made a name for himself by successfully recruiting a West

German software executive, who had gladly sold the secrets that formed the basis of most of Moscow's banking software. This software had also allowed Moscow to tap into the banking systems of many Western European countries and steal their financial secrets. Many of those backdoors were still in place today.

His father's nationalistic pride made the revelation of the mistress all that more puzzling. It wasn't the existence of the mistress that perplexed him. Many men in power in Russia and Belarus kept a woman on the side. It was her nationality, however, that troubled Max. A Swiss? A Western European? The father he knew would never have consorted with a Westerner, much less fallen in love with one. It simply wasn't done where Max's father had come from. Sleeping with a Western woman was cheating on his country, and that was something Max wouldn't have thought possible of his father. Once again, the specter of uncovering his father's true nature concerned him. He flicked the butt out the window, then took a deep breath of the fresh countryside air.

By the time he approached the Belarusian border with Poland, Max had downed four large cups of coffee and smoked his way through one of the packs of cigarettes. At the city of Brest, still on the Belarus side, he exited the highway, then threaded his way through the tiny hamlet. It was getting close to five a.m., and the city was starting to wake up. Delivery lorries bustled through empty streets and Max could see a faint light on the eastern horizon.

He ditched the car in the parking lot of a rundown strip mall, took pains to wipe down the interior and the exterior door handles and trunk latch, then hitched up his bags and started walking. He welcomed the moderate exercise after being stuck in the car for four hours, and made good time down the main road into Brest.

Once in the Old Town section, he made his way to a small inn called the Dancing Boar. He slipped through the front door and found himself in a darkened common room. With a knowledge of the interior from years of experience, he headed toward the back room, then quietly roused the proprietor. After the rotund man gave Max a long bear hug, he pulled back and, with tears in his eyes, conveyed his condolences for Max's father's death. Max sat with the proprietor for a short time, reminiscing about his father, then left him with a large stack of euros. After trying unsuccessfully to refuse the money, the proprietor led Max down a set of stairs into the larder. There he pushed aside barrels of flour and crates of dried sundries, and pulled open a hidden door. With a final word of thanks, Max descended into the tunnel.

It was one of the hundreds of tunnels that had been constructed throughout the old Soviet Union, designed to make transit between countries by the KGB's spy network easier. After trudging almost a kilometer in the dark, Max emerged into the basement of a pub. Not by coincidence, this pub was run by the Dancing Boar's proprietor's son-in-law. Max left another large stack of euros with a protesting young man, then traded another stack for the man's car. Max let himself be fed a massive breakfast of steaming eggs and sausage and fresh biscuits by the young man's earnest wife, then waved farewell. Once back on the highway, he opened another pack of Belomorkanals, lit a smoke, and pointed the car west toward Warsaw.

Julia Meier. He let the name roll around in his mind. Both Julia and Meier were common Swiss names. Almost too common, he thought. He wondered if perhaps the name was fake. Maybe it was an assumed identity, or perhaps Anatoly had been lying about the name. It was probably a cover, Max reasoned.

He wondered how his father and Julia had met. Certainly, his father had spent a lot of time out of Belarus. But for a relationship like that to blossom, Julia would likely have been living in Minsk. What kind of profession would bring a woman from Switzerland to Minsk? Perhaps she was married, and her husband was in banking, stationed in Minsk for an overseas assignment. Or maybe she was in the spy business. Maybe his father had recruited her, turned her, and was both running her and sleeping with her. It certainly wouldn't be the first time.

Max knew one thing for certain: finding Julia Meier was his only lead. Whatever her connection had been with his father, she would be able to shed some light on his father's activities. Max chewed on that as he sped west, toward Frederic Chopin International Airport in Warsaw.

To find Julia, Max needed access to resources he didn't have in Minsk. That was the reason for the late-night departure out of Belarus. When he reached the airport, he left the car in long-term parking and put the keys under the rear bumper where its owner could find them. He tossed the two guns into a waste bin, hiked across the massive flat lot to the terminal, and disappeared into a sea of international travelers. He was betting the reach of the KGB didn't extend to Poland, a country that was desperately trying to leave its Soviet roots behind. Before going through security and passport control, he found a DSL office in the terminal, shoved the duffle with the cash and identities into a box, and arranged for the box to be shipped to Della, his faithful club manager in Paris.

Finally, he settled into first class and accepted a glass of

Champagne from the perfectly-coifed Air France stew-
ardess. It felt good to be going home, but he also felt pensive
about the price he might have to pay for the information he
needed.

EIGHTEEN

Undisclosed Location

Nathan stood in his office, arms crossed, seething, attempting unsuccessfully to hide his irritation. Wing stood next to him, arms also crossed, her brow furrowed in anger. They were both watching a large monitor mounted on the wall of his office, and listening to the two men on the screen talking. One of the men was in charge. The other looked like he was on the verge of a breakdown.

Nathan's mind wandered for a moment, and he considered his diminutive protégé. She was much shorter than him, wore her black hair cut at straight angles, and was dressed in a tailored suit. She looked like a trader on the Hong Kong Stock Exchange. The grey wool hugged her tiny frame and a white blouse was open at the neck. For a moment, his anger was replaced by a sense of pride.

Ten years ago, Wing had been a destitute but promising pupil at Malaysia's state-run university. An orphan since birth, she'd been in and out of institutions and foster homes her entire youth. She'd worked hard in school and had taken on multiple jobs just to afford the tuition. She'd appeared on his radar through a scholarship program Nathan's firm sponsored, targeted at developing the best and the brightest from the poorest families. The program was international, run by a governing body chaired by Nathan himself, and extremely competitive. The scholarship's unpublished objective, of course, was to find candidates worthy of becoming operatives at Nathan's firm.

He had adopted Wing as a daughter, bonding emotionally with her and recognizing her potential early on. Now, he was grooming her to become his successor. She was wickedly smart, tough as nails, and ruthless, just like himself. He figured he'd eventually die from his line of work. He wanted to leave the company that he had worked so hard to build in good hands. This was why he'd put Wing on this assignment. After Ivan's screw-ups, he needed his trusted lieutenant to get it cleaned up. Nathan's own life depended on it.

He knew Wing never failed. This operation had been an anomaly from the start, and Nathan was kicking himself for not putting her on it from the beginning. From the eccentricity of his client to the prominence of the target to the scope of the job, it was fraught with complications. For the hundredth time, he cursed himself for accepting the job at all.

She elbowed him, her arm hitting his hip. "Did you hear that?"

Nathan's mind snapped back to the present.

"No, what'd he say?" The monitor showed two men in a small, cramped room. The room had one table and one chair, both bolted to the floor. The man in the chair had his hands on the table, and looked like he was under a great deal of stress. His white hair was in disarray, and he kept trying to flatten it with shaking hands. His face was red and puffy. Fear was evident in his bloodshot eyes. The second man wore suit pants and an Oxford cloth shirt with the sleeves rolled up. He was hunched over the table facing the older man, pounding his fist on the table while he shouted.

"Walk me through it again. Don't leave out any details. I need to know everything."

Nathan and Wing listened as Anatoly Burov told his tale in its entirety. According to Burov, Mikhail Asimov had appeared at his bedside around one a.m. the previous morning and put a gun in his mouth. Asimov had asked about his father. Then showed Anatoly a picture of a woman.

"That he got from the box in the basement of the butcher shop?" the interrogator asked.

"Yes, I told you that," Anatoly said. He looked exasperated, and his white shirt hung open in tatters.

"This fucking guy—" Nathan muttered under his breath.

Wing hushed him.

"And you'll tell me again and again until I say we stop, you got that?" The interrogator stood and paced. "And the photo showed a woman, correct?"

Anatoly nodded his head. Blood dripped from his nose and down his chin.

"Speak up, Burov. The photo showed a woman, correct?"

"Yes," Anatoly said.

"Describe the woman in the photo again for me," the interrogator said.

Anatoly sighed, then rattled off in monotone, as if from memory, "Blonde hair, wavy. Blue eyes. White, straight teeth. Sitting on a bed, legs bare and outstretched, wearing a man's shirt, unbuttoned."

"Right. Now I remember," the interrogator intoned, then turned and faced Anatoly directly. "And you said you didn't recognize her?"

"Correct. I didn't recognize her."

"BULLSHIT!" the interrogator roared, spit flying from his mouth and landing on Anatoly's forehead. "Tell me her name, Burov, or so help me God you'll be rotting in a Siberian gulag before the night is over."

"I swear, I don't know her name," Anatoly said, his voice going up in pitch.

The strike came so fast that even Nathan, who knew it was coming, didn't see it until Anatoly's head rocked to the side. The interrogator was a tall, broad-shouldered man, whose muscles rippled under his shirt and who moved with the grace and dexterity of a midfielder. He grabbed Anatoly by the shirt from across the table, then hit him again with an open-handed slap. When Anatoly straightened, blood was coming from a split lip.

"Things are only going to get worse from here." He pushed Anatoly back into the chair, then cracked his knuckles. "It's going to be a long, painful night for you if you don't tell me the woman's name."

"I don't know what it is," Anatoly said, his voice soft and wavering. "I can't tell you what it is if I don't know it."

The next strike was a close-fisted punch that landed in the middle of Anatoly's face, splitting his nose open. Blood poured from the wound.

Nathan watched, riveted to the screen. He knew that whoever was in that photo must have meant something to the older Asimov, and therefore might mean something to Asimov's son. If they could get the woman's name, they may be able to reach her before Mikhail Asimov did and lay a trap for their target.

An hour later, the captive broke. As soon as the name was uttered from his bloody mouth, Wing was on the phone to her staff.

Find that woman, Nathan knew, and they'd find Asimov. He let a smile touch his lips for the first time in a week.

NINETEEN

Paris, France

Max exited Charles de Gaulle Airport and breathed in the air of his adopted home. He'd come to love everything about the City of Light, from its timeless architecture and its exquisite cuisine to its world class shopping, and even the acrid stench of the air pollution. For some reason, Paris always smelled like a tinge of floor wax and fresh paint. Still, he loved the intimacy of its many neighborhoods, strung together like a patchwork quilt made of silk. He loved the constant flow of red wine, the seductive allure of the city's women, and the languorous way in which Parisians went about their business. An afternoon siesta was as important to the locals as their next bank transaction. In a world that was accelerating toward more gadgets, more money, and more work, Paris was, to Max, a city daring its citizens and visitors alike to take respite from the hubbub of the world and relish its Old World charms.

Max found a cab and, in perfect French, supplied the driver with exact latitude and longitude points, which the turbaned Sikh happily pushed into his GPS unit. They roared away from the curb, found the Autoroute du N, and headed south toward the city center. Max wished he could make a stop at his favorite cafe; he missed the roasted taste of a properly made cafe au lait. Instead, he cracked the window of the cab and basked in the smells of his favorite city.

He thought briefly of his beloved club, La Caravelle, with its dark and steamy interior, the veranda overlooking the Seine, and its patrons, perfectly primped for a sultry after-hours music experience. Then he reminded himself that he was not on a social visit. He was comfortable that his manager had things under control, and he needed to get back to Minsk as soon as possible. Being away from his sister made him nervous. For a moment, Max felt a tinge of sadness for Arina, who now had to raise a young boy on her own. Then he pulled himself out of it and removed his mobile phone. He tapped out a brief text message, and hit send.

Ten minutes later, Max got out of the cab in a quiet warehouse district on the southwest side of the city. He walked down one street, then crossed over another and angled through a trash-filled vacant field before stopping in front of a small door on the side of a large grey building. He stood at the door and looked up into the eye of a bubble-lensed security camera. Then he waited, feeling a mixture of anticipation and dread. Nothing he'd ever gotten from this woman had come for free.

He knew it was useless to try to call her or even arrange for an appointment. She came out of her shell on her own schedule. Normally, Max would contact her via secure email, outlining what he needed and arranging electronic payments to pay her fees. But she was fickle, and Max knew she couldn't be counted on to get back to him in a hurry. Max was one of the privileged few who knew where she lived, and he knew the only way to get her attention in an emergency was to show up unannounced at her home. No matter what it might cost him.

As if on cue, a small speaker inset into the wall crackled and a husky voice came through. "What the fuck, Max? It's Sunday morning for Christ's sake. Why the fuck are you here?"

Max pushed a small white button next to the speaker and said, "I need something. It's urgent. Can I come in?"

There was a pause. For a moment, Max thought he might be turned away. Then the speaker box squawked. "Fuck. Ok. Hold on." Max stood in the sun for ten minutes, hoping he wouldn't regret what he was about to do. Just when he was about to punch the white button again, he heard a metallic click. He pulled the heavy door open and walked through. In the next room, he removed his mobile phone and put it in a locker by the door. Then he left his overnight bag next to the locker, and approached another door and looked up. He raised his arms as if to say to the video camera, *I'm clean*. He knew the drill. The door clicked and he pushed his way in.

Her home was a hermetically sealed, custom-built structure encased in the warehouse. The freestanding building had two floors and was as large as a suburban house. The difference was, her "house" could withstand earthquakes and was built to shield any tracking technology, heat-sensing devices, and other surveillance technology. Max's phone would be useless behind the home's walls.

He walked down a dark corridor until the hallway opened into a large, modern kitchen with every appliance a celebrity chef might want. Standing in the middle of the room, next to an expansive butcher-block island, was his contact. She wore a short, kimono-style robe made from black silk, and was holding a plain white mug. Max could smell the distinct aroma of Ethiopian coffee, and felt his mouth water.

She was known to him only by her code name *Goshawk*. In real life, a goshawk is one of the largest of the bird-eating forest hawks. The fierce raptor bears red eyes, dark grey feathers, and massive talons, presenting a terrifying appearance to its prey. The goshawk is known to eat live prey as large as a duck.

Max's contact presented a similarly terrifying appearance, albeit with a rabid sexual overtone. At almost six feet tall, she was covered from clavicle to toe in artfully drawn tattoos of horrific and bloody battle scenes. The artwork ranged from gory midlevel battles to elegant samurai sword fights.

"Fuck, Max, you look like shit," Goshawk said, regarding him with a smirk. Her hair color varied from purples to oranges to reds to pinks, depending on her mood. Today, it was stark white and arranged over one shoulder.

Max paused a beat. "Been a rough couple of days."

Goshawk reached across the island, a slow elegant movement that was all flowing silk robe and tattooed arm, and handed him a cup of fresh-brewed coffee. He thanked her and sat down on a stool.

"Damn, Max. You need a shower." She made a point of wrinkling her nose, a gesture that Max found both alluring and irritating. "Why don't you tell me what you need and I'll get to work on it while you get cleaned up. I think you still have a drawer, right? Or did I throw it all away?" The smirk returned. It was a look Max had grown used to, but eventually tired of. He felt like it was a mixture between patronization and a joke known only to her. He tossed the picture of Julia Meier onto the table.

With another fluid movement, Goshawk swept up the photo and studied it, then whistled. "She's a beauty, no? Who is she?"

"That's what I need you to find out," Max said.

"Hmm... Got any more information?"

"I'm told her name is Julia Meier, and that's she's Swiss."

"Julia Meier, huh? That's probably the most common name in Switzerland."

"Exactly. But I know someone of your exquisite talents won't have any problem locating her."

"Which of my exquisite talents are you really here for, Max?" Goshawk said, the smirk returning once again.

Max avoided her gaze and sipped his coffee, savoring the rich and slightly charred taste. He wanted to keep the conversation directed at what he needed. His relationship with Goshawk, once a full-blown romantic entanglement, had turned turbulent over the years as Goshawk's appetite for drugs and other extracurriculars had increased. "I need an address, preferably an email and a phone number. And anything else you can dig up."

"Well, aren't we the demanding one," Goshawk said. She dropped the photo into a pocket of her kimono, then pulled a small, flat leather case from the same pocket and slid it across the counter at Max. It was about the size of a passport wallet, and had a zipper around three sides. The leather was well-worn.

Max knew exactly what was inside. This is what he'd been afraid of. "Can't I just pay like a normal customer?"

"Not this time, Max. You're here in the flesh, unannounced, which is convenient. That's the price." She winked. "Now get your ass upstairs and get cleaned up. By the time you're done, I should have something for you." She turned and left the kitchen, leaving behind the scent of lavender and vanilla. Max could hear the graceful sounds of a Tierney Sutton ballad echoing from the hallway as she disappeared. When not running her lucrative computer hacking business, Goshawk dabbled as a jazz crooner. Max had met her years before when she'd sung at his club; she'd brought the house down, and their stormy relationship had ebbed and flowed since.

Leaving the leather case where it was, Max took his cup and crossed through the large living space, then found a set of wide polished wooden steps framed in burnished metal. Upstairs, he stepped into the bathroom, a large modern affair with white marble, white cabinets, a massive claw-foot tub, and a wide glassed-in shower containing two shower heads. He dropped his clothes on the floor, turned the water on hot, and stepped into the shower, letting the water warm his bones. He stood that way for a long time before slowly lathering up.

When he stepped out and toweled himself off, he could see the nude form of Goshawk sitting cross-legged on the bed through the open bathroom door. The leather case was in front of her, and she was tapping a white powdered substance from a glass vial onto a small mirror.

Max felt arousal creep into his groin as he stared. Then instantly he felt ashamed as a rush of self-loathing filled his mind, memories of past encounters with Goshawk ending in weeks of regret from the usage of the drug.

For a moment, he considered walking out. Then he remembered his sister and Alex, and steeled himself. This was the price he'd have to pay.

Goshawk looked up at him, then dabbed her finger into the white powder. She brushed it across a nipple, leaving a trail of the drug. "Come to mama," she said, leaning back onto the bed.

TWENTY

Paris, France

Max awoke with a start and peered into the inky darkness. For a brief moment, panic welled up in him and he reached under his pillow for a gun, but found nothing. Then he remembered where he was, and what he'd done. The guilt consumed him for a moment, and he had to take several deep breaths to calm his racing heart.

It took his eyes a moment to adjust to the dark. Next to him, Goshawk slept on her side, naked, back to him, her shoulder rising and falling with each breath. Her white hair was spread out on the pillow and seemed to shimmer in the darkness. Their brief but powerful cocaine-fueled sex act came rushing back to him, and he felt both elated and ashamed. Cocaine disgusted him, and his limited experience with it had all been with Goshawk. He hated himself for succumbing to the vice, but the pleasure of the experience always prevented him from saying no. The only consolation to his guilt-addled mind was that he'd done it for his sister and nephew.

He looked at his watch. Its luminous dial showed 5:30 in the morning. Despite the hour, he was wide awake. He'd slept for over fourteen hours. He swung his feet to the floor and padded into the bathroom, where he pulled on his jeans and shrugged back into his shirt and motorcycle jacket. Carrying his shoes, he walked quietly out of the bedroom, down the stairs, and into the kitchen. A minute later, he exited the home into the antechamber and grabbed his bag and phone. As he was pulling open the outer door, a voice came over the intercom. It was sleepy, with a syrupy lilt. "Come back soon, Max. You're always welcome." Max paused, then stepped out and shut the door behind him. He could almost see the little smirk on her perfectly sculpted face.

Despite the hour, the warehouse district was coming alive. Men in trucks made their way to work, lunch pails in hand. Semi-trucks and single-axel lorries trundled and jock-eyed for position in front of loading docks. Max hitched his overnight bag onto his shoulder and made his way toward the train station.

After their session in bed and a long nap, Goshawk had come through for him. She'd managed to pull together a dossier of images and information on a Julia Meier. To be sure it was Julia, she'd run the images through a facial recognition algorithm to compare against Max's photo. As he walked, Max ran down the details in his head.

Just over seventy years old, Julia Meier resided in a small but modern townhouse in a wealthy suburb of Zurich overlooking the Zurichsee. She was un-married, and as far as Goshawk could find, had never been married. The latest pictures showed Julia as an elegant woman about town, frequenting local galas and art galleries. They found records of her volunteering on various boards of education and public health and with a few local charities. Pictures of her turned up on the social pages of newspapers and the websites of art galleries and museums. Her bank records indicated she was quite well off and that her funds had been well invested. Goshawk could find no indication of the source of her wealth.

Max entered the cavernous train station and blended into the endless flow of travelers. The train ride took Max into Gare du Nord, Paris' main station. He switched lines and took a brief ride before he exited and took the north entrance. Back on the street, he turned into a cafe. He waited patiently behind a commuter in a suit, then greeted the barista by name and ordered his usual, a dry cafe au lait and croissant. Recognizing one of his regulars, the painfully thin barista smiled a wide grin. He counted out Max's change, then took his position behind the gigantic espresso machine.

As he pulled the shot, the barista asked, "Did your friends find you?"

Max looked up, alarm bells going off. "What friends?"

"There were two men in here yesterday. They said they were old friends of yours. Showed a picture of you, and asked if I'd seen you around."

"What did you say?"

"Of course I said nothing, monsieur. It is not my place to comment on my customers' lives."

"Good man," Max said, and stuffed a wad of euros into the tip jar. "What did they look like?"

The barista fussed with the machine, then looked up in the air as if trying to remember. He pulled on his thick beard.

"Both of them were tall and broad-shouldered, with tight, perfect hair. Good looking fellas. Youngish, with that fresh, pink look all Americans seem to have."

Max smiled at that. "What were they wearing?"

"Suits, both of them," the barista replied. He finished with the machine and set a perfect cafe au lait on the counter. "Dark blue, I think. They both stuck out like sore thumbs."

"Did they have accents, or speak French?"

"They spoke in French," the barista said, pausing as he cleaned the espresso machine, as if surprised. "Pretty good French, I must say. There was a light accent, but nothing I could place. I've never been outside of France, and don't really care to go."

Max thanked him and took his coffee and the bag with his croissant over to a table by the window. He sat with his back to the wall and watched the street through the window. A block away was his home, a narrow brownstone with a wide stoop and a bright red door. It had a two-car garage off the alley and a garden patio on the top floor with a nice view of the city. Inside, it had a Scandinavian feel, with teaks and stainless steel. It was a four-block walk to his club, where he spent the majority of his time. He'd hoped he could stop at his flat this morning and retrieve a change of clothes. Now, he had different plans.

He sipped his coffee, savoring the taste, and watched the street, his senses now highly tuned to anything out of the ordinary. He wondered who the two lads might be. The description matched the stereotype of the American feds, but Max knew stereotypes in his business rarely held true. Besides, what would the Americans want with him? There was no reason he could think of that he should be on their radar.

He swallowed the last bite of his croissant and washed it down with the remains of his coffee. Leaving the cafe, he headed in the opposite direction of his flat and took a meandering route in the general direction of his club, stopping periodically to check for surveillance. This activity was known in the spy game as a surveillance detection run. He wound his way through several city blocks, then ducked down into the Metro. A stop later, he emerged and got into a cab, noticing an *Uber Go Home* sign on the back window. When he emerged from the cab, he meandered a few more blocks before ducking into his club. He'd noticed no tails.

Max had opened his after-hours jazz club, La Caravelle, seven years ago as part of his strategy to blend into Paris society and to provide a cover. Initially, he'd taken on two partners. As the success of his other business blossomed, he was able to buy out his partners, and he was now the sole owner. He wondered what the fastidious Parisians would think if they knew part of the money to start the club had come from the KGB, and another part from the business of killing people. The club bled cash, but Max loved everything about the establishment.

He walked past the kitchen and emerged in the main room, an intimate, dark expanse with a small stage and tiny round tables arranged haphazardly. One wall was lined with French doors leading to a veranda overlooking the Seine, where patrons could escape the music for intimate conversations. He never got used to the smell of stale beer and cigarettes; for some reason the club reeked of it during the daylight hours, but when nighttime rolled in and the club filled with patrons, the smell disappeared.

"That you, Max?" He heard Della's sing-song voice ring out from the tiny office behind the kitchen. A moment later, his octogenarian Creole manager came out and wrapped him in a bear hug.

"*Bonswa,* Max, where you been?" She pushed him back and held him at arm's length. The large rolls of fat hanging from her triceps shook as she gripped his arms and peered up at him. It was the same greeting he always received when he'd been away, and was usually followed by a heaping bowl of her gumbo.

"Home, Della. Had to go see my sister."

"Everything ok at home?" She held Max tight, concern on her face.

"No, Della. Everything's not alright. I just need to drop some things off, then I might be gone a while again. Everything ok here?"

"*Oui, oui,* of course," Della said. "You're not going to tell me what's wrong, are you, *Zanmi?*" It was her pet name for Max, the word *friend* in Haitian Creole.

Max shook his head, then let himself be led back to the kitchen, where she warmed up a heaping serving of her crawfish gumbo. He dug in, washing the spicy stew down with a draught of Stella from the tap on the bar.

Once they'd caught up on club business, Max said, "I might be gone a while this time, Della. If anything goes wrong, you know how to get hold of me. And you know where the spare cash is upstairs in the safe."

"*Oui, oui, Zanmi,*" she said. Maybe it was something in his tone, but he caught a hint of sadness in her eyes as she turned away to clean his dish.

"Oh, and you should expect a DHL package in the next few days. Please just put it in the safe."

"Of course, of course," Della said.

Max went upstairs, where he kept a small but comfortable apartment. In the office nook, he pulled open a hidden panel in the floor so he could access a safe. Only he and Della knew the safe existed. He spun the dial a few times, then pulled it open. He removed a few straps of euros and a fresh set of identification before shutting the safe and twirling the dial. He tossed the cash and passport into a small backpack and covered them with a few items of clothing.

Before leaving the club, he gave Della a long hug, then wandered through the club's main room. The walls were covered with pictures of every performer that had come through, many of them signed to Max. He looked at each one. When he saw the picture of Sonny Rollins, he smiled. Sonny was his favorite. He wondered how long it would be before he would return to La Caravelle.

He left the club through the back alley and made for the train station, where he bought a TGV Lyria high-speed train ticket to Zurich. An hour later, he was settled into his seat, watching the greens and the yellows of the French countryside speed by, feeling pensive.

TWENTY-ONE

Zurich, Switzerland

Max sat on a park bench listening to the birds chirping. Parked at the curb in front of him was a small but fast BMW motorcycle he'd purchased used for cash. The scene was tree-lined and sun-dappled, like a fairytale. The street was orderly and well maintained, lined with new-looking row homes with large bay windows. Every car was a new variety of German luxury sedan. He guessed the men were all at their banking jobs while the women shopped and lunched. He grimaced at the lack of character. There wasn't so much as a splotch of gum on the sidewalk.

The bench was directly across from Julia Meier's home. He held a recent picture of her in his left hand, printed from Goshawk's computer. He wondered how he'd recognize her among all the other elderly, tall blondes who were parading down the street in track suits. He hoped he didn't look like a homeless man stranded on a Stepford Island of obscene wealth.

On the train from Paris, Max had realized approaching Julia Meier might be problematic. He needed a way to meet her without raising alarms, particularly in this neighborhood where the Cantonal police were just waiting to roust a vagabond from their midst. Without knowing much about her, Max could only think of one way to approach her. So he bided his time, waited, and watched.

Max had been trained by his father to constantly maintain a heightened sense of awareness about his surroundings. Even when he was vacationing in *le Midi*, known to most as the South of France, he was constantly on the lookout for anything out of the ordinary. Today was no different, and he spent his time paying attention to the little things. He saw a young man mowing the lawn with earbuds stuck in his ear. The boy wore a shirt with the emblem of a lawn service on the back. A young lady rode by on a bicycle, her long auburn hair streaming out behind her. A service crew, wearing orange vests, was gathered around an open manhole. The crew's van was parked five meters from the manhole. Every detail went into a vault in Max's mind.

Unlike his own row house, the one belonging to Ms. Meier had its garage in front. A quick tour around the neighborhood showed Max that her unit had a small backyard with an exquisite garden, several shade trees, and new-looking patio furniture. Two blocks over, the neighborhood gave way to Lake Zurich, and it looked like Ms. Meier enjoyed an expansive view of the bright blue lake. Max figured eventually she'd leave her flat, and fifteen minutes later, his patience was rewarded. The garage door to her unit opened and a silver Mercedes station wagon backed out. He put on his helmet, straddled the bike, and took off in pursuit.

The silver car gleamed from a fresh wax job, and Max

had no trouble following as she made her way through the neighborhood's streets and into the city. She made a stop at an outdoor cafe, where Max watched from across the street as she lunched with two women. Then she drove a kilometer, where she parked in a flat lot and entered a museum called Haus Konstruktiv.

As Max pulled into the lot, an alarm went off in his head. Along the sidewalk on the road opposite the museum strolled a young woman carrying a messenger bag over one shoulder. Normally, Max wouldn't have given her a second look, except that he recognized her long auburn hair and noticed she was the same woman who had pedaled by Julia's condo a little over an hour ago. The messenger bag was a new addition to her outfit.

Once is happenstance, Mikhail, his father's voice sounded in his head. *Twice is enemy action.*

Max parked his bike on the street near the museum's entrance and considered his options. Either the woman with the auburn hair was watching him, or she was watching Julia. Max made a show of fussing with the bike and watched the young woman through the smoked visor of his helmet. She continued past the museum's parking lot, then disappeared around a corner on the next tree-lined block. The prudent thing would be to bail and make the connection another time.

Still, it could be a coincidence, Max reasoned. Or Julia might be in danger. Carrying his helmet, he left the bike and entered the museum. A small sign indicated the facility was the only such institution in Switzerland dedicated to the exploration of concrete, constructive, and conceptual art. Max rolled his eyes and walked through the door.

The lobby of the museum was an expansive atrium filled with a jumble of what looked to Max like home construction projects gone wrong. Wood, metal, concrete, plastic, and all other manner of materials had been used to create works of "art." Some hung from the rafters, some lined walls, and others were large enough to take up significant amounts of wall space. Max didn't call them art, although he knew there were those who did.

He noticed Julia Meier standing alone, admiring a particularly hideous-looking structure of wood and plastic. Even from afar, she was a striking woman. Nearly six feet tall, she wore white slacks, silver wedged heels, and a colorful blouse that billowed around her, even though there was no moving air in the room. Her blonde-white hair was made up perfectly and her lips were colored a bright red. A large leather bag was slung over one shoulder, completing the ensemble. She looked just like any other wealthy elderly woman ready for an afternoon of art shopping or museum hopping.

Max walked up to the reception desk and asked for a pen. He took a small flyer and jotted a quick note in German. With the note written, he folded it so it was the size of a euro note folded twice, like one might hand to a bellman.

When he turned back to the atrium, Julia had disappeared. A hasty glance provided him with two options: A sign on a stanchion in front of a corridor indicated it led to two more galleries, or there was a set of restrooms close to Julia's last position, where she could have ducked in. Max gambled, and started down the corridor. As he walked, it occurred to him that Julia might have been in the spy business. Perhaps she was an operator, and that's how she'd met his father. Perhaps she'd been a member of the Swiss Military Intelligence Service, or maybe was even an agent for East Germany during the Cold War. Zurich might simply be where she'd retired after a long career behind the Iron Curtain. He cautioned himself to be careful about a casual encounter.

He walked down the bright, open corridor and stepped left into another large gallery. This one was filled with red and blue interconnected constructs of tiny pipes, similar to the Lincoln Log toys he knew children enjoyed. The pipes and tubes wound their way through and around the room like gigantic snakes. Overhead, a ceiling of glass let the midday sun shine through, creating a kaleidoscope of shadows on the white marble floor. Max didn't see his quarry, and had started to turn back toward the corridor when he felt a sharp jab in his upper ribcage.

"That's a pistol," he heard a light voice say in his ear. As she spoke, Max caught a whiff of perfume. "And I'm not afraid to use it. It's pointed directly at your heart. It's only a .380, but at this range, that'll put you down. This place doesn't get many visitors. You'd be dead and I'd be on my way long before anyone knew what happened. Now who are you, and why are you following me?"

TWENTY-TWO

Zurich, Switzerland

Max raised his hands slowly, holding the note in the left hand and his motorcycle helmet in his right. In a pinch, he knew he could use the helmet as a weapon. He hoped it wouldn't come to that. He tried to turn, but he felt another sharp jab in his side.

"Don't move. Talk. You have about five seconds to tell me who you are and why you're following me. I've killed men for less."

Max was instantly angry at himself for underestimating his target. That was an error he knew could get him killed.

"I'm not following—" he started.

"Bullshit," the woman said. "I saw you from the moment I left my house. You paced me into the city, then watched while I ate lunch. Now you're shadowing me here. Do you honestly expect me to believe you came here to appreciate the crap in this museum?"

"No, ma'am," Max said, realizing he'd better be quick.

He decided honesty was the best policy. "I wanted to meet you, that is all."

"Bullshit!" she said again. "You're down to two seconds before I pull the trigger."

"Take the note from my left hand," Max said. "Also, I have a photo of you in my pocket I'd like to show you. I believe you knew my father."

Max felt the note jerked from his hand. The gun was still jammed into his ribs. He started to move his left hand toward the inner pocket of his jacket. He felt another sharp jab and she said, "Don't move. I'm going to back up a pace. Slowly drop your jacket to the ground, take a step forward, then lie face down. Do you understand?"

"Yes, ma'am." Max said. His instincts told him to speak to her with respect. "Can I place my helmet on the floor?"

"Yes, slowly," she said. Then he felt the pressure in his side disappear and heard a heel on the marble floor. He bent and put the helmet down, then shrugged out of his jacket.

"On the floor," her voice commanded. Max dropped to his stomach and lay still.

A minute later, he heard a gasp, then silence. Finally, she said, "Well, I'll be damned. You must be Mikhail."

———

"We have a small complication," Max said.

She'd permitted Max to stand and was staring at the picture like it was an artifact from a time capsule, which Max surmised wasn't far from the truth.

She looked up and said, "What kind of a complication?"

Max explained the woman with the messenger bag. "There was also a service crew in front of your place this morning, and if I put that together with the girl, I'd surmise you are under surveillance."

Julia's eyes narrowed. "Why do you assume it's me that's under surveillance, and not you?"

"Anything is possible. I have a lot to catch you up on. But before we talk, I think we need to shake these guys."

"Agreed," Julia said. "Are you armed?"

Max shook his head.

With an exasperated sigh, she said, "Your father must be rolling in his grave." She tossed him the pistol. "You're probably a better shot than I am." Then she turned on a heel. "Follow me."

———

For an older woman, Julia was more spry than she looked, and Max had to jog to catch up with her. He checked the pistol as he moved. It was a SIG Sauer P238, with six in the mag and one in the chamber. The .380 rounds were slightly smaller than 9mm bullets, and the gun would be useless past about ten meters, but it was better than nothing. "Has this thing ever been fired?" he called out.

She made a left turn and pushed through a set of folding doors into a back hallway. "Of course. I've put a couple hundred rounds through it. It's clean. Untraceable."

Max followed her through a maze of offices, then saw her dart over to one and rummage. Then he followed her to a tiny kitchen. A young woman sitting at a table eating a salad called out, "Hi, Julia!" Julia waved at her, then paused in front of an exit door. "I'm on the board here," she explained.

"So you do call this art," Max said.

She ignored him. In a hushed voice, she said, "We'll

leave both our vehicles here. Outside this door is the employee parking lot. Annette's BMW should be about five paces away."

"BMWs are notoriously hard to break into and hotwire," Max said. "We should pick a different—"

Julia waved a set of keys at him and winked. "I'll drive."

"Are you sure—?" But before he could finish, she was out the door. Max sighed, and followed. It seemed Julia's energy belied her age. She was quickly proving a capable operator.

A glance showed the parking area empty of people. Julia had already unlocked the car with the fob and was sliding into the driver's side. Max walked around the car and jumped into the passenger seat. Before the door was shut, the car was in motion. He settled into the buttery leather seat and glanced around.

"My town. I drive. You shoot," Julia said.

"If I didn't know better," Max said, "I'd think you were enjoying this."

"I can only do so many museum tours and luncheons and charity events, Mikhail. I was getting bored."

She drove with an aggressive self-assurance, hands at ten and two, moving through the gears with precision and controlling the sedan with the clutch and shift. Max was pretty sure she hadn't yet touched the brakes. They skidded through a green light, narrowly missing a bicyclist, the sedan's engine growling in second gear.

"Not sure we need to call attention to ourselves," Max said. "Perhaps a more stealthy approach is warranted? I don't see anyone behind us."

The car slowed. "Sorry. Got carried away," she said.

"Can you get us to the Zurich Cantonal branch on Lintheschergasse?" Max asked.

"Yes, of course. Why?"

"My go-box," Max said. "I need a proper weapon. Something other than this rubber-band shooter you have here."

The car made a sudden turn left, and Julia accelerated onto a large boulevard. "Hey, at least I had a gun," she said.

Five minutes later, she double parked. "Make it quick, Mikhail," she said, her eyes lingering in the rearview mirror. "I'm a sitting duck out here."

He jumped from the car and moved across the sidewalk to the entrance of the bank. He groaned when he saw the line in front of the service manager's desk. Looking around, Max spotted an attractive blonde woman in a smart blue suit hurrying through the lobby. Her name tag gave her away as an employee of the bank. Max hailed her in German.

"Ma'am, might I trouble you for a minute?"

She looked up, startled, then smiled at Max. He smiled back.

"I'm late for my flight," he said. "But I need access to my box to retrieve my mother's power of attorney," he said, putting a baleful look on his face. "She's not long for this world, I'm afraid."

The blonde instantly put her hand on his arm. "I'm so sorry," she said, "is there anything I can do?"

Max turned slightly to gesture at the line of people, then made a show of looking at his watch. "I don't want to risk missing my flight," he said. "I'm afraid if I don't get there tonight, she may pass away before I've gotten a chance to see her."

She smiled knowingly. "Of course. I'm so sorry to hear about your mother's health. Please follow me, Herr—?"

Max just smiled and held up his thumb. His favorite

aspect of the Swiss banking system was the anonymity. A twelve-digit number he'd memorized combined with his thumb print would gain him access to the box without having to reveal his identity.

"Of course," she said. Guiding him by the arm, she led Max toward a large door built in the style of a massive vault. Ten minutes later, he was exiting the bank with a SIG Sauer P226 in the small of his back and two 15-round magazines. Each mag was filled with 9mm hollow points.

"Feel better?" Julia asked as she pulled away.

Max removed the SIG and put it on his lap. "Yes, although I'd feel even better with an assault rifle. Know where I can get one?"

Julia ignored his question. Max glanced over, and saw her eyes glued to the rearview mirror. "We've got company," she said.

TWENTY-THREE

Zurich, Switzerland

"Fuck, that was fast," Max said, turning in his seat. He double-checked the action on the SIG.

"The white van pulled out at the same time we did," Julia said.

Max easily picked it out of the traffic. He activated the automatic window. "Roll your window down," he said.

"Why?"

"If the shooting starts, we don't need broken glass flying everywhere." Max said.

"If the shooting starts?" she said. "Out here in broad daylight?"

"Apparently, they want me dead pretty badly," Max said. Julia was slowing down for a yellow light. "Don't stop for the light," Max said. He felt the car accelerate, then swerve as Julia moved into the vacant left-turn lane to get around a car that was already stopped for the light. Horns blared and tires screeched as other cars made evasive maneuvers to avoid their BMW. Max felt the car's big engine growl as they accelerated down the long boulevard. Turning in his seat, he saw the white van emerge from the intersection and come after them.

"Why do they want you dead so badly?" she asked.

"I don't know. That's what I was hoping you could tell me," Max said.

———

"Don't lose them, goddamn it," Cezar growled. He had a machine pistol on his lap and was holding onto the handle of the passenger side door.

"Relax," the driver said.

"Don't tell me to fucking relax," Cezar said. Abrams had put a team-wide bounty on Mikhail Asimov's head, and the individual who actually killed Asimov would get a large cash bonus. Cezar, as the team leader, would get an even larger bonus. This job had gone on long enough in his mind. Despite the risks out here in broad daylight, Cezar intended to take down Asimov while he had him in his sights. "Shut your fucking mouth and drive the van," he growled.

———

The attack, when it came, took Max by surprise. He'd been tracking the white van, and didn't see the silver sedan slide up next to them on the passenger side until it was almost too late. From the corner of his eye, Max saw a muzzle slide from the rear driver's side of the sedan.

"Floor it!" he yelled at Julia, and she hit the gas.

Bullets hit the rear passenger side of the BMW, shattering the window and sending bullets into the backseat. A split second earlier, and Max's head would have been splattered over the interior of the car.

Remarkably, Julia's demeanor remained calm. They shot through an intersection and onto a broad, tree-lined boulevard, with both the van and the sedan in pursuit.

"Something tells me you've been in this kind of situation before," Max said.

"You could say that," Julia said. She had one hand on the wheel and the other was moving through the gears like a Formula One driver.

"So how did you and my father meet?" Max asked. He craned his neck, looking for the white van and the black sedan.

"You want to talk about that now?"

"Why, do you want to make small talk for a while?" Max asked.

The silver sedan was catching up to them. To Max's utter surprise, he saw two muzzles protrude from the car's windows, one on either side.

"Incoming," Max yelled. Then he saw flashes, and shots began hitting the rear of the BMW. The rear window spider webbed as bullets hit. Julia weaved the car and bullets flew wide.

"Intersection," Julia said. "Hold on!" She downshifted, worked the clutch, turned the wheel, and the BMW easily wove around two cars and shot through the intersection.

His view was obstructed by the shattered safety glass. Max crawled into the backseat and kicked at the window. After a few strikes, he managed to dislodge the broken window and kick it into the street.

"Can you get us onto a highway? We need to get to a more sparsely populated area. Otherwise some civilians may get killed." He felt the car heave to the right as Julia swung them onto a freeway entrance ramp, then the big car seemed to settle as she pushed the pedal down. They shot onto the expressway, then wove to the outer lane.

"You're a pretty good driver," Max said. He watched the white van emerge onto the freeway, shimmying and weaving from the abrupt movements at top speed. The van's driver was no slouch. Then he saw the silver sedan shoot out from behind the van and pass it, attempting to close the gap.

"For an old lady, you mean," Julia said, giving him a look.

"For anyone," Max said. "When I say now, hit the brakes, okay?"

"Are you out of your mind?"

"Trust me," he yelled. Max knelt on the backseat facing the rear, the SIG clenched in a two-handed grip, braced by the car's back deck. "Now!"

The BMW slowed, and the silver sedan closed the gap in an instant. Max saw two muzzles emerge from the passenger windows. *Hold on*, he told himself. *Steady. Just one more half-second.* When the silver car was about ten meters away, he started firing.

Holes appeared in the silver sedan's windshield. It spider webbed, and Max saw blood spatter.

"Curve," Julia yelled, and Max felt the car yaw to the right. He kept firing, emptying the magazine. When the slide locked out, he used a practiced motion to eject the empty magazine and slapped in a new one.

He immediately saw he wasn't going to need the new magazine. The silver sedan, its driver dead, went straight as the highway curved, hit the guardrail, jumped, rolled, landed on its top, then burst into flames.

"Hit the gas, Julia," Max yelled. "The van will never be able to keep up with us." He felt the big car surge forward, and watched as the white van turned into a distant speck.

———

Cezar saw the silver sedan with half his team jump the guardrail and explode. Then he watched as the black BMW widened the gap between them until it was gone. He slammed his fist on the dashboard, then removed his mobile phone, dreading the call he was about to make.

———

"We need to get off this motorway and ditch this car," Max said. He was still watching out the back for the white van, but had lost visual. They were heading south on Route 3. To the left, he could see the bright blue Zurichsee surrounded by a ring of mountains. Julia swung onto an exit ramp and they found themselves in the tiny hamlet of Kilchberg. Julia drove through the town, then found a viewing area where cars could pull off and look out over the water. After wiping down the interior, they left the BMW in the parking lot and hiked back into town. Ten minutes later, they were on a bus heading north toward Zurich.

———

Max spent the first half of the trip filling Julia in on his story. When he got to the part about his parents' house blowing up, she gripped his arm.

"I'm so sorry, Mikhail," she said. "I'd heard he'd been

killed, of course. Frankly, I'm surprised he lived as long as he did."

"I need your help, Julia," Max said finally, after he'd finished the entire story. "Is there anything you can tell me? Anything at all that might help me understand who hated him enough to want his entire family dead?"

Julia looked out the window for a long time. When she turned back, her eyes were moist. "My relationship with your father was a long and complicated one," she said. "It was both the best part of my life and the worst, if you know what I mean." Max nodded his head. "He was the love of my life. I was the love of his. But we couldn't be together." Julia wiped a tear from her cheek, and looked back out the window. "Someday, Mikhail, maybe I can talk about it. I just need a little time."

"I understand, Julia. But I'm at my wit's end. Is there anything you can tell me? Anything recent, where his behavior was odd or he did things that seemed out of character?"

She thought for a moment, still staring out the window, then started to shake her head. Max was beginning to think this had all been pointless. Then, she turned to him and said, "There could be one thing, but it's very minor. It could be nothing."

"What is it?"

"Well, it was one of the last times I saw your father, only several months ago. We rarely met in Minsk, but your father was desperate to see me, so we arranged for me to fly in for a night. He picked me up and we'd planned to stay at the Hotel Minsk. On the way, we stopped at a hole-in-the-wall pub for a bite to eat and a drink. We usually stuck to out-of-the-way places, you see—"

"Yes," Max said, not wanting to hear the details of how they'd avoided his mother. "Go on."

"Well, we walked in and found a small table near the bar. We ordered, and caught up over a drink. Halfway through our dinner, a man walked through the door, and then went behind the bar like he owned the place. As soon as he walked in, your father's face went chalk white. I mean, it was like the blood literally drained out of his face. He threw a few rubles on the table, grabbed my hand, and we left. Right in the middle of eating. I remembered thinking that perhaps your father had seen someone who would care that he was having dinner with a strange woman in a strange bar."

"Was it characteristic of my father to be afraid of any man?"

"Not at all. That's what was so odd about it. I'd never seen him like that."

"How many years did you know him?" Max asked.

"Are you interrogating me?" Julia said, a sudden edge to her voice.

Max put up his hands in a signal of defeat. "I'm sorry if it came off that way. No harm intended."

She seemed to take that at face value.

"Did he tell you what the encounter was about?" Max asked, as gently as he could.

"No, he wouldn't tell me. He just said that it wasn't good for us to be seen in public together. I remember at the time not believing him."

"What did this man look like?" Max asked.

"I don't remember much. My memory isn't what it used to be. There was a time when I could walk into a bar and instantly be able to describe everyone there. But not any longer. I do remember he was an older man. I recall he was

somewhat stooped. And he had a few strands of white hair
—" Her voice trailed off.

"Anything else?" Max asked.

"Oh, I remember his hands. Gosh, yes. His hands were
knotted and gnarled, like he had advance-stage rheumatoid
arthritis. Because I remember wondering how he was able
to bartend."

"Gnarled hands," Max said.

"Right. They were very bad."

"Do you remember the name of the pub?"

She looked away and seemed to be thinking. "There
was an animal in the name. A bear? Maybe a boar?"

"The Black Bear Pub?" Max asked.

"Yes, that's it. The Black Bear," she said, as if the
memory was hard to contemplate.

They rode the rest of the way in silence, Max desperately wanting information, but deciding not to press her. At
the bus terminal, they hugged and she flashed him a smile
that made him realize how beautiful she must have been
when she was younger. He could see how his father might
have fallen hard.

"Don't be a stranger, Max. I've enjoyed meeting you.
You're a good listener and very polite. I hope we get to talk
again someday soon. We have more in common than you
might think." She pressed a card into his hand. "That's my
number. I'm going to leave Zurich. It's time for a new scene.
I'm bored with Switzerland. Time for somewhere new."
Her eyes twinkled, and she turned on a heel and
disappeared.

TWENTY-FOUR

Minsk, Belarus

Max knew the Black Bear Pub well. It was located in an industrial district on the edge of Minsk, and was popular with warehouse workers and over-the-road truckers. It was a ramshackle building that looked like it could fall down if someone leaned on it wrong. A single window in the front was boarded up and covered with grime and soot. The door had a single neon sign over it that read *Black Bear*. There was no picture of a bear anywhere to be seen. Parking was in the rear. It was the kind of place you didn't venture into unless you were either a regular or you knew how to take care of yourself. It was a curious place for Max's father to bring a date, but perhaps he'd figured they would have privacy. Besides, if there was anyone that could handle himself in a room full of thugs, it was his father.

Max pushed the door open and walked inside. It took a moment for his eyes to adjust to the dim light, and when they did, he saw a room full of overweight men in working clothes drinking beer and digging into baskets of food. A tired-looking waitress swung her ample hips as she slung drinks and cleared glasses. When Max walked in, the entire room seemed to look at him and activity slowed for a moment. Then life resumed and the patrons seemed to ignore him. Max figured that would change.

Max knew he could be an imposing figure. He looked capable, and he walked in with a confident stride that sent the message that he belonged. Still, he toyed with a set of brass knuckles in the pocket of his leather jacket. He was confident, but not stupid. *The devil is always ready to rock the cradle of the saint who sleeps,* his father would say.

He made his way through the room and took a seat at the end of the bar. He sat with his left arm on the bar's rough wooden surface and his back to the wall, and ordered a Krynitsa, a local working-man's beer made in Belarus. The bartender, a hulking young man with no neck, slapped the beer down and accepted a few rubles in payment. Max sipped it as he thought about his meeting with Julia.

Max hadn't known what to expect, and had come away with a positive impression of Julia Meier, if indeed that was her name. She and her father had clearly been in love, and Max was still shocked at how long their relationship had gone on. He had memorized the number on the card, then disposed of it and made a mental note to look her up again. He realized he liked her, and wanted to learn more about her. They shared a curious but strong tie.

Max became aware of a presence at his shoulder. He turned to find a mountain of a man standing to his right. A long beard hung from a face that had seen its fair share of violence. The man wore a black watch cap and a worker's shirt with the name of some mill or factory on the breast pocket. A large chain ran from his belt to his back pocket.

That didn't take long, Max thought. The man stood close enough for his enormous belly to touch Max's elbow. He became aware that the entire bar had grown quiet, its attention on the two men. The bartender had disappeared into the back.

"Can I help you?" Max asked.

"You can help yourself by running your ass outta this bar. We don't like strangers in here. Especially when we're trying to enjoy our dinner."

Max could smell the borscht and onions on the man's breath. He almost expected him to start cracking his knuckles.

"I'm just having a beer, trying to wind down from my day," Max said.

"Why don't you drink it down right now, then get the fuck outta here."

Max noticed another behemoth of a man had sidled up to his new friend and stood behind him, just to the first man's right. *Still not a fair fight,* Max thought. "I don't think so. I'm going to enjoy this one, then I'm going to have another one. Then I'm going to enjoy some food. Then I'll probably—"

He didn't get to finish his sentence. The man closest to Max grabbed him by the front of his leather jacket and ripped him out of his seat. Next thing he knew, he was standing face-to-beard with the big man.

Big mistake, thought Max.

Max grabbed the man's head between his hands and forcibly brought it down. At the same time, he flung his forehead forward, and connected with the bridge of the man's nose. He knew he could easily kill someone with a head butt if cartilage from the victim's nose was pushed into the brain, so he restrained the force of the blow.

The man's nose gave way with a sickening crunch and blood spattered onto Max's face. The man howled in pain, put his hands to his nose, and tried to move back. Max held onto his head, forcing it down. At the same time, Max brought his knee up and connected with the man's mouth with a crunch. Teeth fell to the floor and the man howled a second time. Max shoved him, and he fell back into a table. The table crashed to the floor, taking food, beer, and the attacker with it.

Max turned and faced off with the second man. Not as large around as the first man, the second attacker had an equally full beard and the ruddy cheeks and nose of a hard drinker. Max slipped his right hand into his pocket and found the brass knuckles. He heard the *chink* of a switch-blade opening and saw the dull glint of sharp metal.

With his back to the wall and the bar to his left, Max didn't have a lot of room to maneuver. The man lunged with the knife. Max shifted his weight to the right and used his left arm to guide the knife away from his body. The attacker lost his balance for a moment and fell toward Max. Brass knuckles in place, Max brought his right fist around toward the side of the man's head, landing the roundhouse on his temple. The attacker fell hard to the floor and didn't move. Max kicked the switchblade away and looked around.

The room had grown silent. Several of the larger men had risen to their feet, but weren't moving. The first attacker was still on his back, covered in food and blood. Max was hoping no one had a gun. That would even the fight in a second.

From the corner of his eye, Max saw a third man moving fast around the bar, carrying what looked like a baseball bat. He wore the white apron of a cook. The man had the speed of a midfielder and the build of an Olympic lifter. He faced off with Max for second, then came at him with a flurry of swings. Max was caught off guard by the man's speed, and he felt a dull pain as a blow glanced off his shoulder. He was ready for the second swing, however, and deflected the bat with his right forearm. He jabbed the man with a left, putting him off balance, then crushed a right uppercut with the brass knuckles to the man's jaw. He felt bone and ligaments give way as the cook crashed to the ground. Max suspected he would be eating through a straw for a month.

Then Max saw what he'd been dreading since the beginning of the fight: The bartender came up from behind the bar with a short, evil-looking shotgun aimed directly at Max's face. He could see barbs on the end of the gun from the saw used to cut the barrel off close to the magazine. The stock was securely braced against a meaty shoulder. Max knew he was done. Sawed-off shotguns were useful for close-quarters combat and in cases where the shooter was untrained. The shorter barrel made the shot disperse in a wider pattern, regardless of whether it was loaded with birdshot or buckshot. He knew the bartender couldn't miss.

Suddenly a voice roared out, "What the fuck is going on here?" A stooped man appeared from somewhere in the back, his sparse white hair flying in all directions. The man's cheeks were caved in, and his face was pockmarked and grizzled with white stubble. He rounded the front of the bar, grabbed the bat from the floor with a pair of misshapen hands, and swung it with surprising force at Max's knees. A shooting pain went up the back of his legs, and he lurched sideways. *Never bring a knife to a gunfight, my son,* his father said in his ear. Then the bat came down on his head, and his world went dark.

TWENTY-FIVE

Minsk, Belarus

Max was snapped into consciousness by a whiff of smelling salts. As his awareness returned, he felt a dull throb in the back of his head where the baseball bat had hit him. Silver tape held his wrists to the arms of a wooden chair. He ignored the pain, blinked his eyes, and tried to take in his surroundings.

He was no longer in the bar. Instead, he was in a large room with high ceilings. Tall windows were blacked out with dark sheets. The wood floor was scratched and gouged. The expansive room was piled with jumbled equipment, boxes, clothing, furniture, and other assorted junk.

The far end of the room caught his attention, and he stared in amazement. The opposite wall was filled with pictures, news clippings, and printouts, all taped or tacked to the wall. He looked closely, then tried to strain forward. Suddenly, his stomach turned. The pictures were all of his family. In the center, he could see several photos of his father taken through a telephoto lens. Pictures of his parents' home were next to images of his mother at the market. On the left side of the wall, he saw shots of himself as a young man in the Russian Army and during his years in the KGB. On the right side were pictures of his sister and his ten-year-old nephew. Max was stunned to realize he was looking at the surveillance photos of a killer's targets.

A slow voice came from the corner, near a stove. "The fly comes home to roost, eh, Mr. Asimov?"

The voice came from the gloom to Max's left. The words were cracked and rough, like the speaker had smoked too many cigarettes. Max turned and saw the same stooped man who had knocked him unconscious. A tattered and frayed corduroy jacket now hung on his drooping shoulders, replacing the white apron he'd worn earlier.

"I think you mean the *chicken* comes home to roost," Max said. He turned his head, and tried to take in the rest of the room. A long table ran down one wall, holding a mess of equipment. Looking closely, he saw handguns, tools, ammunition, and what appeared to be parts for making homemade explosives.

"Whatever," the old man said. "I never did care for Western idioms."

"Is this where you made the bomb that killed my parents?" Max asked, turning back to look at the old man.

"It's where I made part of it. But you probably know that a bomb that size requires vast amounts of RDX. The fuses were made here, along with the blasting tubes, but the rest of the bomb was made out back." The stooped man walked toward him carrying a steaming mug.

Anger surged in Max's blood. He tensed, flexing his arms against the tape, and making blood vessels bulge in his forearms.

Behind him, a voice growled, "Might want to conserve your strength." A man appeared from behind Max's chair. Max recognized him from the bar. He'd been by the front door. Short and stout with a beer belly protruding like a pregnant woman's, he was pointing a pistol at Max.

The old man then produced a pistol with a long silencer and trained it on Max with a surprisingly steady hand. His swollen knuckles made it difficult for his finger to fit into the trigger guard, but he somehow managed.

"I want you to meet my close friend, Mikhail," the old man said. "His name is Sergei. Now, what makes you think you can just waltz into my bar and start beating up my patrons?"

"They started it," Max said. "I was just drinking a beer." He feigned nonchalance, but the images on the far wall worried him. Why would the bomb maker, or assassin if that's what the old man was, have pictures of him and his sister and nephew on the wall, along with his parents? The logical progression of thought made his blood grow cold.

"I doubt that, Mr. Asimov. The question is, how did you find me?"

Max's mind was reeling from everything he'd seen on the wall. He stayed silent.

"Who was it, Mr. Asimov? I need that information before I kill you."

Max struggled to regain focus. He made a calculated guess, watching the old man's reaction.

"Victor Dedov."

The old man hesitated for a moment, then laughed. A loud guffaw came out of his mouth and rolled around the large room, echoing in the open space.

"Bullshit," the old man said, taking a sip of his tea. "You'll tell me soon enough. Imagine my surprise, Mr.

Asimov, when your father walked through the doors to my pub only weeks before he was due to be executed. At first, I thought maybe he was on to me. But if that were the case, he wouldn't have ordered dinner and brought a date. At that very moment, the bomb that would later kill him was under construction out back in this very parking lot, only a couple blocks from the pub. Coincidence, Mr. Asimov, makes the world a more interesting place, don't you think?"

Rage took over and Max heaved at the tape holding his arms. For a moment, he wondered if he could break free from the chair and cross the two meters of space in enough time to strangle the old man before bullets ripped him to shreds.

The old man laughed again and set his coffee mug on a table. He pulled a smartphone from his pocket, tapped the screen, and held the phone to his ear. After a moment, he said, "Guess who appeared at my front door?" A pause. "No, you'll never guess... The target of operation Albatross... I know, he's under control... Yes, I'll take care of it and let you know when it's done... Yes, we're still on track for the other thing... Right. Then we'll be done." The old man snapped the phone shut and slid it into his pocket.

"Sergei, prepare the plastic. I'll cover Mr. Asimov here."

Max watched as Sergei rummaged in a corner and emerged with a folded piece of plastic sheeting. He unfolded it, then laid it out on the wooden floor behind Max.

"Now let me tell you how this is going to go, Mr. Asimov. You're going to tell me what I want to know. Then I'm going to shoot you, wrap you in that plastic, then have Sergei here drive you to the outskirts of the city and dump you in a field. But your death will be quick, and perhaps you'll eventually have a nice burial, if that's what you prefer. If you don't tell me what I want to know, I'm going to have Sergei cut you up into tiny pieces and flush you down the toilet, one piece at a time. Have you ever seen a human carved up, piece by piece? It's an agonizing death, let me assure you."

Max was silent. In the space of thirty minutes, his world had changed. Before, he was hell-bent on one thing: finding his parents' killers and exacting swift justice. Now, Max was more concerned with keeping his sister and nephew alive. He guessed the *other thing* referenced by the old man was a bomb meant for Arina and Alex.

Sergei was covering him again with a pistol. The old man had let his own droop while he sipped his tea. When the old man talked, he waved the gun around for emphasis.

"So tell me, Mikhail, who told you where to find me?"

Max heaved at his bonds, struggling against the tape. The chair creaked, and he heard a small crack. The tape cut into his wrists. "Go fuck yourself," he managed through clenched teeth.

"Sergei, please." The old man waved his pistol in Max's direction.

Sergei pocketed his pistol, approached Max, then threw a roundhouse right. Max tried to duck, but the punch connected with his cheek, sending sparks through his eyes. The power of the punch pitched him backward onto the plastic sheeting. Sergei stood over him and delivered a kick with his weight behind it, connecting with Max's ribcage. Pain shot into his chest. Three more kicks connected as he tried to pull himself into a fetal position.

Finally, the old man said, "Get him up, Sergei. Perhaps he's come to his senses." Max was pulled upright. He could feel a piece of the chair poking him in the wrist. The wooden arm holding his right wrist had broken. He managed to work his wrist free, but held it in place.

"Who told you where to find me?" The old man's voice was more forceful this time.

Max stayed silent. The old man waved his gun, and Sergei punched Max again. This time, Max saw the punch coming and heaved himself to the side, falling to the floor. Sergei kicked at him. Max wrenched his right arm free and grabbed Sergei's leg, pulling hard. Sergei tumbled forward. Max let go of the leg and wrapped his arm around Sergei's neck, gave his arm a violent twist, and felt the man's neck break. He let go and grabbed at Sergei's gun, pulling it from the man's pocket. Sergei's dead weight was between Max and the old man. He heard a gun discharge. A bullet passed next to his shoulder and embedded itself in the wood floor.

In the melee, the old man had started circling, trying to get a bead on Max. He fired again, aiming for Max's head. The bullet hit Sergei's chest instead. Max raised his gun, pulled the trigger, and hit the old man in the stomach, pushing him backward. Somehow, the old man was able to keep his gun arm up and fire another shot. This one went wide as the old man's hand wavered. Max pulled the trigger again and hit the old man in the left hip. The old man's gun arm sagged, and he fell to the floor.

Blood pooled under the old man as Max heaved Sergei's dead body onto the floor. Max saw the old man struggle to pull his smartphone from his jacket pocket, then jab at the screen. The phone fell to the floor with a *thunk*.

Max scrambled on his hands and knees to the old man's side, where blood was spreading out in a wide circle.

Fuck, don't die, Max thought. *Please don't die.*

TWENTY-SIX

Nathan Abrams' mobile phone buzzed. He looked at it with irritation, then inwardly groaned when he recognized the caller. It was a man Abrams loathed with all his being. Yet, a man he couldn't seem to rid from his life. Perhaps one day, he would do the world a favor and kill the man himself. For now, though, he seemed to be stuck with the bomb maker like a spiteful Siamese twin.

"Abrams," he answered. Most of his irritation stemmed from the bomb maker's refusal to work with Nathan's staff. The man thought that since he and Nathan had shared time in the army, he was entitled to call Nathan directly. Nathan's irritation grew as he heard the caller's voice.

"Guess who appeared at my front door?"

"I don't know, Travkin, stop playing games and tell me why you're calling," Abrams said.

"No, you'll never guess."

"I'm hanging up now," Nathan said, about to pull his phone from his ear.

"The target of operation Albatross," Travkin said. That caught Nathan's attention.

"Congratulations, Travkin," Nathan said slowly, hiding his glee. "That's quite a catch. Is he secured?"

"I know. Yes, he's under control."

"Well, don't fuck around. Take care of it immediately before you fuck it up. Then send me a picture."

"Yes, I'll take care of it and let you know when it's done," Travkin replied, now sounding irritated himself.

"Are we still on track for the rest of Albatross?" Nathan asked.

"Yes, we're still on track."

"Then we're done, correct?"

"Right, then we'll be done."

Nathan hit End on his phone and dropped it into his pocket. He walked to the large, floor-to-ceiling windows that overlooked his operations. The room below resembled mission control at a space station. An impressive array of computers lined rows of tables, each manned by a member of his staff. Spread around the walls of the room were massive flat-panel monitors that showed the status of each of their operations. To the right, a team was working on an operation centered in Bahrain. To the left, another team was running an operation in Northern Africa to rescue the kidnapped son of a wealthy oil tycoon. On any given day, he had teams working across the globe at all hours of the day and night. Directly below him, he could see Wing at her own work station.

Despite his continued annoyance with old Travkin, Nathan had to admit he was effective. Trained by the KGB, then employed by the Russian government in a capacity even Nathan couldn't uncover, Travkin had become Eastern Europe's most renowned bomb maker. His bombs had killed scores of people over the past three decades – some foreign dignitaries, some enemies of the Soviet Union, and some enemies of Travkin's himself. He was a dangerous man, and Nathan didn't trust him any further than he could throw him. He seemed to take a perverse pleasure in the act of destroying things and people. Travkin's psychopathy gave Nathan the creeps.

Nathan was reaching for the intercom to give Wing an update when his phone buzzed again. He pulled it from his pocket and looked at it, startled. There was an alert on the notification screen – one he'd never expected to get. The kind of alert operators often set up as a backup, but seldom used. It took Nathan a minute to remind himself of the protocol. Then, anger set in and he reached for the intercom and punched a button. A second later, Wing's voice came through his speaker.

"Yes?"

"Who do we have left in Minsk?" he barked.

"Just about everyone was in Zurich," Wing replied. "We have Wild Boar, of course. And we have one sleeper, code-name Wolverine. Cezar and what's left of his team are still en route from Zurich."

Nathan's heart sank. The alert had come from the man codenamed Wild Boar, also known as Travkin. The alert meant Travkin needed assistance. Nathan's gut told him Asimov had somehow turned the tables on the old man.

"Fuck. Ok, activate Wolverine. I'm coming down."

He opened the glass doors to the office and the din of his operations center flooded in. Nathan took the wide stairs two at a time, found Wing, and hovered over her station. The tiny Malaysian was yelling into her headset. "I don't

give a fig how much you've drunk. This is a code-alpha acti-
vation. You need to move NOW." For some reason, Wing
wouldn't swear. It was usually endearing. Today Nathan
found it irritating. Lately, he was finding a lot of things
irritating.

He yanked the headset from her head and jammed it
onto his own.

"Wolverine, this is Command. What's your status?"

"Scrambling now, sir. What's the situation?" The voice
that came over the line was slightly slurred.

"I need you to activate immediately. Take weapons and
backup if you have it. I'm going to send you a picture while
you're en route. Wing is providing coordinates now. If you
find the man pictured at this location, I want you to shoot
him on sight. Am I clear?"

"Yes. I have three other men here with me."

"You need to move fast. If you kill this man, there is a
large bonus waiting for you. Keep your wits about you. He's
highly dangerous. Shoot first, ask questions later."

"Boss, I'm at least twenty minutes away from that
location—"

"Be there in ten, goddamn it," Nathan barked. He
severed the connection and tossed the headset back at
Wing, then paced in front of her station. He tuned out the
din of the command room. He was close to nabbing Asimov,
Nathan knew. He could feel it in his bones.

"Send him a picture of Asimov," he told Wing. "The
latest one." He kept pacing, calculating the scenarios. Could
this be the break he needed? Nathan chewed on a hangnail
while he waited for Wolverine to get to Travkin's residence.
He wondered if Travkin was dead, and had to admit the
thought appealed to him.

TWENTY-SEVEN

The old bomb maker was sprawled at an awkward angle on the wooden floor in front of the couch. A crimson pool of blood was seeping into the caramel-colored wood. Max kicked the old man's gun away. The old man's eyes were closed and his breath came in ragged heaves. He was losing blood fast, and Max knew he wasn't long for this world.

"Who hired you?" Max growled. He pressed the man's jacket to his stomach to try and staunch the flow of blood. The effort seemed futile. The stomach wound bubbled with every ragged breath. "Goddamn it, don't die on me. Who hired you?"

"Go...fuck...yourself," the old man managed. Blood and foam sputtered from his mouth, the pool of blood spreading fast. "You're...a...dead...man, Asimov..."

The old man's head lolled backward and his breathing finally stopped. Max fingered his neck, but found no pulse. He wiped his hands on the man's jacket and tore the remnants of the tape from his own wrists. Then he plucked the phone from the floor and put it in his pocket, and patted the old man down. He found nothing else.

Max stood and looked around. A second doorway led from the back of the room. A quick examination showed a flight of stairs down, leading to a doorway. He made sure the door was locked. Next, he checked the action on Sergei's gun. It was an older-model Makarov, with six 9mm rounds left in the magazine. He slammed the magazine back into the handle, then racked the slide to put a round into the chamber. He stuck the gun into his belt at the center of his back.

He knew he shouldn't linger. Although the old man's gun had been silenced, Sergei's had not. The two shots might draw attention. Max peeked out the window from behind one of the dark shades. A light rain was coming down and the window was steamed over, casting a blurry haze over the glistening street.

Max turned back to the room and cursed to himself. The whole purpose of tracking down the old man had been to get information. Now he was dead, and Max was no closer to finding out who had ordered his parents' death.

On the ceiling, duct work was exposed against a ceiling lined by wooden beams. A large, distressed desk covered in papers sat underneath the wall of photos. In the back corner, a pile of dirty laundry sat next to a small cot with unkempt sheets and blankets. The small kitchen was over-grown with dirty dishes and scraps of moldy food. A large pile of cardboard boxes was stacked in one corner, like the old man had never unpacked.

Max strode to the far wall and examined the pictures. A lump rose in his throat as he saw dozens of surveillance photos of his father and his parents together. The photos showed them exiting their car, waiting at stop lights, entering and exiting restaurants, and lounging in the yard of their home. The whole thing made him feel ill. It was evident the bomb maker had been tracking the Asimov family for a long time. Newspaper clippings featuring Max's father were taped to the wall. Max peered at a shot of his mother cut from the newspaper. It looked like it had been taken from the society section. She was wearing a gown, like they'd just been to the theater. His mother had been a beautiful woman, with long dark hair, strong cheek-bones, and large eyes that hinted at mischief. His father said often he'd been a lucky man to catch her. He had always told his friends she was a beautiful woman who'd born him two children, who loved to cook, and took no shit from the men of the house. In the field his father had been king, but at home he'd always said it was his mother who ran the oper-ation. For a moment, Max regretted he hadn't had a closer relationship with his mother. Then the memory came flooding back to him – the one that always seemed to stick in his mind.

Max stood in front of the broad front porch of their home, wearing the regal uniform of the Red Army, gazing at his parents. He had finished military school two weeks ago, and was off to officer training in Moscow. It was to be his first opportunity to start applying his lifetime of training. A duffle bag sat at his feet. A sedan waited in the driveway to ferry him to the airport.

"Son, I'm proud of you," his father said, a broad smile on his grizzled face. Then he saluted, and Max's chest puffed out in pride as he saluted his father in return. "I've taught *you everything I know," the elder Asimov said. "I'm expecting great things."*

Max looked at his mother. During his stay, she'd been distant and reserved. He found himself wondering if she'd been avoiding him. He smiled at her and waved. His smile disappeared as he saw her turn and walk back into the house. No goodbye. No hug. No wave. She'd simply turned her back on him. With sadness in his heart, Max climbed into the waiting car. He stared forward as the car wound down the driveway. He wondered what he'd done to turn his mother against him. He wondered if he would ever know.

Choking the memory back, Max turned away from the wall. Now she was dead, and he'd never have a chance to reconcile their relationship. He'd probably never know why she had been so cold to him. Turning from the wall, he went to the desk and began rifling through papers. He was amazed to find complete Moscow FSB personnel files for him and his father. He looked at them a moment, then tossed them back on the desk. Their presence confirmed that the FSB had some kind of role in his parents' death. The top of the desk was piled with more surveillance photos and wrinkled maps of Minsk. Under a phone book, Max found the blueprints to his parents' house, as well as copies of their car registrations, passports, and drivers' licenses. Max was stunned by the amount of information.

He walked to the far end of the room and went through the man's clothes, finding nothing of interest. Max moved to the long table in the center of the room. He found a mess of blasting caps, detonators, blocks of C-4, rolls of detonator cord, piles of mobile phones, remote devices, and other bits of bomb-making equipment. Another section of the table contained a stack of laptop computers and tablets. Next to the computers were a pile of Makarov pistols, clips, and silencers in various states of disassembly. He found two magazines, each filled with 9mm bullets from a box on the table, and stuck them in his pocket.

A sound from outside startled him. Max went to the window and pulled the black sheet over an inch and looked out. Rain was falling harder, puddles forming in the street. To his right, he saw red lights from the tail end of a bus pulling away from the curb. The street was empty of people. Max watched for another few minutes, then let the sheet fall back into place. He knew he should leave, but he needed to find a link between the hitman and his employer. The stakes had just risen. Someone wanted him and his sister dead, and wanted them dead very badly. Instead of vengeance, Max was now fighting for their survival.

TWENTY-EIGHT

Minsk, Belarus

Max checked the street one more time, and found it empty of both pedestrians and vehicles. Any moment, he knew authorities might knock on the door, called by some earnest neighbor who thought they'd heard gunshots. The smell of blood filled his nostrils and a haze of gunpowder still hung in the air.

There was an alarming amount of information about his family in this flat, and his mind wandered to who might have assembled it. One man couldn't have taken all those surveillance photos. The personnel files must have been provided by someone at the Belarusian KGB, or at least someone with access to its files. His first thought was of Anatoly.

Max's father had been a product of the old-school KGB, an organization that prided itself on knowing more information about its citizens and enemies than any other clandestine service. As the assistant director of the Belarusian

branch of the First Chief Directorate, the division responsible for foreign espionage, his father had been in a position
of extreme power and influence. Staunchly nationalistic, he
had been quietly disgusted by the actions of the Second and
Fifth Chief Directorates, the divisions responsible for
internal political control and censorship against internal
dissidents, artists, and activists. In 1991, the KGB in Russia
was disbanded along with the rest of the Soviet Union, and
replaced by several smaller organizations of more limited
scope, including the FSB. But many of the men in charge of
the old KGB still remained in positions of power, and their
influence still ran deep in Russian government and society.
If his father had alienated one of those men, or a group of
those men, Max knew his enemy was indeed a formidable
opponent.

Max looked around the large room and found a mili-
tary-issue rucksack under the cot. He tossed it on the table
and placed both of the KGB files in the bag. Next, he
began a methodical dismantling of the room. He started
with the tiny kitchen, emptying every drawer and examining the undersides. Then he pulled everything out of
the small freezer and refrigerator. He pulled apart the
cabinets and drawers, turning the kitchen into a pile of
rubble. He moved to the tiny bathroom, where he pulled
down the mirror, looked into the toilet tank, and
rummaged through the wastebasket. Back in the main
room, he rifled through the stack of boxes. The last box,
buried in the corner, wasn't a box at all. It had the bottom
cut out of it and had been used to hide a safe. *Bingo*, Max
thought.

The small, steel safe was about a two feet square, and
had two beefy external hinges, a dial, and a hand-sized lever
for opening the door. He hefted it and carried it over to the

long table, surprised at the weight. His muscles strained with the effort.

Before tending to the safe, Max checked the window again. Finding the street quiet, he went over to the wall showing the photos of his family and began ripping them down. He paused at the head shot of his mother from the newspaper article. He pulled the photo from the wall, folded it, and stuck it in his pocket. He resumed ripping the remaining photos and maps from the wall, then paused, his eye catching something on the far edge of the materials. He looked closer, his stomach dropping, then pulled the Polaroid from the wall. He flipped it over. The back was devoid of writing. He turned it back over and stared at it.

The photo was yellowed with age, and showed a tall, graceful-looking woman in a flowered summer dress, leaning on a pipe railing. Her smile was glorious, wide and full of white teeth. Her eyes were locked on the photographer. In the background, glorious in its own right, stood the Eiffel Tower. The woman in the photo was Julia Meier. He shoved this picture into his pocket as well.

He ripped the rest of the papers down and deposited them in the middle of the floor. He emptied the desk's contents into the pile and searched the drawers. He found nothing.

Surveying the room once more, he resigned himself that whatever clues he might find were either in the hitman's phone or in the safe. Nothing else was hidden around the room.

Max had been well trained in the use of explosives. He made regular use of them in his work and was an accomplished bomb maker in his own right. He examined the C-4 and saw it was in good condition. Using a knife he found on the table, he carved off a small chunk of the plastic explosive, then rolled it in his hands until it was a long strand about two millimeters in thickness and a foot long. He pressed the strand of C-4 into the crack where the door met the wall of the safe, and folded the ends around the two door hinges.

Max sorted through the pile of blasting caps. There were a variety of the multicolored devices. He found a package of the older fuse-style caps among a larger pile of the more common match-type caps. He pulled one of the fuse caps and saw that the fuse had already been crimped into place in the cap. He used the knife to cut the fuse short, then gently shoved the elongated metal stick of the blasting cap into the end of the C-4 he'd molded into the door of the safe. The trick was to use enough explosives to separate the door from the safe, but not so much that the explosive would damage the inside.

The last thing Max did before he blew the door was to dowse the pile of papers on the floor with lighter fluid he'd found on the table. He emptied the can onto the papers and the wood flooring around the pile.

The bang from the C-4 rattled the windows of the room, and the table jumped several inches off the floor. He waved away the smoke and used a pair of gloves from the table to pull the smoking door from the front of the safe.

Inside, Max found a jumble of items. The bottom shelf contained stacks of euros and American dollars in large denominations held together with rubber bands. Many of the bills were charred from the explosives. He dumped them all into the rucksack. On the top shelf he found several fake passports in various nationalities along with corresponding credit cards and other identification. Most had been damaged by the C-4. Those he tossed onto the stack of fuel-saturated papers on the floor.

In the back corner of the safe, Max found a small metal box. He knew time was running out, but curiosity got the better of him. He pried open the lid. Inside, he found a small plastic baggie, the type one might find holding a dose of meth. Through the plastic, he could see a tooth. Words on the outside of the bag had been written in ink. It looked like N. *Abrams*.

A noise from outside startled Max. He shoved the plastic bag with the tooth into his pocket and hurried to the window, pulling open the curtain. Outside, a dark panel van had slid to a stop on the street below. Four men were exiting the van. His time had run out. Max grabbed his leather jacket from the couch and shrugged it on. The familiar smell of the leather felt welcome among the room's stench of blood and death.

He shouldered the rucksack, then dropped a match onto the pile of papers. It went up with a *whomp*. The room was instantly filled with thick, black smoke. He heard heavy boots pounding up the front stairs. Pulling the Makarov from his pocket, he darted down the back stairs and exited into a heavy rain, moving fast. He turned left and started running, the rucksack banging off his back.

Then Max heard a shot, and a chunk of brick flew from the wall next to him, hitting his cheek. He turned on the speed.

TWENTY-NINE

Minsk, Belarus

Max ducked left, trying to keep his footing on the wet pavement. Another bullet ricocheted off the corner of the building where he turned. He pumped his legs, but the rucksack weighed him down. As he moved, his mind raced. The black van that had pulled up had no markings. The men had not identified themselves as law enforcement. They were shooting first, not asking questions. Somehow, the bomb maker had gotten word out to someone. Then it dawned on him: The bomb maker must have sent a signal using his mobile phone as he lay dying. Max zigzagged across the empty street and disappeared down an alley. He felt two more shots sing past his head.

He had to find shelter, and try to even the odds. Four men with high-powered assault rifles vastly outgunned him. If he didn't find cover fast, he was a dead man. He willed his legs to move faster and tried to keep the pack from bumping against his back with his left hand. In his right hand, he held the bomb maker's Makarov.

Max had grown up in Minsk, and although it was a city of two million people, he knew every nook and crevice. As a child, he'd run with a group of boys who had explored the alleyways and back lots in his neighborhood. When he was older, his father would drop him off in remote parts of the city and challenge him to get home on his own. In his teens, he and his father would play games of cat and mouse, practicing surveillance and counter-surveillance tradecraft throughout the city. This industrial neighborhood had provided a playground rich with challenges.

He came to the end of the alley and found it blocked with a chain-link fence. Hoping no one had fixed the hole in the fence he remembered since childhood, he hunched down and pushed at the metal links, feeling it give. With a sigh of relief, he ducked through, and found himself in a parking lot adjacent to an abandoned factory. Cutting to the right, he hugged the side of the building and made for the main entrance.

The factory was a massive concrete bunker of a building constructed in the early 1940s to support the war. In its heyday, the factory had supplied parts for Soviet-era aircraft, including the Ilyushin DB-3 and DB-4, long-range bombers responsible for dropping the first Soviet bombs on Berlin in 1941. Later, the factory had been converted to manufacture parts for more modern craft. It finally closed after an industrial accident left thirty workers dead. It seemed no one had the heart, or the funds, to convert the facility for modern use. As a child, Max and his friends had snuck in and explored every inch of the building.

He ducked through an opening in another fence, then zigzagged through the litter-strewn yard in front of the factory's offices. Graffiti covered the concrete walls, dulled by time and weather. He sidestepped through a broken doorway and entered the main office. The inside was a jumble of trash, concrete, broken tile, and smashed furniture. Along one wall were several stained mattresses. Drug paraphernalia and condom wrappers were strewn on the floor. He stepped carefully through the offices and entered the vast main room of the factory.

Most of the equipment had been removed, and the cavernous space echoed with Max's footsteps. He found refuge behind a row of hulking and rusted machinery along the back wall and considered his options. From his vantage point, he could see the entrance he'd come through. To his right were a set of metal stairs leading up to a row of offices. Behind him, a door went out into a storage yard.

He heard footsteps coming from the direction of the offices. Peering out from behind the equipment, he saw a man stick his head into the main room. Max gripped the Makarov and held his fire. He wasn't yet ready to give away his position.

Max heard hushed voices, then a man appeared and hugged the wall as he moved down the length of the room. He wore paramilitary gear and carried an assault rifle at the ready. He moved like he'd been well trained. Max considered his options. A pistol was a weapon best suited for close combat. On a range, with good lighting, no wind, and his own weapon, Max could plunk bullets into the center of a target from thirty meters. He could easily injure a man at forty meters. Most of his shooting records from his KGB training still stood. He estimated the man was about twenty meters away, with dull light and an unfamiliar weapon. Max aimed the gun and squeezed the trigger twice in rapid succession. The pistol popped twice and the man went down. Casings pinged off the cement floor.

Max ducked back behind the machinery and took the stairs up two at a time. Shots from a silenced semi-automatic rifle plinked off the metal machinery and the stair's guardrails. He turned to look as he ran and saw the shadows of two men use the cover fire to move into the main room. Three against one. Better odds, Max thought to himself as he disappeared into an office at the top of the stairs.

————

The commandos were no stranger to close-quarters combat. Trained in the Red Army, with battlefield experience in Afghanistan and Chechnya, and later, operational experience with the Spetsnaz, they were well-versed in room-to-room combat. Although in their forties, each man had stayed in shape and had built careers selling their services to the highest bidder. Having operated together for two decades, they could almost read each other's minds. They didn't know who their target was, but with one of their men down, it had now become personal.

Wolverine, their unofficial sergeant, squeezed his fist together, then waved a finger forward. He started squeezing single shots toward a fast-moving shadow behind machinery at the far end of the room. Taking advantage of the covering fire, his men moved into the room, around the machinery, then followed the shadow up the stairs and into the office at the top. Flashlights attached to their automatic weapons illuminated the way. On the other side of the office, a hallway stretched out in both directions. Wolverine made a decision and turned them to the left.

He didn't see or hear the form that dropped from the

ceiling behind them until he heard his men fall to the ground. The shots had found each man in the neck or back of the head. Wolverine turned and pulled the trigger instinctively, holding it down. His silenced gun bucked and spit, the bullets chewing up the wall and floor of the hallway behind him. The man had disappeared.

Wolverine cursed and moved slowly forward. Three of his men were down. Men he'd come to know as brothers. He stalked forward, gloved hands steady on the rifle. Turning the corner, he sprayed bullets down the hall and up into the drop ceiling. He methodically searched all the offices, firing rounds into each panel of the office's ceilings. His target seemed to have disappeared. He made his way back down the stairs and out onto the main factory floor.

Wolverine had come to believe he'd live forever. Having survived scores of conflicts and special operations jobs, he'd seen many men die, but never thought he'd be one. When his moment finally came, he didn't see the man who ended his time on earth. He simply felt a searing pain in his neck, and his world went black.

THIRTY

Undisclosed Location

Nathan looked around wildly for something to hit. He wanted to hurl his headset to the ground, then find a cricket bat to beat on a table – or perhaps an underling. But he contained himself and got control of his emotions. He hadn't risen to this position of success and power by flying off the handle at every little setback. Besides, this was why he didn't keep a cricket bat in his office. Later, there would be enough time to take out his aggression on someone. Perhaps that person would be Mikhail Asimov himself.

Next to him, Wing was talking animatedly into her headset. "You need to get control of the situation over there. It would be bad for you if your police force found these bodies." A pause. "I don't care what you have to do. You need to get to those bodies and make them disappear, you hear me? Or the next body disappearing will be yours."

On the screen overhead, Nathan could see a live feed from Belarusian television showing fire trucks responding to a scene. In the background, he saw the charred husk of a still-smoldering building. Fire teams doused the embers with a chemical spray from long hoses while a pretty young reporter talked animatedly into a microphone, periodically gesturing behind her.

For a brief moment, Nathan consoled himself with the fact that Travkin was dead. It was almost sweet justice that the bomb maker had finally met his death – especially since the work Nathan had hired him to do was complete. A final bomb made by Travkin was in place, ready to finish what had been started months ago. Someday, Nathan might need to find a new bomb maker. When he did, he was certain that person would be more pleasant to work with than old Travkin. Maybe the blackmail evidence Travkin had on him had gone up in flames with the rest of the building.

Wing was still talking. "I don't give a fig how far this goes up the food chain. This is why we pay you. Go earn your money and make those bodies in the factory disappear." She tossed her headset down and looked over at Nathan. "What a flippin' mess. The body count is starting to pile up."

Nathan ignored her comment. "Where do we stand on Blackbird?" He didn't give a fuck about the commandos. They were hired help. He only cared about one thing, and that was catching and killing Mikhail Asimov. If it didn't happen quickly, they were going to have much larger problems on their hands.

"Blackbird is ready to go, sir."

"Cezar?"

"He's in place, sir."

"Good. Let's hold off for twenty-four hours. Asimov may have just found out that the rest of his family is a target. He'll most likely surface again and try to get them to safety.

Let's wait until his head pops up, then take them all out at once. Then we can get on with our lives."

————

The Stranger had his secure satellite phone pressed to his ear. From his vantage point on the roof of a three-story warehouse, he could see smoke coming up from a building to the north. Despite the rain, the building had been almost entirely destroyed. Fire trucks were gathered and the news media were making themselves a general nuisance. With his other hand, he held a pair of night-vision binoculars to his eyes, facing the southeast, watching a peculiar scene unfold. A windowless van had backed up to the front doors of an abandoned factory. As he watched through the grainy green lens, a group of men loaded what looked like bodies into the back of the van. What struck the Stranger as odd was that the men doing the loading were wearing the uniform of the Minsk city police. No other authorities were around. No floodlights had been set up. No ambulances or other emergency vehicles were in sight. If he didn't know better, he'd think this crew was trying to conceal a crime scene.

"Go," came the female voice on the other end of the phone.

"Our boy almost got himself killed," the Stranger replied. "This thing is heating up quicker than a tATu concert in Red Square."

"Report."

"I picked him up when he arrived at the airport after getting the alert from Zurich Station. He took a cab from the airport and holed up in a fleabag motel, the kind you can rent by the hour. Around nine p.m., he appeared and took a cab to a dive bar called the Black Bear. I did not follow inside. I would have stuck out like a sore thumb among that clientele. Inside, there was some kind of altercation. Eventually, ambulances showed. Our boy was not among the injured. The tracking device led me to a two-story loft-style warehouse, where I arrived just in time to see it engulfed in flames. A gunfight erupted outside and I saw our target make a dash for freedom, pursued by four commandos. He disappeared into an abandoned factory. Now I'm watching the police remove four bodies, presumably the commandos. Our target's tracking beacon is moving north from the scene at a steady pace."

"It's time." The woman's voice came through strong and sure of herself. "I'm sending backup. Foster and McKey are on their way."

"Foster? That insolent prick? Couldn't you have found someone else?"

"This isn't a democracy. You need muscle, and he's the best I've got. You're to rendezvous with them at the Renaissance Hotel at 0600. Then grab Asimov and bring him in."

The line went dead.

THIRTY-ONE

Minsk, Belarus

Arina's neighborhood was silent, save for a few birds chirping their morning greeting. The narrow street was lined with rows of apartment buildings interspersed with leafy trees that rustled in a light wind. Cars of mostly foreign make lined both sides of the street. The apartment buildings were only four stories, and were newer and well maintained. Each unit allowed for wide balconies, and many tenants had built flower-box gardens on their railings and had strung up flowering plants along the balcony ceilings. It was a pleasant, upper-class neighborhood where university professors lived alongside senior government officials. Arina's husband had held a midlevel position in the Belarus KGB.

Max was sitting low in a rusted Renault he'd broken into and hot-wired not too far from the airplane factory. He was parked along the street, about a half block from the front entrance to Arina's apartment building. He could see the building's doorman emerge periodically and sweep the sidewalk or gather newspapers.

Since his flight from the abandoned factory, Max had been addled by a low-grade anxiety that dominated every thought. Just hours ago, he'd been hell-bent on finding his parents' killers. Now, he was focused on an entirely different task: saving the lives of Arina and his nephew Alex. Whoever had hired the bomb maker to prepare the bomb that had killed his parents was also focused on killing Arina, Alex, and himself. For some reason, that person, or group, wanted the Asimov family erased from the planet. Max didn't yet have a plan, but he needed to act quickly to get his remaining family to safety.

There were two logical places bombs might have been placed to target Arina and Alex. The first was Arina's car. Since her van had been destroyed, she had been driving her husband's Toyota Land Cruiser. Max wondered how the family afforded the vehicle, but then figured perhaps their father helped. The second most likely location for a bomb would be in the apartment itself. Either bomb, Max thought, would probably be detonated by a radio-controlled device activated by a human with some visual proximity to either the Land Cruiser or the apartment.

As Max watched, he toyed with the bomb maker's mobile phone. It was a Japanese Android phone, and it seemed to be locked with thumbprint security. Max realized it would be a dead end without the right equipment. He tossed it on the passenger seat.

He scanned the street in both directions. A man with a remote detonator could be anywhere. There were several vans parked along the street. He could also be hidden in any one of the apartment buildings in the immediate area.

Max knew he needed to get his sister out of the neighborhood, but that would be tricky. Their last conversation had not gone well, and Max had done what he'd always done, simply disappeared and avoided the family drama. It wasn't a habit he was proud of, but he just didn't want to deal with the conflict. He preferred life to be drama free. Arina was strong-willed, and wouldn't go without a good reason. Also, getting into the building without being seen by a man holding a radio-controlled transmitter would be difficult. He knew there was a back entrance where vehicles came in and out of the garage, but that would likely be watched as well.

The doorman came out of the building and began to clean the outside of the plate-glass door with a cleaning solution and a rag. He wore a uniform consisting of an over-coat and a cap that resembled a nautical captain's hat. Max sized him up, then was struck with an idea. After a moment to work through the details in his mind, he started the car, moved out of the spot, and drove two blocks down the street, where a corner store was just opening for business. Max parked, got out, and wandered through the store until he found a tiny, cramped restroom in the back. Then he approached the old woman behind the cash register, handed her a large stack of euros, and said, "I need your store for an hour. Can you disappear?"

After the old woman had shuffled out, he grabbed a burner phone from a wall display, dialed information, and asked for the number of the main desk at Arina's apartment building. Then he dialed the number. After two rings, the doorman answered. Max identified himself as Arina's husband, and said in a brusque voice, "Would you be a sport and run down to the corner store and grab us a quart of milk and some eggs? We're trying to get the kiddo ready for school and we're out of food."

Ten minutes later, the doorman was tied up, gagged, and locked in the bathroom. Max had the doorman's coat over his own, and was wearing the man's hat. He hoped it would be enough to trick an observer from a distance. He carried a bag of groceries and walked back toward Arina's apartment.

He used the doorman's key to gain entrance to the building through the front, then tossed the groceries behind the desk and found the stairs down to the garage. He was moving fast now, needing to finish before the doorman was either discovered by the store's proprietor or someone realized he was missing. Max took the cement steps down two at a time and shoved the door open to the underground parking. The Land Cruiser was not in its spot. Where would Arina be at this hour of the morning? He knew she didn't leave to drop Alex off at school until eight a.m.

Cursing to himself, he dashed over to the elevator bank, then jammed his finger on the number four, the top floor. He kept jabbing at the number until the car arrived. A minute later, he was exiting out onto the forth floor, composing himself, trying to act like a doorman. He made his way down the hall to number 405 and paused, listening. It was just after seven a.m. and he reasoned they should be awake. He heard nothing through the door.

Standing back, he rapped his knuckles on the door. "It's the doorman, ma'am." Then he knocked again, louder.

He heard nothing.

Anxiety turned into panic. Had they been killed in their sleep? Were they even still alive?

Max pulled out his wallet, removed a set of lock picks, and went to work on the door lock. When the last tumbler fell, he pulled out the Makarov and pushed the door open. He was prepared to be devastated.

The first thing that struck him was the floral scent of a cleaning agent. He stepped through the door. The kitchen was to his left, off the entry hall, and he peeked in. The kitchen's white linoleum and cherry cabinetry gleamed in the morning light. Not a dish was in the sink. The counters were clean and empty of food or trash. He stole down the hallway into the living room. There, he found the room in perfect order. The blanket he'd used to sleep with was folded and draped over the back of the couch. The coffee table was empty and the glass surface clean and dust free. None of Alex's toys were around. Max stayed away from the living room windows, not wanting to alert anyone who might be watching that he was in the apartment.

He moved down the hallway to Alex's bedroom and looked in. When Max had stayed over, the room had been a tidal wave of toys and computer equipment and games. Now, it was clean and everything had been put away. The bed had not been slept in. Max hurried down the hall to the master bedroom, and found the same thing. A clean room. A made bed that hadn't been slept in.

Where on earth were his sister and nephew?

THIRTY-TWO

Minsk, Belarus

His alarm increasing by the second, Max dashed back to the kitchen. He examined the inside of the oven, the refrigerator, and all the cupboards. He wasn't sure what he was looking for, maybe some sign of life, or maybe a bomb hidden among the appliances, maybe some kind of surveillance device. Instead, he found canned goods and boxes of food all neatly arranged. The oven was empty. The refrigerator had been cleaned out. It looked like his sister and nephew had flown the coop.

He moved into the living room and stopped to think. Would his sister have taken her own safety and the safety of her only child into her own hands? Would she have felt threatened, and disappeared on her own? If that were the case, he would have thought she'd have left a message for him. He glanced around the kitchen one more time. It looked like she'd cleaned up and prepared to be away for a long period of time. And the car was missing. Max checked his phone, but found no email from his sister.

One side of Max's brain was screaming for him to get out of there. He felt like a bomb could go off any moment, taking him with it. But he needed to find a clue, a lead. Something to help him figure out his next move. What he was seeing didn't add up. There had to be something that could give him a hint as to what had happened to his sister. Or where she'd gone.

Moving quickly, he started searching the apartment. He opened up the hallway closet and pulled the contents onto the floor. Winter boots and jackets tumbled out. He yanked the items down from the closet shelf. Hats, scarves, gloves, and children's mittens fell onto the floor. He rooted through all the clothing, looking for anything out of the ordinary. He found nothing. If she was on the run, she hadn't planned on going anywhere cold.

He glanced around the hall, about to move back into the kitchen. Something caught his attention near the front door – something he'd missed earlier in his haste to get into the apartment. The paint around the doorjamb looked fresh. The walls were an off white, almost eggshell-colored. The trim around the door was more of a pure white. But as he looked, he could see that some of the pure white had been painted over the eggshell, like someone had been in a hurry and neglected to tape the wall when they painted the trim. He touched the paint and found it tacky to the touch. Then he examined the lock, where the bolt went into the door-jamb. It looked new. The brass was shiny and the bolt mechanism worked flawlessly. He looked out into the hall at the neighbor's door. The lock was dull, tarnished, and scratched.

Max could think of only one reason for the retouching,

and it didn't make him feel very good. Someone had forcibly gained entrance to the unit, and wanted to disguise the fact.

He went back into the apartment and into the kitchen. He fought back panic. It was looking more and more like someone had taken Arina and Alex.

Max rifled through the entire kitchen, starting first with the pantry, then moving on to the cupboards. He pulled food items out onto the floor, not caring about the mess he was making. He found nothing, other than dishes, pots and pans, canned goods, and boxes of cereals and pastas. The refrigerator was completely cleaned out. Pictures of Alex and Arina's late husband and herself were on the refrigerator, and showed them at a park, hamming for the camera, taking selfies. Various pieces of children's artwork, presumably from Alex as a younger child, lined one side of the refrigerator. Max opened the freezer. It was packed with containers of frozen vegetables and other food items. He rummaged through the contents looking for something out of the ordinary, and found nothing. With growing frustration, he tossed a bag of frozen peas back in and slammed the freezer door.

Perspiration had formed on his forehead, and he felt overheated. Max shed the heavy overcoat and tossed the hat aside. He moved into the living room, taking care to stay away from the windows, where the open shades allowed the morning sunlight to stream in. He could see the balcony from inside the living room and noticed it too was clean and tidy. A set of chairs was lined up next to a compact, round, glass-topped table. The plants in the small window boxes perched on the railing were green and healthy.

He rummaged through the seat cushions of the couch, and found nothing. The coffee table was cleared of the normal everyday stuff that accumulated on such pieces of furniture. He bent down and looked under the couch and chairs, finding nothing but dust bunnies on the oak wood floor.

Finally, he moved back toward Alex's bedroom. A quick search uncovered nothing of significance. Then he searched the master bedroom. When he reached the master bathroom, he stopped short. All the normal men's products and shaving tackle were in place. He saw deodorant and nail clippers next to one of the sinks. But the second sink was clean and devoid of items normally found in a bathroom. All the women's grooming products and equipment were missing. He saw no hair dryers, shampoo, fragrances, lotions, or makeup. He yanked open the medicine cabinet and found it completely empty. There were no pill bottles or tubes of ointment. Suddenly, he knew they had left of their own volition. Arina was fastidious about her looks, and even if she'd left in a hurry, Max could see her shoving her beauty accessories into a duffle bag and running out the door with the bag over her shoulder.

Max was tense as he returned to the living room. If his sister and nephew had indeed fled Minsk under their own power, finding them would be a relatively easy task. Arina couldn't get far without leaving a sign somewhere on the grid, whether through the use of a credit card or a passport scan. That meant it would be easy for Max to trace her. His fear stemmed from the fact that if it was easy for Max to find her, it would also be easy for their enemies.

As he walked into the room from the hallway, he noticed the gas fireplace. A dozen tall candles rested on the inlaid tile surrounding the hearth. In the center of the fireplace mantle was an ornate clock. He paused, looking at it. He didn't recall the clock being on the mantle when he'd stayed here last week. He remembered being distinctly drawn in by the fireplace, with its ornate inlaid surround tile and all the candles. He'd lay on the couch after the bombing, unable to sleep from the ringing in his ears and the trauma he'd just witnessed, staring off into space. The fireplace had been directly in his line of view. He was certain the clock had not been there last week. He stepped toward it with growing trepidation.

THIRTY-THREE

Minsk, Belarus

In a vacant apartment half a block down from their target, Cezar jolted awake from a fifteen-minute power nap. The naps were one of his trademarks, a skill that allowed him to go long periods without sleep. He glanced at the set of monitors in front of him, fast forwarded through the last fifteen minutes of footage, then looked at his watch. He walked across the empty living room, his hard-soled boots ringing out on the hardwood floor, and threw open the sliding door to the balcony. Using a pair of binoculars, he scoured the street in front of the target's apartment. He watched for a few moments, seeing residents leaving the building. Oddly, the residents were working the door themselves. He waited for a minute, but didn't see the doorman appear.

Then he scanned the street in front of the building, looking closely at each car. Cezar had a photographic memory, one of the many traits that made him a success at Nathan's firm. Born in Tunisia, Cezar had left as a young teenager, and had never returned. Now he considered Italy his home, and was currently only tolerating his post in Minsk. He couldn't find good food to save his life and the women were as cold as a Peroni, his favorite Italian beer. He took note and realized that three cars he'd seen before were no longer on the street: a Honda, a Renault, and a Lada. The street was emptying as the neighborhood's residents left for work.

"Anything?" his partner asked. The young man was from Albania, and early on had shown himself to be a bigot toward Muslims. Cezar loathed the man, but knew he couldn't always pick his team. Still, Nathan would be lucky if Cezar didn't kill the Albanian before this operation was over.

"Nah," Cezar said, still looking through the binoculars.

The Albanian tipped his chair back and picked his teeth with the tip of a combat knife. "This thing ain't happening," he said. "Shitty deal. He ain't gonna show up here. He's too smart for that."

Cezar put the binoculars down and lit a cigarette. The less time he spent with the young idiot, the less likely he'd kill him, so he kept to the balcony. He put the binoculars back up to his eyes and scanned the street. Then he saw the tall man in the distinctive doorman's jacket and cap walking hurriedly down the street, toward the building, carrying what looked like a bag of groceries. He watched as the doorman entered the building, then he resumed scanning the street. He was looking for any sign of their target, one Mikhail Asimov, a man whose face and mannerisms Cezar had memorized. A man who had killed many of Cezar's operators. A man Cezar was becoming obsessed with defeating.

He took his time with the cigarette, watching the street below him. As he took his last drag, he heard the young Albanian shout out, "Hey, look at this!"

Cezar dropped the butt and ground it out with this foot, then picked it up and put it in his pocket. He stepped back into the living room. The idiot was probably watching cartoons on his phone. Cezar strode over to the monitor and gazed at the subject of the young Albanian's attention. It instantly caused Cezar to forget his loathing for his partner. The grainy monitor showed the doorman standing in the target's living room.

Cezar's mouth opened, and he quickly closed it. Why was the doorman in the Asimov woman's apartment? They watched as the man moved away from the living room and down the hall. A second camera picked him up as he glanced through the door into the master bedroom, then they saw him pull back. A second later, he walked back through the living room and toward the kitchen.

Cezar cursed his rotten luck. Suddenly he wished they'd put a camera in the kitchen. He stood rooted to the monitors to see when the doorman would reappear.

Then, Cezar's mouth dropped open. The man walked back into the living room and shed the doorman's jacket and hat. Cezar was staring directly at Mikhail Asimov. "Fuck! I'll be a—" he cursed, then fumbled for his mobile phone and hit a speed-dial button. He watched as Asimov methodically searched the living room. A moment later, a woman's voice came over the line.

"Wing here."

"We got him," Cezar said.

"Asimov?"

"Fuck yes," Cezar could barely contain his excitement. "He's in the woman's apartment right now."

"The woman and child?"

"Not present."

There was a brief pause. Then, "What's he doing?"

"Searching, it looks like. He was disguised as the doorman, which means he's probably on to us."

"If he were on to you, you'd be dead," came the reply. Cezar's blood instantly chilled.

"Can we detonate?" Cezar asked excitedly.

"Do you have confirmation that it's Asimov?"

Cezar swore, then turned on the phone's speaker and held it out to the young Albanian. "Confirm it's Asimov," he demanded at the youngster.

"It's him alright. I can confirm it." The Albanian looked as excited as Cezar felt.

"Then go," Wing said. "For fig's sake, go!"

Cezar pulled the detonator from his pocket. It was an old cellular phone, the kind made before flip phones and smartphones. He pushed the on button and let the phone come to life, continuing to watch the monitor, praying to Allah that Asimov wouldn't flee the apartment before he could push the button. Then he saw Asimov come back into the living room from the direction of the bedrooms, and stare directly into the monitor. It was as if the famous assassin were staring right at him, able to see directly into his mind. It gave Cezar a chill. Then he felt excitement run up his spine as he realized he was about to become known for taking down the great assassin, Mikhail Asimov.

He took one last glance at the monitor and saw Asimov's face up close to the camera lens, as if he were examining the ornate clock in which the lens was hidden. Then Cezar dashed for the balcony, wanting to see the explosion in all its glory. He stepped through the sliding door and pushed the send button on the detonator, bracing himself for the concussion wave.

THIRTY-FOUR

Minsk, Belarus

The clock had a design reminiscent of the Baroque period. It was grotesquely ornamental and intricately carved out of tarnished brass or gold, Max couldn't tell which. The clock's face had inlaid round white marble pieces etched with roman numerals. The hour and minute hands were woven strands of gold, and were not moving. The piece was so out of place in his sister's modern apartment, that Max was sure he'd have remembered it. A gift from someone, perhaps? Maybe she resurrected it from storage, something she liked but her husband had banished to the closet? Maybe it was something their father or mother had loved? Max doubted it. His sister was not a packrat. And it didn't seem like something his parents would like, either.

More likely, Max thought, someone had placed it here deliberately. He peered more closely at it, then picked it up to examine the back. The underside was unremarkable, but the rear of the clock had an ornately carved, round access panel. Max pulled at the tiny tab with his fingernail, and the door came open.

He didn't know whether he expected to see a bomb or clockworks. Instead, he saw several wires and a familiar-looking electric device. It took him only a moment to recognize it. A tiny transmitter and a micro-lens camera were attached to the direct center of the clock face. Suddenly, being in the apartment didn't seem like such a good idea.

He dropped the clock and lunged toward the door. His thoughts were consumed by one thing, and one thing only: Get out of the apartment. He yanked the door open and lurched out into the hall. If he could get down the hall and around the corner, he might be safe. As he sprinted away from the apartment, he was suddenly picked up off his feet by a blast wave and propelled through the air. He was hurled the length of the hallway until he was thrown into a wall. Then, he blacked out.

———

The blast was so devastating that first responders were shocked at the extent of the damage to the apartment building. The entire top corner of the structure was gone, leaving only shards of concrete and bent tailings of rebar exposed to the air. Rubble and charred personal effects had been blown out into the street, and cars, trees, and sidewalks had been covered with thick dust. Windows had been shattered for a block around the explosion and several car alarms had been triggered. When the dust cleared, three units in the building had been completely destroyed and six others would need major repairs.

Investigators would later conclude that the bomb had been constructed from an RDX-filled mattress in the master bedroom. That the building was still standing was a surprise, based on the amount of RDX calculated to have been used. Investigators would also be stumped by the lack of human remains in the debris. Although the target seemed to have been the daughter and grandson of the late Andrei Asimov, also recently killed by an RDX bomb, the lack of a body indicated the bomb had failed to achieve its goal. Perhaps it had simply been a warning, investigators surmised.

None of that explained, however, why Arina or Alex Asimov were never seen or heard from again. Eventually the investigators would close the case with a final report indicating the bomb had injured no one, but that Arina and Alex Asimov's whereabouts remained unknown.

THIRTY-FIVE

Undisclosed Location

The dog sat on its haunches, long swollen tongue dangling from its mouth. A thick string of drool ran from its tongue to the ground. Foam had formed around its mouth and the canine's eyes were bloodshot. A short rope around its neck led to a stake stuck in the arid ground, ten meters from where Max stood.

The hot sun beat down on Max's head and his hand was perspiring, making it difficult to hold the heavy gun with his teenage hand. His father had supplied him with something new this time. "You can't get too used to any one kind of gun," his father admonished. "You never know what you're going to run across while in the field." This one was a Nagent M1893 seven-shot .38mm revolver, a weapon that had been produced in Russia since 1895. "A gun so sturdy," his father said, "you could fix it with a hammer." Max tried to aim the weapon at the dog, but the heat and the moisture in his hand combined with the fear of killing a live animal caused the barrel to waver.

"Keep it steady, son," his father called from the chair where he sat smoking. Despite the heat, his father wore heavy wool pants and a long-sleeve shirt. "Remember what I said. Just think of the dog as already dead."

Max knew the dog was a stray that had advance-stage rabies, and would likely die within the next twenty-four hours anyway. He tried to tell himself that he was doing the dog a favor. Still, at age thirteen, he'd never killed anything. His finger trembled on the trigger.

"Pull the trigger, damn you!" his father bellowed.

Startled, Max pulled the trigger, hitting the dog in the shoulder, causing the animal to let out a tiny yelp. Shame rose in his face, and he pulled the trigger again, this time hitting the dog in the head. The animal fell over, dead.

Max jolted awake and sat upright, the dog's plaintive cry from his dream ringing in his ears. Sweat streamed from his face and body, and he instantly lay back down as a bone-crushing pain enveloped his head. His perspiration had soaked the sheets, and he threw off the wool blanket and top sheet in an attempt to cool down. He broke out in goose bumps; it felt like the cold air was freezing the perspiration directly onto his skin. He ignored the pain in his head and reached down to pull the blanket back over him. It looked like he was in a hospital room.

It was then that he felt the pain in his side. Moving the blanket, he peered down and saw a large bandage covering the right side of his torso. In his career, he'd been shot three times and been cut with knives more times than he could remember, but the pain of those injuries paled in comparison to the pain he now felt in his right oblique. He peeled back the dressing and grimaced when he saw the hole that had pierced the muscle. He felt around with his hand and found a similar wound in his back. It looked like a large-caliber bullet had passed cleanly through. He probed at the wound with his finger, feeling for any sign of remaining shrapnel. It felt like the wound was clean.

"I wouldn't do that if I were you." The voice came from the corner, out of the darkness. Looking around, Max realized he wasn't in a hospital room after all. A dim light was shining from a dusty bulb high overhead. Sheets of plastic had been strung from wires forming three walls of a makeshift room. The fourth side opened into darkness, and Max couldn't see much past the perimeter of the little room. He was lying on a cot. An IV drip stood next to the cot, attached to his right arm. The voice continued. "We're not exactly in the most sanitary of conditions. You don't want to get it infected."

The man speaking materialized out of the gloom and took a seat on a camp chair next to Max's cot. The first thing Max noted about him was his pronounced limp. He moved as if he needed a hip replaced. The rest of him was unremarkable, except that he looked like a university professor. He wore a tweed jacket with actual patches on the sleeves and a dark green turtleneck that had seen better days. His face was leathery, and Max made out a deep set of crow's feet next to his sparkling eyes. He placed the man at about fifty-five years old. Something about him seemed familiar to Max. Like he'd seen the man before.

"Who the fuck are you?" Max said.

Just then, another man pushed aside the plastic sheeting

and entered the makeshift room. He wore a white lab coat and carried a tray with medical equipment. This man had the blue eyes, thin red lips, and prominent cheekbones of a native Russian. That told Max he was probably still in Belarus, or maybe Russia.

"Dr. Rabinovich here is going to sew up those holes you were just prodding. When he is done, we'll start our conversation." The professor moved to get up from his chair.

"Talk now," Max said. "Who the fuck are you and what am I doing here?"

The professor seemed to consider this for a moment, then sat back down in the chair. "Very well, let's talk. I'm the one who just saved your life. Left to lay where you were, you may have bled out from the rebar that had blown through your side. Or perhaps the bombers may have returned to finish the job. You were very lucky, Mikhail, unless of course you die from infection."

Max considered his words. If what the professor said was true, he may owe him his life. It took more than that to earn Max's trust, however. "You still haven't told me who you are."

"Who I am may become known as time progresses, depending on how the next few hours go. Until that time, you'll just have to play along."

Wrong answer, Max thought. He didn't enjoy games, and this was adding up to being some kind of mind fuck. He winced as the doctor inserted the needle and started yanking thread through his skin. "Am I held here captive?" Max asked.

"Not in so many words," the professor said. "But I think you will remain here at least for several hours. We are providing this medical care *gratis*, so the least you can do is to hear us out. Right now, the building is surrounded by armed guards. Their job is to keep your enemies away and to keep you in here. We are on your side, I assure you."

What side is that, Max wondered to himself. Aloud, he said, "So I am a prisoner."

"I prefer not to think of it like that. I prefer to think of it as, you are incapacitated by your injuries and in a position to hear us out. If at the end we both agree that our relationship is not mutually beneficial, then you may go on your way."

The doctor indicated Max should roll over. A second later, Max felt another jab as the needle went into his back.

"Your injuries are no longer life threatening," the professor said.

"Good to know," Max said, his face pressed into a pillow. "You seem to know my name. Can I at least have yours?"

A pause. "You may call me Mr. White."

"That's funny," Max said. "You don't look like Harvey Keitel."

"Who?" White asked.

"Forget it," Max said. "So talk."

The doctor tossed the needle on the tray and announced he was satisfied with the results. He instructed Max to leave the stitches in at least ten days. Max grunted his thanks and the doctor made his exit. Max sat up, and found a large plastic cup with a straw on the floor. He grabbed the cup and took a sip, found the water refreshing, and drained the entire cup.

"What if I were to leap from this cot and snap your neck, then take that pistol in your ankle holster and shoot my way out of the building?" Max asked. He was pretty sure he was too weak from his injuries to even move off the cot, but he wanted to hear the response.

White laughed. "You'd be subdued by Tasers by the two rather large gentlemen standing just behind me." As if on cue, two linebacker-sized men in paramilitary clothing moved into the light, showed Max the Tasers in holsters on their belts, then moved back into the darkness.

"You'll need at least two," Max said. Getting no response, he asked, "So where exactly are we?"

"This is a facility we use from time to time when we don't want to be disturbed. We keep basic medical supplies here in case they're needed. I must say, your injuries strained our capabilities here. You were quite close to death."

"You don't say," Max said. "Can I get some more water?"

White looked momentarily perturbed, then got to his feet and took the plastic cup and disappeared. The footsteps faded into the darkness, and Max tried to count the steps. Eventually, they vanished completely.

A few minutes later, White returned carrying the cup along with a deli sandwich and a package of cookies. "Apologies for the fare," he said. "Best we could do on short notice."

Max discovered he was famished and ate the sandwich in five bites. He declined the cookies and went to work on the water.

"Watching your weight, I see," White said. "How admirable."

While White had been away, Max had been thinking, his mind going around the possibilities. Clearly White and whomever he was working for wanted Max alive, otherwise he would already be dead. That meant they must want something from him. If they wanted something from him, the best way to accomplish that was to come up with some leverage. He put two and two together, and the notion that entered his mind chilled his blood. When he'd washed the sandwich down with several gulps of water, he glared at White and said, "So what did you do with my sister and nephew?"

THIRTY-SIX

Undisclosed Location

Nathan knew well the telltale signs of an approaching migraine. He'd been getting them since childhood. It started with brief flashes of light, usually in his left eye, but sometimes in both eyes. The flashes lasted several seconds to a minute. Then his left leg would turn to pins and needles, like he'd been sitting on it at an awkward angle too long. He'd try to walk it off, but the sensation would remain for several minutes. Eventually, a crushing pain would start on the left side of his head and sometimes his vision would blur. When he was younger, the attack might be so severe that he would vomit. Usually the migraine would last several hours, after which he felt drained and often had to take a nap or go lie down on the couch in his office.

Right now, flashes of light were appearing in his vision. He cursed to himself. He knew from many years of experience that nothing could stop the onslaught. In a few minutes, he'd have to go lock himself in his office and remain there until the pain passed.

Nathan was standing next to Wing's desk, watching as she talked animatedly through her headset. The flashes of light in his eyes made him impatient, and he jabbed at the speakerphone button. The caller's voice jumped out of the phone. Wing tossed her headset onto the desk and leaned back, her arms folded.

"— no sign of survivors," Cezar was saying.

"So is he dead?" Nathan asked, impatient.

The caller's voice took on a more measured tone. "Sir, it's too early to confirm. All we can do is assume. The amount of RDX in that apartment was substantial, but as you know, only a nuclear bomb can vaporize a human. We'll need to wait for the forensics report."

"Fuck. Ok," Nathan said. "But we can assume at this point, right? I mean, you hit the button as soon as you saw him in the apartment."

"Just about, sir."

"Just about? Or exactly?" Irritation was rapidly turning to anger.

"Well, sir, I was instructed to get confirmation of the sighting, which I did. Then I detonated the bomb. So there were a few seconds—"

"Ok, fine – but unlikely, right? I mean, unlikely he could escape something of that magnitude?"

"Correct, sir, I would say extremely unlikely."

"Excellent," Nathan said. Numbness was creeping up his left leg. He knew his failure to kill Asimov, and the pressure he was about to experience from his client, were the cause of the impending migraine.

"What about the sister and the boy?"

"They both left the apartment yesterday morning on

schedule. She always dropped the boy off at school before going to work. She and the boy never showed up at either."

"Damn it to fuck," Nathan said. "How could they just disappear like that? Speculation, both of you."

Silence. Nathan rapped his knuckles on the table. "Come on. Two people don't just disappear in a town where we own everybody. Wing, what about the KGB?"

"I've checked. Initial reports are they know nothing. Our source is researching and will get back to us. But there is no reason the KGB would pick them up."

Cezar chimed in. "Maybe they flew the coop by themselves. Or maybe Asimov helped them."

Nathan shook his head. "The video clearly showed him gaining entrance to the unit through clandestine means. He knew, or guessed, the building was being watched, and was either looking for something or needed to talk with his sister. We know there has not been any communication between the two since that night."

"That we know of," Wing said. "They are the children of a spy—"

"Still, the most likely scenario is they haven't talked. He came for a visit, and found the apartment empty. The surveillance footage seems to be clear on that point."

Cezar said, "Agreed. So the woman and kid flew the coop themselves."

"Fuck," Nathan said. He knew that after all other options had been eliminated, the only remaining answer – no matter how unlikely – had to be the right one. "You're probably right. Let's get our teams and the KGB on all points of exit."

"It's a little late, sir," Wing said. "They disappeared twenty-four hours ago."

"Fuck. So who dropped the ball on reporting their

disappearance?" Nathan demanded. Blood was pulsing in his forehead and he knew the migraine was about to become full-blown.

"It took a while to notice they were gone, sir. We didn't have someone on them twenty-four-seven," Wing said. "That was the operational plan we briefed you on and you signed off on."

"Fine," Nathan said, knowing she was right. "We got Asimov, that's a huge step in the right direction. A woman and a child with limited means can't hide too long. We'll find them, wherever they went. Then we'll take them out, just like we took out Asimov." He hit the end button on the phone, severing the connection. To Wing he said, "I'll be in my office with a migraine. Unless the world starts to end, I can't be disturbed."

"Even if our client calls?"

"Especially if our client calls. Tell him I'm off the grid. You'll think of something." The pain was pulsing through his cortex and cerebellum now. The light and noise from the operations room had set him on edge. He knew he needed to get out of sight before he took off someone's head. He made for the stairs, took them two at a time, then rushed into his office and slammed and locked the door. He dropped the blinds on the windows overlooking the operations room, then found the earplugs he kept on hand for this sort of thing. He lay down on the couch, pulled a blanket over himself, put on a pair of eye shades, and tried to focus his thoughts on his son.

Instead, they focused on his own father. Born in a Jewish enclave in St. Petersburg, Russia, Nathan's father had moved his family west after the Russian revolution, settling in Berlin. There, Nathan had blossomed as a top student, mastering several languages and showing remarkable acumen in his business classes. His father, however, struggled, failing to hold jobs or establish a name for himself. Finally, one evening his father came home and put a revolver to his own head, leaving Nathan to care for his mother and two sisters. Nathan later learned that his father had been taken advantage of in a shady business deal, and left behind crippling debt. When Nathan witnessed a pair of men who came to threaten and collect from his mother, he vowed never to let himself be vulnerable. Those two men had been his first kills.

Now, as the pain took over, a vision materialized in his mind. Nathan was kneeling at the feet of his client, who was wearing an executioner's hood. The client was pointing a pistol at Nathan's head and laughing maniacally.

THIRTY-SEVEN

Undisclosed Location

"So what did you do with my sister and nephew?" Max asked.

White's brow furrowed at the question. "Well now, the answer to that question depends entirely on you, Mr. Asimov."

Blood pounded through Max's chest and head as fury rose to the surface. He set the cup down and started to get up. "You fucked with the wrong guy," he started to say. As he sat up, a wave of nausea struck him and he had to stop. Still in a half-upright position, he said, "Where is she? She better be ok, or I'm going to find you when this is all over and kill you, kill your family, and kill your friends. Then I'm going to find your boss and kill him, then kill everyone who works with your boss. Do you hear me?"

If White was shaken by the threat, it didn't show. He said, "Mr. Asimov, please do not make us restrain you. Lay back down and rest. Do not overexert yourself. You need rest to heal properly. An infection at this point would be most inconvenient for both of us."

"Where is my sister, goddammit?" The wave of nausea had passed and Max yanked out his IV. He swung his legs down and started to get up.

"Oh my," White said.

Immediately the two paratrooper-bouncer types stepped in front of White. The one on the left, a barrel-chested soldier with a blond flattop, demanded, "Lie back down before we make you lie down. If we have to make you lie down, you'll wish you'd done it yourself."

"B`lyad," Max cursed in Russian. He felt tired and drained, angry and helpless. It seemed for the moment that White had him by the balls. He lay back in the cot with a groan.

"That's better," White said. "Now, why don't we have a little chat, and then we can see if there is an agreement in our future."

"So chat," Max said, reaching down for the water. His mouth had gone bone dry. He seemed to have no other alternative but to play White's game.

White folded himself into the camp chair and crossed his legs with obvious effort. "Let's start with your child-hood," he said. "You were trained by your father from a very young age to be a spy, correct?"

"Wow. You jump right to the point, don't you? You must already know the answer," Max said.

"You excelled in grade school, then were sent to a special military prep school in Moscow, isn't that also correct?"

Max stayed silent. His history was a closely guarded secret. How far did White's knowledge go?

"At the prep school, I forget its name now, you were a

star forward on the soccer team, and also excelled at rugby and shooting. As the son of a famous spy, you were destined for greatness. Upon graduation, you were sent to military training, also in Moscow. Then you did a stint in the Red Army, although that was short. You were quickly singled out for special operations training. Then things get a little fuzzy. We assume you were moved into an intelligence training program, where you were trained in the fine arts of spycraft, espionage, and perhaps assassination, although it's possible that came later. Finally you entered the KGB. You were placed in the First Chief Directorate, also known as Foreign Operations and Foreign Espionage. You were stationed with the Moscow KGB instead of the Belarusian branch in Minsk, which displeased your father greatly. Am I right so far?"

Max said nothing. He suddenly realized he could only be dealing with a foreign intelligence agency, perhaps the CIA or MI6. It was hard to get a read on White's ethnicity and background. He could easily have been British using an American accent. But he seemed at ease in the East, as though he'd lived here a long time. There was a slight possibility that he was Israeli Mossad, but Max doubted it.

"We know a lot, Mr. Asimov. The Russian KGB in Moscow kept you for their own purposes because you were such a valuable asset. They saw great potential in you. For a period of time after your initiation into the First Directorate, there is a gap in our information. You presumably lived in Moscow and trained with the KGB, perhaps performing operations behind the Iron Curtain. Then, in 1991, the Soviet Union collapsed and the KGB was split into two groups, the Federal Security Service – the FSB – and the Foreign Intelligence Service. You were placed with the Foreign Intelligence Service, and almost immediately sent into Western Europe as a field operative. This also displeased your father, who preferred you remain behind in the Soviet Union. How am I doing thus far?"

Again, Max said nothing. He didn't have the energy to deny the facts. But he also wasn't going to give White the satisfaction of admitting to the truth. He tried to keep the concern from showing on his face. In reality, Max was reeling from the fact that this person, this agency, knew so much about him. He'd spent most of his life hiding in the shadows, protecting his true identity. He was supposed to be a ghost. This exposure of his personal history made him very worried. "Cut through the crap and get to the point," Max said.

"You were stationed in Paris, directed to establish a cover vocation that would allow you freedom of movement and ample income, and told to wait until contacted, presumably to conduct assassinations on European soil. You opened a jazz club for cover. The specifications of your operations for the KGB in Europe are unknown, but contact grew less frequent, perhaps because of the chaos surrounding the dissolution of the Soviet Union. It was almost as if you'd been forgotten. You grew accustomed to your comfortable life in Paris. You went native."

Max stayed silent. His body was tense, his eyes boring holes in White's forehead.

"But while living in Paris, you weren't letting your skills go to waste. In fact, you'd established your own little side business, capitalizing on the skills the KGB taught you. You started to take on freelance assassination work. This much we know. What we don't know is your list of targets, although we have enough information to guess at some of them. Over the years, you managed to develop quite a repu-tation for yourself, although your true identity remained a mystery to the various law enforcement agencies around the globe. Interpol has been chasing you for years, but to this day, they have very few clues to go on."

"Who is we?" Max asked. He felt like a caged animal, but couldn't see a way out other than to listen.

"Now, to present day," White said, ignoring his question. "You return to your parents' house after years of being away. Tragically, a bomb explodes in your childhood home, killing both of your parents, your sister's husband, and destroying the entire building. I am truly sorry for your loss, Mr. Asimov."

"Go fuck yourself," Max said, his voice low.

White ignored him again, and posed his first question. "Did you ever wonder why the bomb exploded so close to the time of your arrival?"

In fact, Max had wondered about this. At first, he'd assumed it was a coincidence. After his experience with the bomb maker, though, he had put two and two together. He stayed silent.

"Did it occur to you that the bomb was meant to include you, your sister, and your nephew?"

"It occurred to me that the bomb was meant for me," Max said. "But it doesn't matter. The bomb did what it did, and I'm going to find out who killed my parents if it takes me to my grave. Do you know who it was?"

"But it does matter, Mr. Asimov," White said, continuing to ignore Max's questions. "It matters very much."

"Who killed them, goddamn it? Tell me!"

White shifted in his chair, wincing as he rearranged his long legs. "We don't know for certain, but we have a good idea."

Suddenly it dawned on Max – whoever White represented wanted a trade. "Tell me. I'll do whatever you want."

"Patience, Mr. Asimov, patience—"

Max interrupted. "Call me Max. You're driving me insane with this formal name bullshit."

White laughed. "If you'd prefer that, I'd be happy to. Now, about your sister—"

"Where the fuck is she?" Max asked, growing weary of the game.

"She's safe. With us. For the time being."

"What does that mean, *for the time being?*"

"As I said before, Mr. – er, Max. That depends entirely on you."

THIRTY-EIGHT

Undisclosed Location

Max thought he was going to lose his mind. He briefly wondered if this were some new form of torture: Play with a person's mind until they snapped and killed the interrogator, then was Tasered to death. Mentally, he took an inventory of his body. His legs were tired. He felt a great deal of pain in the right side of his torso. His arms and hands felt as if they were made of lead. His head pounded like a jackhammer. Overall, he felt a fatigue like he'd contracted mono. It occurred to him he may have been drugged.

"I'm just going to lie here and meditate while you prattle on, White. You're not doing anything other than trying to get into my head. Well, it's worked. You're now so far into my head that your nose is sticking out of my asshole."

The older man regarded Max in silence. Max looked around, trying to take in more of his surroundings. It was then he noticed the camera. There was a pan-tilt-zoom security camera hanging down from the ceiling above White's head. Max was not surprised that their conversation was being recorded. He wondered who was on the other side of the camera.

"Ok, I'll level with you on a couple of things, but then I want some information in return."

Max said nothing, preferring instead to close his eyes and focus on his breathing.

"First, we believe your entire family is being targeted for extinction."

At that, Max opened his eyes.

"Thought that might get your attention. We don't know any details, but we do know that your father made someone, or some group of men, angry enough to put out a contract for your entire family to be killed. Whatever your father did, or knew, was important enough for this group of men to get very nervous." White paused.

"I'm listening," Max said.

"The bomb at your parents' home was intended to do just that. If I'm not mistaken, you, your sister, and your nephew are all that's left of the Asimov family. The team that detonated the bomb made a mistake and let you and Arina and Alex live. Since then, that group has been trying to rectify their mistake."

"What group?" Max asked. His attention was piqued now. He forgot about trying to meditate.

"That's all I'm going to say for now," White said. "Except to tell you that we're on your side, Max. We want to help keep you and your family alive. You need to trust me on that." White let that hang in the air for a few beats. Then he said, "Now you need to talk. Tell me why you never returned to Moscow and instead remained in Paris, away from your father and the KGB?"

"Why do you want to know that?" Max asked.

White said, "Just answer the question."

"Fine. I fell in love with Paris. What can I say? I grew to love the art, and the cuisine, and the wine, and the lifestyle. It was a much more pleasant way of life. Parisians are friendly and warm, especially if you know the language. I also grew to love my club. It's fun to run a well-known nightspot. It fits my lifestyle."

White nodded his head, as if he'd expected the answer. "But Russians, and I assume Belarusians by extension, are very nationalistic. Very patriotic. And very honor-bound. Did you not feel that pull, that responsibility to return?"

"Don't confuse Belarusians with Russians," Max said. "Yes, there are a lot of similarities, but as a Belarusian, returning to Moscow was not an attractive proposition."

"And how did that sit with your father? The man who had groomed you to work beside him?"

Max glared at the older man. "Let's leave my father out of this. How is that relevant?"

"Let me worry about what's relevant," White said, leaning forward and resting his elbows on his knees. He stared at Max.

"Fine," Max said. "He didn't like it. He wanted me to return to Minsk and work with him at the KGB there."

White smiled. "Isn't it true that your real reason for not returning had nothing to do with preferring the comforts of Paris to your native Minsk?"

Max stayed silent.

"The truth was, you'd come to resent your father's influence over your life. He'd trained you to be a killer, and you'd come to resent him for that."

"Fuck you," Max said. He wanted to beat the smug look from White's face.

White leaned back in his chair. "Do you prefer the Soviet Union pre-1991, or do you prefer the switch to democracy – the post-1991 Russia?"

"First of all, Belarus is not free and democratic," Max said, glad the subject had been changed. "Belarus is known as the last European dictatorship for a reason. Its president is very authoritarian, and is directly aligned with Moscow." Max paused, then added, "Also, do not get confused about Russia post-independence in 1991. It is not a democracy. It is not a free economy. It is an economy dominated by a few corrupt businessmen, criminals, and politicians. You should think of Russia now as a criminal state, a criminal economy. They have essentially traded a corrupt communist economy for a corrupt elitist commerce economy. Why would I want to return?"

White nodded his head again. "Do you see any irony in an assassin complaining, or judging, another criminal enterprise?"

Max stared at White for a moment. "Do you see any irony in a kidnapper judging another morally questionable endeavor?"

"Is that what you call assassination?" White said. "A morally questionable endeavor?"

"There may be irony, but I'm not confused about my values. The targets I kill deserve to die. In my line of work, the ends justify the means. My targets do not include innocent civilians. The criminal enterprise you call Russia milks every last dime from its citizens, suppresses free speech, and willfully distributes propaganda to create its own false truths. It's hardly appropriate to compare what I do to mass authoritarianism."

"So you believe the ends justify the means in your own carefully crafted value system?"

"I do."

"Then you are acting as judge, jury, and executioner." White stated.

"Correct."

"Who gave you the right to take on those roles?"

"I did," Max said. "Much as someone takes it upon themselves to start a charity to promote cancer research, or start a business that distributes shoes to poor people."

"It doesn't bother you that it's against the law?"

"No. In fact, the legal systems in many countries are particularly incompetent at enforcing the law. They're mired in bureaucracy, ineptness, and corruption. Especially when it comes to international law. What legal jurisdiction is equipped to catch, prosecute, and execute a known gun runner who is providing weapons to warlords in Africa?" Max paused. White stayed silent at the rhetorical question. "The answer is no one," Max continued. "So why not enable a lone individual or small teams who are equipped to track down such criminals and eliminate them?"

"How do you know they're guilty?"

"Determining guilt is often far simpler than tracking down the individual."

"Especially when you're not burdened with laws preventing the invasion of privacy and violation of an individual's civil rights."

"Precisely," Max said. "One could argue that an individual running guns to African warlords gave up those rights when they decided to commit the crimes."

"So an individual is presumed guilty until proven innocent?"

"No," Max said, starting to enjoy the conversation. This line of questioning was a topic he had spent many hours contemplating. "An individual is guilty when an individual is proven guilty. The moral question is what constitutes proof? If I have proof, is that enough? Perhaps the proof I have would not hold up in a court of law because it was obtained illegally, but the proof is irrefutable. And the proof I have is enough to convince me the individual is guilty."

"So what about the sentencing? How do you, as a lone individual, determine the proper sentencing for the guilty individual? Where do you draw the line between life and death?"

"That one is simple. Would the world be a better place without that individual in it?" Max sensed White was enjoying the conversation as well.

"I see," White said. "What about, say, the life of a nuclear physicist who is selling reactor technology to Iran?"

"That's easy. He, or she, should die. There is no plausible argument for why Iran, a rogue Islamic state known to finance terrorism, should attain nuclear status. Also, that individual is violating international law for his or her personal gain. No moral ambiguity with this one for me. They should die."

"Instead of, say, being locked away in a prison?"

"Instead of being put through a corrupt, expensive, and inefficient legal process, only to find that the individual is released on a technicality, a plea, or jammed into an overcrowded prison and supported by overburdened taxpayers."

"So the international law you mentioned a second ago was imposed by one doctrine, a Western doctrine. If you take the point of view of, say, Islamic clerics living in Iran who disagree with the law, then who are you to say the Western law is to be upheld?"

"But doesn't every dissenter, by the nature of their actions, disagree with a particular doctrine or law?" Max smiled at White.

"Ah, now you're answering a question with a question."

"But the point is valid. History has shown that mankind, individuals, should not put blind trust in authority. I think it was Ben Franklin who said, 'It is the first responsibility of every citizen to question authority.'"

"So you're an activist?"

Max heard a buzz. White reached into his pocket and withdrew a smartphone.

"You could put it that way. I think the morals are the same," Max said. "Although that is not how I behave. Instead of activism, it's probably more accurate to simply call it action. Activism is acting out to make a point. If you tie yourself to a tree to prevent it from being cut down, you're protesting deforestation. But are you actually doing any good? Eventually that tree will be cut down. Activism, in most cases, is a narcissistic act. It's usually designed to call attention to something the activist disagrees with, or to make the activist feel better. Action, on the other hand, is simply doing. I'm doing what the law enforcement, legal, and judicial systems of this world can't do, or choose not to do."

White looked at his phone's screen, then put it back in his pocket. He abruptly stood and walked out of the makeshift room and into the darkness. Again, Max tried to count his footsteps, but eventually they faded away.

Then there was silence.

THIRTY-NINE

Kate Shaw removed a pair of noise-canceling headphones and shook out her long curly hair. Adjusting her glasses, she continued to stare at the monitor set up in front of her on a folding table. She watched intently while the man on the screen lay motionless on the cot. She wondered what he was thinking. The conversation she'd just choreographed hadn't really been an interrogation. Rather, she thought of it as a seduction.

Kate Shaw ruled her world with an iron fist. Those who worked for her revered the ground she walked on. She treated her team fairly, but expected them to wring blood from stones. Those who opposed her were usually crushed under her sharp wit, her ability to wield power, and her uncanny command of office politics. She was usually the smartest person in the room, and didn't hesitate to use that power. To her, you were either on her bus, or an obstacle to be run over. At this moment, she was wondering whether Mikhail Asimov, aka Max Asimov, was going to get on her bus.

She continued to gaze at the monitor while she waited for her agent, Spencer White, to make the long walk through the warehouse from the makeshift hospital room. She watched as the man on the monitor lay still with his eyes closed. Perhaps he was meditating. Perhaps he was sleeping. He didn't look or behave like a caged man. He looked like a man preserving his strength. For a moment, she appraised his appearance. He was tall, rugged, and handsome, although she might appreciate his looks more if he'd let his hair grow. For a moment, she pictured him with dark wavy hair. She wasn't fond of bald men. His physique was remarkable for a man in his mid-forties: no body fat, well-defined muscles, and broad shoulders. His large hands were interlaced and resting on his abdomen. His breath was slow and even.

The door to the dingy office opened and Spencer walked in, shutting the door behind him. Kate moved away from the monitor and leaned her back against the far wall, careful not to smudge her pantsuit. She was known around the office for wearing only charcoal-grey suits. It was a uniform she'd settled on that allowed her to minimize energy devoted to trivial tasks like getting dressed, something she'd learned from reading Steve Jobs' biography. Simplify the rest of your life in order to focus all your energy on the important things.

"Well?" Spencer started. "What'd you think?"

"You first," she said.

"Classic psychopathic tendencies, as found in most assassins. His are overlaid, however, with a defined moral compass. He has deep conviction of his beliefs. A singular focus, to the detriment of his personal life. Although I think recent events have jolted him from the carefully structured life he's created for himself into a chaotic mess of intangibles. He's hell-bent on vengeance for the death of his parents, and now presumably conflicted by the urge to save the lives of his sister and nephew. I imagine he's confused by these thoughts and emotions, and therefore he's in a more vulnerable state than he might otherwise be."

"Good. I agree," Kate said. "What else?"

"If what he says is truthful, and I do believe him, he has little allegiance to the Russian or Belarusian governments. He seems to have morphed into a Westerner over the past seven years of his life. He's grown to appreciate the quality of life in the West and is prioritizing that over family, duty, and allegiance. That means he's come to terms with himself emotionally and as an individual, and is valuing that over the collective good of his people. That could be either good or bad for us."

"Agreed. Do you think he could be compelled to act against targets in the Russian or Belarusian governments?"

"Russian, yes, as long as the rationale for the target matches his value system. Belarusian targets might be a different matter."

"Why?"

"He's loyal to Belarus, his home country, but disgruntled by its authoritarianism and its connections to a corrupt Moscow."

Kate took a deep breath and pushed away from the wall. She began to pace, another trait she was well known for. This, she'd admit, came directly from her boss. She found it a useful way to think.

"How violently will he react to the leverage we have?" she said. "And will he take the offer?"

"Those are the million-dollar questions," Spencer said. "I think the odds are in our favor. But his demeanor is unpredictable, given the emotional strain he's under."

"I agree. Only one way to find out," Kate said. With that, she turned toward the door. "Let's go."

FORTY

The woman who walked into Max's makeshift hospital room cut an impressive figure. She was tall and athletic, with wild curly hair and a sharp grey suit straight out of a tailor's shop in London. She looked like a lawyer ready to negotiate a billion-dollar corporate deal. She wore a pair of tortoise-shell glasses that softened the hard edges of her face. The eyes that regarded him were steely, and Max guessed there was an intellect there that might have given Einstein a run for his money. He was instantly alert. The stakes were about to go up.

White followed her and remained standing while she took a seat on the camp chair. She crossed one leg over the other and flashed some kind of fancy shoe, with high heels and a black and white pattern that resembled a maze. Max guessed the shoes cost more than White's entire wardrobe.

"How are you feeling?" she asked, regarding Max with a smile that belied her cold demeanor. The smile showed a row of perfectly straight, white teeth. Max got the feeling she didn't give a shit how he was feeling.

"Who the fuck are you?" Max asked, ignoring her question.

She regarded him for a moment and the smile disappeared. "I'm the fucker who controls your life right now, Mr. Asimov. Your life, and the lives of your sister and nephew, are directly in my fucking hands."

"So we can finally cut the shit and get down to business?" Max asked. He decided he didn't want to be lying down. It made him feel more vulnerable. He shifted his weight and swung a leg to the floor, then levered himself up so he was sitting. The doctor had cut off his clothes and he was naked under the blanket. When he shifted, the blanket moved so it covered only his midsection. The woman's eyes stayed centered directly on his face.

"The shit that you so eloquently prefer we cut through is very necessary to our burgeoning relationship, Mr. Asimov," she said.

Max nodded. Despite the fact that he was completely at this woman's mercy, he grudgingly admitted he liked her. Any woman who so freely cursed was a woman after his own heart. He felt like she would chew up and spit out just about anyone who dared cross her path. "So you know my name. Who are you?"

She hesitated, then answered, "You may call me Kate."

"Kate what?"

"Just Kate for now. Let's see how the next ten minutes go, then we can decide whether we're going to swap spit."

"Fair enough," Max said. "Where are my sister and nephew?"

"White, will you get Mr. Asimov some more water?" Kate said. Then, to Max, "Are you hungry?"

Max shook his head. "But I'll have to pee in a minute if you give me any more water."

If Kate found that humorous, she didn't crack a smile. White walked off, his footsteps fading into the darkness.

"Your sister and nephew are safe and comfortable, you can be assured. They're very well looked after." She fished in her jacket pocket and produced a smartphone. She scooted the chair closer to Max and held the phone up so he could see the screen. Max caught the faint hint of some floral scent he couldn't place. On the tiny screen was a video feed that looked like it came from a camera mounted in the corner of a shabby room. It showed a small boy sitting on the floor in front of a large television screen playing a video game. A woman who looked a lot like Arina was leaning back on a couch reading a book. Every few minutes she took a sip of something from a Starbucks cup.

"Where are they?"

"Safe. To tell you more would put their lives in danger."

"How so?"

"Because depending on how our conversation goes, you may be back out on the street in the next hour. If you are, you'll get picked up by Abrams' team. He'll torture you until you reveal where they are hidden. Then he'll kill you, and come find Arina and Alex. Then he'll kill them."

Max perked up at the name she'd just dropped. His mind immediately went to the plastic baggie he'd found in the bomb maker's safe. "Did you say Abrams?"

Kate ignored him. "Let me propose a deal, Mr. Asimov."

"Call me Max," he said. Just then, White came back into the room with the plastic cup filled to the brim with water. He handed it to Max. Max took a sip, then set it down on the floor.

"Ok, Max," Kate said. She lowered her voice and

slurred her words. "I'm going to make you an offer you can't refuse."

Max looked at her, surprised. "Is that supposed to be Brando?"

She shrugged. "I'm still working on it."

Max said nothing. Then she said something he hadn't seen coming.

"We want you to come work for us."

Max didn't know what he'd expected to come out of her mouth, but that sure hadn't been it. He tried to keep his face passive, then reached down for another sip of water.

"You what?"

"I don't think I stuttered, Max. We've been watching you for a while now. We've done our background on you. You're very good. I have use for a person of your unique skill set on my team."

Max played for time by drinking more of the water. "And what team is that?"

Kate paused for a moment, then said, "Let's just say I work for a Western intelligence agency."

"No shit, Sherlock," Max said. "That much I figured out. But which one?"

"Does it make a difference?"

"Absolutely."

"You'd rather risk the extinction of your entire family than agree to work for me, sight unseen?"

"Of course," Max said. "Some things are nonnegotiable."

"For instance?"

"You say you're Western. But that could mean a lot of things. Or you could be lying. I wouldn't work for Iran or any of the Islamic countries. They're too non-secular. Also,

I wouldn't work for any of the Asian countries, nor many of the countries in the former Soviet Republic."

"Fair enough, but let me state the terms of the deal."

Max said nothing. Right now, he was thinking he'd take his chances on his own. Especially now that he knew the name of the man who was after him. That knowledge was enough to give him an edge. He trusted his skills to take care of the rest.

"I want you to come work for me as a contractor, exclusive to us. I'll provide a lucrative retainer, enough so that you won't need to work for anyone else. You'll retire very well off." She let that sink in.

Max was silent; he knew there'd be more.

"I'll also put the three of you in protective custody. New identities, facial reconstruction, and a safe place to live. Your sister and nephew can have normal lives. Alex can get a great education. Most importantly, your family will be safe."

"They won't be safe until the people who killed my parents are dead," Max said.

"That may be so, but we can provide them with the best protection. You won't find protection like ours anywhere else."

Then he knew – it had to be the Americans. No one else would be this confident of their ability to protect his family. Fuck. The Americans. Unbelievable.

"Tell me about Abrams," Max said, again stalling for time.

Kate paused for a moment. "Well, we don't know much," she admitted. "But we do know that he runs a private business called The Firm that does work for very wealthy clients. Basically, he makes the problems of the ultra-rich disappear."

"He's a fixer," Max said.

"Correct. A fixer on the wrong side of the law. We don't know the size of his organization, or really much about it. We don't know where it's located. He's been on our list for a while, but frankly until you got involved, we weren't paying much attention to him."

"When I got involved?"

"We've been watching you closely for about a year. As you know, recruiting a foreign agent takes a long time, and a lot of investment. If your parents hadn't been killed, and you hadn't been pursued by Abrams, we'd still be watching you, and waiting for the right moment."

"So this is a recruitment," Max said.

"You could say that."

"Do you always recruit using extortion?"

"Not always. But sometimes. I'll admit this is a grey area, but the situation couldn't be helped. The reality is, we scooped up your family and put them in a safe place. They're a little unsure of what's happening, but that's to be expected. We saved your life by providing medical attention. The only forcible thing we did was to keep you here long enough to have a conversation. When we're done, if you choose not to participate, you're free to go, and we'll deliver Arina and Alex back to Minsk."

Max looked at her. "The fucking CIA."

Kate shrugged her shoulders.

"How long do I have to decide?" Max asked.

Kate looked at her watch. It was a large, clunky, men's diver-style timepiece. Maybe a Rolex, but Max couldn't be sure. "About five minutes."

FORTY-ONE

Undisclosed Location

Nathan sat at a large, ornate oak table, the kind one might expect to find in front of the bar in the House of Lords. The immense room opened up in front of him and culminated in a tall apse capped with a dome covered in frescos and gilded baroque. Stained glass let in the afternoon light, but prevented him from seeing out. A foot-high dais spanned the apse in front of him. The room reminded him of the interior of a church with the altar and pews removed, except the walls were covered in renaissance art by the masters. He picked out a Brunelleschi and a Donatello. Each time he appeared in this room, he wondered if the art had been stolen.

He was tired of waiting. To his right was a man he knew only as Mueller. Tall and thin, with a head of short-cropped salt-and-pepper hair and a light grey suit, Mueller could easily have been a German industrialist. Mueller had the emotions of a chunk of granite and the personality to match, and Abrams hated him with a passion. Six armed guards in black suits stood around the perimeter of the room.

Unlike their previous meetings, Nathan's client didn't keep him waiting long. A motorized wheelchair rolled out from the shadows onto the dais carrying a primly dressed man in a charcoal suit and black tie. He had the pinched and sunken face of a malnourished hospital patient. His patent leather wingtips shone brightly in the light from the stained glass windows. With all his resources, Nathan had yet to determine his client's identity.

Nathan's disorientation was palpable, and he hated himself for feeling anxious. In the twenty years he'd been running his business, he'd never been afraid of anyone, especially a client. But as he sat there waiting for the old man to speak, he could feel his armpits growing damp.

"Report please, Mr. Abrams," came the voice from the man in the wheelchair. The voice was low and rough, and belied a strength that didn't mesh with the old man's physical appearance.

Nathan stood, took a deep breath, and started. It had been two weeks since his last verbal report. "The primary target is deceased," he began.

"I'm aware," the client's voice rang out. "The primary target was only part of the contract, Mr. Abrams."

"Correct, sir," Abrams said. It galled him to use the word *sir*, but he forced a smile. "As I reported, the target's wife and son-in-law were also taken out in the first bomb—"

"You're stalling, Mr. Abrams. I know all this. Where are we on the last three targets?"

Nathan sucked in his breath at the rebuke, then swallowed and started again. "We completed an operation that we believe took out target number four. We're waiting on confirmation from our contact in the Minsk police force."

"Excellent. And the remaining two?"

Nathan cleared his throat and looked at Mueller, who simply stared back at him with the expression of an obelisk. "Well, sir," Nathan paused to clear his throat. He felt like someone had poured cement in his mouth. "The remaining targets have disappeared. It looks as if they've run. I can assure you—"

Nathan was cut off. "Disappeared?"

"A temporary setback, sir. I'm 100 percent confident that I'll find and terminate them within a week. We have agents around the globe, connections in many customs jurisdictions and embassies. I have people monitoring financial networks. They'll cross a border somewhere, or use a credit card, and they'll turn up. When they do, we'll be there waiting for them."

The man in the wheelchair was silent. Nathan's armpits were getting clammier by the minute, and he was thankful for the suit jacket over his shirt. He continued. "This is why you hired us, sir. We have the largest network of resources available in the world. They—"

"I know why I hired you," the man interrupted. "I hired you to erase the Asimov DNA from the face of the planet. I hired you to do it in one massive, catastrophic event. You've failed at that, and now you're running around cleaning up your mess. The group of men I represent have no tolerance for failure, Mr. Abrams, and neither do I."

Nathan screwed up his courage. He wasn't going to go down without a fight. "Sir, let me remind you that the contract only stipulates the elimination of the six targets. It does not stipulate in what manner, nor within what time-frame. It simply says *with all due haste.*" Nathan tried to swallow, but his throat was dry.

A pause. Then a chuckle. "Very good. You are correct, Mr. Abrams."

Nathan breathed out, and glanced again at Mueller. Mueller's expression showed nothing. For a brief, giddy moment, Nathan had a fleeting vision of punching Mueller in the face hard enough to elicit some kind of reaction.

"However," the client said, "I elect to amend the contract, as is my right under section 11.4, subsection C."

Nathan's heart sank.

"I am imposing a time limit on our contract of seven days from today. If you are unable to complete the contract within exactly seven days' time, I will activate the failure clause. Do you remember that clause, Mr. Abrams?"

Nathan clenched his fists. "I remember—"

"It states," the old man said, as if reading from a contract, "'upon failure to complete the mission or in the event Contractor attempts to ascertain the identity of Client, clause 6.2, subsection B will go into effect.' Do you remember clause 6.2, subsection B, Mr. Abrams?"

Nathan's outrage spread from his fists to his chest, and he felt his face grow warm. He was too angry to speak.

"Let me refresh your memory," his client continued. "Clause 6.2, subsection B reads thusly." Once again the old man spoke as if reading from a contract. "'Breach of Contract. Upon breach of contract, Client is entitled to a full refund of monies paid to-date, and has the option to notify Interpol of the identity and location of Contractor.'" The old man continued. "Failure to complete your mission in the next seven days will invoke clause 6.2, subsection B. You will spend the rest of your life in the court system at The Hague. You will lose everything you've built. Your son will be forced to talk to you through bars for the rest of your life. Seven days. That's all you have. Mueller will provide you with an updated contract on your way out." The old man turned his wheelchair and Nathan could hear the whir of the electric motor as he disappeared from the dais.

Mueller stood and tossed a black piece of material at Nathan. "You know the drill," he said.

Nathan was seething inside, but tried not to let it show. The violent anger he'd felt when his client had first issued the threat two months ago had returned. Not only had the threat been renewed, but now there was a time limit. Nathan had no doubt his client would follow through on that threat.

Nathan ran the world's most renowned services firm specializing in fixing problems for ultra-high-net-worth clientele. He'd worked for sheiks, billionaires, high-ranking diplomats, leaders of the world's most preeminent criminal organizations, and CEOs of the largest corporations. They paid him millions to make their problems go away. Many fixes required Nathan's team to operate outside the law. If Interpol was alerted to Nathan's identity and location, his life would end as he knew it.

He swatted the piece of material out of the air. It was a black hood made of soft velour, and he was indeed familiar with it. He glared at Mueller, then put the hood over his head and allowed himself to be escorted from the room.

As always, he tuned his senses into his surroundings as he walked. His heels clicked on what felt like slate or porcelain tile, and the sounds echoed in a large chamber. He walked down a ramp, as might be used for a wheelchair. A breeze ruffled the hood, and he was guided into a vehicle smelling of leather and fake pine. The car ride was silent for a stretch, then the sounds of a city came through the hood. Eventually, he was helped from the vehicle. He caught the familiar smell of jet fuel, rubber, and asphalt, and was guided to a set of stairs, which he knew from experience was the gangway to a private jet. Once on the jet, the hood was removed and he sat in a wide, plush leather seat. The window shades were all down. Mueller sat in the opposite seat, staring at him. A minute later, the jet was airborne.

The flight was short, so Nathan guessed his client resided somewhere in Western Europe. Before today, he had known his client was eccentric, private, and probably a paranoid delusional. Nathan never took a job without knowing more about the client than he knew about the target; it was a rule designed for his own preservation. This job, however, had been different. He had been blackmailed into taking the job, and threatened away from doing his normal research. At first, he hadn't worried. The job was well within the capabilities of his team. Now, however, the rules had changed.

He reached over and, in defiance of instructions, pulled the shade up. The window filled with blue sky. A layer of white fluffy clouds grazed the bottom of the plane's wings. Mueller cleared his throat and Nathan shoved the shade back down.

Nathan wouldn't go down without a fight. Not for the first time, he realized that the man in the wheelchair had him by the balls. Even if Nathan was successful on this job, he would either be forced to perform other tasks or would simply be turned in. The real threat came from the fact that Nathan was unable to use his considerable research power to learn his client's identity. It wasn't clear how the old man would know if Nathan's team started researching him, however. Maybe it was time to test his client's defenses. One piece of new information had come out of the meeting: His client represented a group of presumably powerful men. There were only so many such groups in existence. Find the group of men, and Nathan would find his client.

As the Gulfstream sliced through the air at Mach 1, Nathan's anger was slowly replaced with smug contentment. It was the satisfaction of an upcoming challenge. He knew he'd find the girl and her son – that would be easy. But now he had a new challenge: find, then terminate, his client.

He glanced over at Mueller and shot the man a casual smile. Mueller just looked at him in stony silence. Maybe Nathan would add Mueller to the list just for fun.

An hour later, Nathan was unceremoniously handed his mobile phone, watch, and fountain pen. He stuck the pen back in his suit jacket pocket, fastened the watch onto his wrist, and started checking his messages as he walked across the tarmac to his waiting vehicle. Halfway back to the armored Range Rover, he stopped mid-stride. He was listening to a voicemail from Wing. She had both bad news for him and good. The bad news was that somehow Asimov had escaped the bomb. The good news was that they knew where he was. Nathan clenched his teeth as he climbed into the car.

His secretive client could go fuck himself.

FORTY-TWO

Undisclosed Location

Max stared at Kate. She stared back at him steadily. He guessed there wasn't much in the world that scared her. He took her in again. No wedding ring. No jewelry of any kind, except for the watch. Only a trace of makeup. Her hands were bony and veiny, and her fingers were long, with a French manicure that had seen better days.

She consulted her watch. "Four minutes."

Something Kate had said a minute ago bothered Max. "Time out," he said. "Tell me more about this Abrams person and his company. If he runs a firm that specializes in removing problems, then my real enemy isn't Abrams. He must have a client who wants us dead."

"Bingo," Kate said. She looked at White. "I told you he wasn't stupid."

"So what do you know about this client?" Max asked.

"Nothing," Kate said. "I've got people looking into it, but so far, nothing. We can't even find out much on Abrams' company. So far, we know that he is in high demand, that he's very selective about who he works for, and that he charges more money I'll ever see in my lifetime." She looked at her watch. "Three minutes."

Max's head was spinning. The stakes had just gotten higher. If it really was the KGB that wanted him dead, they wouldn't have hired an outside firm. They'd simply do it themselves; they had plenty of trained thugs and enough of an intelligence network to do the job. Hiring an outside firm would mean admitting weakness, and would necessitate going outside the family. That wasn't the KGB's style.

He felt instantly relieved at that thought, but also knew that Abrams must have people on the inside of the KGB. How else to explain the copies of their personnel files he'd found at the bomber's residence?

"Two minutes," Kate said.

Fuck, thought Max. This woman was serious.

His mind turned to the prospect of working for the CIA. Twenty-four hours ago, the notion would have been ridiculous. It was one thing to shun his old service by living in Europe and taking the occasional side job. It was quite another to go to work for the sworn enemy. If he agreed to this deal, his life would change forever. The Russians loathed traitors. He'd never be able to return home without fear of being executed. His father would roll over in his grave, and Max would shame the old man's legacy.

"One minute," Kate said.

The odds were stacked against him, he realized. An unknown and unseen enemy with a reach far inside the Russian government and seemingly unlimited resources. If Max was able to neutralize Abrams, his true enemy would simply find another assassin to come after him and his sister. For that matter, Max realized, his enemy may have hired additional assassins or put a contract out on the street, tempting every huckster with a sniper rifle to come after them. Even if he agreed to witness protection with Kate, he'd still have a set of enemies out there looking for them. He watched as Kate shook her watch back under her sleeve and prepared to stand up.

"Counter proposal," said Max.

Kate's eyebrows went up. "I don't see how you're in much of a place to bargain."

"Bullshit," said Max. "You've been tracking me for over a year. You've got a lot of money invested in your operation. You're not going to let me get away this easily. You'd be foolish not to entertain a counter proposal. I'm too valuable a resource for you."

Kate paused, then sat back down. "Ok, shoot," she said, looking amused.

"I'll come work for you, but on a contract basis only," Max said. "You put Arina and Alex into protective custody. New names, social security numbers, US passports, a house in a location of our choosing. They go on a large stipend. I don't want Arina working a government job. They get protection around the clock."

Kate stared at him.

"When I'm not on a job for you, I have free latitude to continue pursuing my parents' killers. You provide me research and logistical support from the CIA, and stay out of my way. The rationale being that you don't want one of your best resources constantly at risk. If I continue to be pursued, it hampers my ability to move freely around the globe to complete your missions."

Kate rocked back in the camp chair and regarded Max over folded arms.

"I can't give you carte blanche access to CIA resources,"

she said finally. "That's a blank check that I can't authorize. Your status with us would be top secret, known only by a handful of top officials in our agency, and POTUS. For obvious reasons, we don't keep resources such as yourself on payroll. You'd be off the books. But I agree that this risk to your life poses an unwelcome threat to our operations. It's an enemy that could theoretically put you, and us, in a weakened position."

"You mean if I get caught and interrogated."

"Precisely," Kate said. "So I agree to your counter proposal, but with limited support from us."

Max couldn't believe he was considering agreeing to this deal. Finally, he realized he was doing it for one reason only: He had come to realize how much his own father had influenced his life, both for the better and now for the worse. Alex now wouldn't have that experience, unless Max stood in as a surrogate father. Suddenly, Max realized that's what he wanted. He wanted to raise Alex as his own son. In much the way his father had provided Max with the skills for survival, Max wanted to do the same for Alex. The difference being that Max would train Alex for life as a civilian, not as an operator. He'd do all the good things his father had done for him, and none of the bad. It would be Max's way of atoning for both his and his father's sins. Maybe his father would forgive him. Holding the blanket up with his left hand, Max stood and offered his right hand to his new boss.

Kate stood and took his hand in hers. It was a firm grip, with a cold, dry hand that didn't pull back.

"There is one more thing," Max said. Her stance shifted, and she cocked her head with a wry look.

"I get first right of refusal on my targets." Her expression changed to one of annoyance. She tried to pull her hand away, but Max held on tightly.

"Fuck you, Max," she said, staring him in the eye. "White, let's go. Obviously Max here would rather fuck around than protect his family's life." She pulled her hand free, then spun on a heel and walked out. A second later, she and White disappeared into the inky darkness.

For a moment, Max felt utterly alone, then he felt shame. All his life, he'd put his own needs and wants ahead of his family, ahead of his friends. He'd shirked responsibility by avoiding long-term relationships and commitments. There was a reason he didn't have pets, or want children, or even really maintain friendships. He was afraid of what those commitments might require him to give up. As a result, his life up until this point had been hollow. Now, just when he'd been afforded the chance to do something good, he'd fucked it up, unwilling to subvert his own moral code for the greater good of taking care of Alex and Arina.

A vision ran through his mind. It only took a split second, but it changed everything. He saw his nine-year-old nephew's face peering down at his, as he woke from being unconscious after the bombing of his parent's house. *Wake up, Uncle Max, pleeeease?*

Max shouted for Kate to come back. "Ok, I'm in." His voice filled the darkness and echoed off the unseen walls and ceiling. "We have a deal."

Just then, a series of explosions sounded from the opposite end of the building.

FORTY-THREE

Undisclosed Location

Light flashed and two explosions sounded in the darkness. Max heard the distinctive sounds of Kate's heels and White's wingtips running toward him. The two guards materialized out of the darkness, and to Max's complete surprise, one drew his Taser and fired directly at Max. The yellow-tipped electrodes shot from the hand unit and two of them struck Max in the chest. The sudden jolt of 50,000 volts froze him in place. Electricity coursed through his body and he keeled over onto his front, falling hard to the cement floor.

Through the din and the pain, he heard shots fired. Then the electricity from the Taser was cut off. Gradually, Max's senses returned. Arms pulled at him.

"Come on, Max, let's go." Kate was urging him up. He was still trying to get his bearings after the shock of the Taser. It was dark all around them. Somehow the single light bulb had been extinguished. He felt something metal pressed into his right hand. He gripped it and felt the familiar impression of a gun's handle.

"Glock 21, .45 caliber," White said in his ear. "Thirteen in the mag."

Max's instincts started to kick in. The gun's heft felt reassuring in his hand.

"What the fuck is going on?" Max hissed. He saw flashlights moving in the distance, playing around the interior space. He counted at least four.

"Come fucking ON," Kate hissed again. She threw aside the plastic sheeting and yanked Max away from the hospital unit. He heard loud bangs coming from their last location, then automatic rifle fire.

A few seconds later, he stood with his back to a cold, metal structure that felt like an exterior wall to a large warehouse. His fatigue and weakness were instantly forgotten, replaced by surging adrenaline. For the first time since the action started, he remembered he was buck naked. As his eyes became accustomed to the dark, he saw Kate standing next to him, a pistol clenched in both hands. White was nowhere to be seen. Max heard more gunfire. It sounded like a large-caliber pistol.

"Preserve your shots," Kate hissed at him. "Spencer is going to draw them over there," she pointed with her forehead. "We're going left. There's a van in the far corner."

"Who's Spencer?"

"White. Fuck. Just follow me."

She took off along the wall. Max followed. He tried to ignore his nakedness. He felt both silly and self-conscious. Then his military training kicked in, and he put it out of his mind. In KGB training, the recruits had been stripped naked and dropped onto the tundra, kilometers from civilization. Those who survived and found their way back to base moved on in the program. One man died of exposure. Several others washed out. Max was the first of his class to return – fully clothed, armed, and well fed, setting a new KGB record.

Max heard more gunfire and saw a shape loom up in front of them, flashlight bouncing up and down. He and Kate fired at the same time and the figure went down. Their shots echoed through the large chamber and seconds later shots plinked around them, ricocheting off the cement floor and putting holes in the thin metal walls. For a split second, Max considered trying to grab the fallen attacker's clothes, but the shots singing around them made him think twice. Kate grabbed his arm and pulled him further along the wall. When she came to the corner, she stopped. The hulking outline of a vehicle was visible in the dim light.

"Get in the van," she hissed, pushing Max forward. He pulled open the side door and stumbled in. She followed him and jumped into the driver's seat, cranking the ignition.

"We can't leave White behind," Max said.

"We're not," Kate said. "Leave the side door open."

The van lunged forward. Max was hurled to his left and he slammed against the side of the van's cargo compartment as Kate made a tight, screeching right turn. Pain shot through his torso. Max peeled himself off the floor of the van and lunged, and managed to grab the handle on the van's open side door. He held on with his left hand and focused on aiming the pistol with his right. He looked over and saw Kate's hair flying as she wrestled with the wheel. Her glasses were gone, and she had a deep scratch along the side of her neck. Blood ran down onto the white collar of her blouse.

"You hit?" Max yelled.

"Just a graze," Kate yelled back.

"I'd rip up my shirt and use it to stop the bleeding, but I'm not wearing one," Max called out.

"Shut up and hold on," Kate yelled. She wrenched the wheel and the van skidded right, causing Max to almost lose his grip. He saw a figure partially hidden behind a row of palettes. The form leveled an assault rifle and started firing. Max squeezed off two shots, but the careening of the vehicle made his shots go wide. Still, the form receded. The van skidded to a halt. He saw Kate stick her gun out the window and heard her firing. The pops were deafening in the confined space. Then a tall, lanky form emerged from a small door and lurched toward the van. Max recognized the limp. It was White.

"Come on," Max urged. Bullets started hitting the side of the van, and he heard Kate squeeze off more shots. Her gun's slide locked out and she tossed it aside. "Move it, Spencer!" she shouted.

White was moving as fast as he could, limping across the open space. If Max hadn't already known about the limp, he'd think the man had been shot. Max feared he wouldn't make it.

Max jumped from the side of the van, sprinted to White's side, and wrapped an arm under his shoulders. Max swept him up, dragged him along, and hurled him into the van. "Go! Go!" he shouted.

The van's wheels spun, then grabbed purchase on the concrete as Kate floored it. A bullet sailed through her open window, shattering the other passenger side window. Another hit the front window, causing it to spiderweb. Shots were hitting the back doors and Max pressed White's body into the floor of the van. A second later, the van lurched as Kate plowed through a closed roll-top door and out into the night.

The volley of shots ceased.

"Anyone hit?" Max yelled.

There was a brief silence. "Not me," Spencer said.

"Me neither," Kate said. She was wrestling with the wheel with two hands.

Max pushed himself up and moved to the front seat. They had left the warehouse's parking lot and turned onto a dark, narrow lane. The weeds along the side of the road whipped by at a blur. Max saw the speedometer pegged at 160 kph.

He crossed his legs and looked at Kate.

When she looked over, she laughed. "Put some fucking clothes on, will you?"

"Give me your jacket," Max said.

"This is a $2,000 Armani," Kate said. "No fucking way."

"Give me your jacket, Kate. If you don't get that neck wound cauterized, you're going to lose a lot of blood."

She looked at him, and the van slowed as she held the wheel with her knee and shrugged out of the jacket. Her white blouse was soaked red. Max ripped off one of the jacket's sleeves and tied a bandage around Kate's neck as she drove.

"Looks like a fashionable scarf," Max said.

"Probably the most expensive fucking bandage ever," Kate said. "Spencer, anybody following? It'll only take a few minutes for them to saddle up."

"I see lights in the distance," he said. He was peering out the broken back window, his pistol held ready.

"Fuck," Kate said.

Max felt the van surge forward as Kate hit the gas.

"Want to tell me what happened back there?" Max asked. Spencer tossed him a small duffle bag. Max opened it and found his old pants, his phone, and his other belongings. He pulled the pants on.

"We had to cut your shirt off. Sorry," Spencer said.

"Looks like we were compromised," Kate said, still wrestling the wheel with both hands. "The two men guarding you must have been in on it. As soon as the entry took place, one of them covered the other with his pistol while the first guy shot you with the Taser."

"Why didn't they just kill me?" Max said. Something about the whole scene didn't make sense. If they wanted him dead, they could have just shot him on the spot.

"When the entry happened, Spencer and I ran back toward your location, and saw you being Tasered and the other guard on one knee, his weapon pointing at us. We both must have thought the same thing – that there was no scenario where they would have Tasered you unless they were working for Abrams. So we put them down. Not sure why they didn't just kill you."

"I think they're gaining," Spencer called out from the back.

Max looked back, and thought he could see that the headlights had gotten a little brighter. Up ahead, he could see the lights of downtown Minsk. He wondered how stubborn these guys were. Would they pursue them into the city?

Suddenly a thought occurred to him, and his blood went cold. "What about the safe house where Arina and Alex are? If we were compromised, could they be compromised as well?"

Kate looked over at him with fear in her eyes.

FORTY-FOUR

Undisclosed Location

"Phone!" Kate barked.

Spencer scrambled to the front and handed Kate a mobile phone. Driving with her left hand, she punched a speed-dial button and pressed the phone to her ear. To the east, Max could see a pink light bleeding over the horizon. He'd lost all track of time, and was aware enough to know that adrenaline alone was keeping him alert. His side ached, but fatigue hadn't set in yet.

"Let me drive," he said. "This is my town."

Kate nodded, the phone still plastered to her ear. She motioned with her left hand. Max moved up close to her and took the wheel with his left hand. He could still smell a floral scent from Kate's hair as she ducked under his arm. Then he slid into the seat and jammed his foot down on the accelerator. The van shot forward as Kate fell back into the passenger seat.

"Come on, pick up," she urged.

Max executed a left, then a right as he approached the city. The facility where the CIA had held him was out in an old industrial complex, not far from the abandoned factory where he'd fought off the four paramilitary mercenaries. It was a part of town left over from the old Soviet military industrial complex. As they drove, the streets turned into civilian neighborhoods, full of small, cinderblock pillbox-style homes and the low, squat cement apartment buildings the Soviets had built to house workers. Max pushed the van hard and wound through the neighborhoods at top speed. He hoped that no early risers were wandering the streets. It was all he could do to keep the van upright.

"I think we lost them," Spencer said. He was glued to the rear window, holding his gun.

Kate pulled the phone away from her ear and looked at Max with wide eyes. "I can't get them," she said.

"Where is the safe house?" Max asked.

She gave him an address, not too far from their present location. It was in the center of a middle-class neighborhood, one Max knew from his childhood. With grim determination, he put the van on a beeline toward the address, running red lights and ignoring stop signs.

———

Kate's mind was spinning, fearful that her carefully planned year-long operation to recruit one of the world's most effective assassins was going to crumble before her eyes. She punched at the speed-dial button again and held the phone up to her ear. While it rang, she watched Max from the corner of her eye. His face was set in a grim look of determination as he flung the wheel to the left and then the right, urging the vehicle to move faster. His hands clenched the wheel as if he were going to rip it from the steering column. Only one thing seemed to be consuming him, and that was the safety of his sister and nephew.

The phone rang incessantly, with no answer on the other end. She told herself that maybe Chuck was just on the throne or in the shower. She ended the call and dialed another number.

When she'd found out about Max's identity over sixteen months ago, she'd had long debates with the director about how to capitalize on the information. He'd argued strongly for bringing him in and leaning hard on him to milk every ounce of information about the KGB from his brain, then leaving him in some rotten hole in the ground as a military combatant. Something about Max had told her there was a better way, and she'd argued for a more measured approach. She wanted to watch him, learn from him, and gather intelligence. She'd argued vehemently for this approach, and finally won. Now, however, she was out on a limb. She had to prove her plan was worth the risk.

"No answer?" Max asked.

Kate ignored him, her mind turning to the possibility of a mole in her team. Foster and McKey had both turned out to be working for the other side. How that was possible concerned her. They both had been key members of her staff, and their defection was alarming. Then her thoughts went to the men who were risking their lives by protecting the two Belarusians. She hoped this asset was worth it.

———

Max toed the brakes and swung the wheel hard, and the van skidded into a driveway. Before they'd come to a complete stop, he was out the door, Glock in hand, racing up the front stoop.

The house looked like all the rest in the neighborhood. It was a single-story cinderblock with small windows and broken-down fencing around the backyard. The homes around it were surrounded by dilapidated cars, rusted oil drums lying on their sides, and laundry fluttering in the breeze, either from rear windows or on lines in the back-yard. A rusty washing machine lay on its side in the front yard.

Max knew there was trouble the moment he saw the front door. It was open and damaged from some kind of large object, like a battering ram. He paused with the Glock held in front of him. Sensing both Spencer and Kate behind him, he pushed the door open the rest of the way, already knowing they were too late.

FORTY-FIVE

CIA Safe House on the Outskirts of Minsk

The smell that hit him as he pushed through the door was the overpowering stench of gunpowder intermingled with an acrid smell of blood and death. The only sound was silence. Max had been witness to the aftermath of many gun battles, and he knew he was walking into one now. With his stomach in his throat, he stepped into the foyer, gun outstretched. His only hope was that somehow Alex and Arina were not among the bodies he knew they were about to find.

The foyer led toward the back of the house, where Max could see a large kitchen area. To his left was a living room. The first body he saw was sprawled among the glass shards and broken metal from a smashed coffee table. The body looked like a corn-fed young man from the prairie, with rosy cheeks and blond hair. He wore blue suit pants and a white shirt. The shirt was riddled with bullet holes and soaked with blood. Blood spatter was everywhere.

"Fuck me," he heard Kate say under her breath.

Spencer had bypassed the living room and moved to the kitchen. Two possibilities had entered Max's mind. The most likely scenario was that Alex and Arina were lying in a pool of blood somewhere in the house and the attackers were gone. The other likelihood was that the enemy was lying in wait somewhere, still in the house, or had left a trap. Max needed to move quickly, but with extreme care.

He entered a side bedroom, and found an unkempt bed and a small duffle bag on the floor. He moved to the second bedroom, and caught his breath when he recognized his sister's jacket hanging on the doorknob. A roller bag was on the floor next to the unmade bed. Max kicked his foot through the contents and found a pile of women's clothing and undergarments. The other two bedrooms were in a similar state, but contained twin beds and bags of men's belongings. The bathroom was empty save for sets of towels and other personal products.

"Clear," Max heard Spencer yell from the direction of the kitchen.

"Clear back here," Max yelled. So far, his sister and nephew were nowhere to be found. He could only hope they were somehow still alive. He made his way toward the kitchen.

"Clear!" he heard Kate yell from the backyard.

When Max entered the kitchen, he saw nothing but carnage. Three more bodies were sprawled in a wide pool of blood. The wooden kitchen table had been shattered and playing cards and poker chips were intermingled with blood spatter, shell casings, and spilled snack foods.

"This is a fucking slaughter," Kate said, stepping back through the sliding door in the kitchen that led to the backyard.

"Any sign of Arina and Alex?" Max asked. Adrenaline was surging, and he felt antsy. He didn't know if finding their bodies would be better than living with the terror of not knowing their fate.

"None," Spencer said, looking at him with compassion.

"Is there a basement?" Max asked.

Kate just shook her head. She seemed to be in a daze. "These were good boys," she said. Max saw her slump against the frame of the sliding door.

"We need to move," Spencer said. Of the three of them, he seemed to be the least in shock. "An attack like this would be loud, and draw attention. The authorities might be on their way."

———

The three of them were silent as Spencer drove. He kept the vehicle at a slow pace through the neighborhoods as he made their way toward a main road.

A thorough search of the house had revealed little else. It was evident the attackers had come in hard, a group through the back that had destroyed the sliding door and a group through the front. The CIA men's weapons, watches, wallets, computers, and phones were all missing. Kate surmised the attackers had been looking for intel. After the search, the three of them had dragged and lifted each of the bodies into the back of the van. The four dead men now lay under a tarp, blood pooling along the metal flooring. This accounted for Spencer's careful driving.

Max knew Arina and Alex must have been terrified by the violence. A small part of him hoped they'd been able to escape, but he knew the most likely scenario was that they were now captives of Nathan Abrams, likely to be used as bait to capture Max himself. The thought of them as help-less prisoners, alone and scared, caused panic to almost overwhelm him. He fought off the wave of fear and forced his heart rate to calm. He knew the only way to control the panic was to focus all his energies on finding them. He wouldn't rest until they were safe.

"Now what?" Max asked.

"South," Kate said. "We have a friendly border crossing into Ukraine. From there we'll get to Kiev, where we can hop an Air Force C-130 to Ramstein and ex-filtrate. Before the border, we'll need to stop at a hardware store and get materials to get these bodies cleaned up and bagged for transport. We have to get them back for a proper burial. Two of these guys were married with children—" Kate's voice trailed off.

"I'm not leaving," Max said. "You can drop me off here."

"The fuck I will," Kate said, swinging back to look directly at Max.

A slow burn started in his eyes and quickly consumed his face and chest. "I don't give a fuck about your operation, Kate." He spat out her name like it was a curse. "We had a deal: Protection for my sister and her son in return for my employment with you. Well, guess what. You can't seem to protect my family, so the deal is off. Let me out here, and we'll call it good. I have to find them."

Kate's eyes blazed with fire. "I've lost six good men trying to protect you and your family," she said. "Six hard-working boys who just wanted to defend their country and make it a place where Arina and Alex can live safely. Six men who had spouses and children and parents and houses and pets that they loved. Six families who just lost men. Those men put their faith in me, so don't lecture me about pain and loss and suffering, Max. These guys were working for you."

"Two of those guys were working for the enemy, Kate," he said, but his voice was softer. "The reality is, I'm not doing anything until I find and rescue my sister and nephew. While I appreciate your help to this point, I'm better off alone. Maybe you'll be able to get your house in order and somehow prove to me that you can provide my family with adequate protection. Until then, I'm more than capable of operating on my own. Stop the van, Spencer. Let me out."

Kate had turned back forward while Max spoke, so he couldn't see her expression. Spencer kept the van moving and looked at Kate, as if waiting for the order.

"Stop the van, Spencer," Max said again. "Or I'm going to jump out while it's moving."

"Wait a minute, Max," Kate said, turning back to look at him. "I have something on Nathan Abrams that may help you. But before I tell you what it is, you have to agree to two things."

It was all Max could do to refrain from wrenching open the side door and jumping from the van. But something told him to wait. He knew he needed all the help he could get. If he left now, he had no leads. He'd be waiting around for Abrams to contact him. Then he'd have to willingly enter into Abrams' trap. If Kate could help him, he owed it to Arina and Alex to hear her out.

"No guarantees," Max said.

Kate stared at him for a second. "Fine. First, you need to help Spencer and me get these four bodies ready for transport. We can't do it ourselves." She paused.

"What's the second thing?"

"You agree to take Spencer with you."

———

It was noon by the time the three of them had adequately prepared the four dead bodies for over-land transport. When they were back on the road, Kate turned and said, "Nathan Abrams plays hardball, Max. There are a couple things you ought to know about him."

"I'm listening," Max said. He wanted to hear what Kate had to say, but was still on the fence about whether to bring Spencer. While he seemed capable, Max was used to working alone.

"Abrams has a large staff of highly trained goons working for him. Each of his people are leftovers from previous careers in a number of foreign intelligence services, including MI6, Mossad, and the KGB. These are people who wanted better pay, or who had been blackballed by their prior employers. He's got armies of computer hackers around the world, and is tied into most nations' immigration, banking, and tracking systems. If someone in the world moves, he knows about it. In addition to operatives and computer people, he's got an army of paramilitary types. Mercenaries with long years of experience in various hot zones around the world. He's got an army, Max. An army of weapons and men who are specialists in urban warfare, counter-terrorism, intelligence gathering, and the like. He basically runs a rogue intelligence agency with the resources of a paramilitary organization, all under one roof, available to the highest bidder." She paused.

"Is this what you had to tell me?" Max asked. "Because I already surmised all of that."

"I'm just warning you to tread carefully, Max. He's basically got a team of people just like you."

"Not just like me," Max said.

"Maybe not," Kate conceded. "But collectively, they are a force to be reckoned with."

"You've made your point. Now what's the angle you have on him?"

"Do you agree to take Spencer with you? You're going to need all the help you can get."

Max hesitated. His mind was screaming at him to refuse, but his gut won out. "Yes, I agree."

She told him.

FORTY-SIX

Undisclosed Location

Nathan did everything he could not to let the glee show on his face. In front of his staff, he'd remain stoic, professional, and even angry. He'd force his dissatisfaction to show through. He needed to keep the staff on their toes. He wanted them walking on eggshells. But deep inside, he was celebrating. Capturing the Asimov daughter and grandson was a coup of the largest proportions. He now had two chips he could play; chips that guaranteed Mikhail Asimov would stick his head up. And when he did, Nathan would chop it off. Then it would be a simple matter to execute the remaining two, wiping that family from the face of the earth and releasing Nathan from his indentured servitude. *Then I go hunt my client*, Nathan thought, suppressing a smile.

Outside the massive airplane hangar, a steady rain beat down, creating pools of water on the grease-stained cement apron. He'd ordered the two enormous doors to remain open, and his staff were wearing overcoats to ward off the cold. He could feel the mist and humidity from the rain saturate his own jacket and he fought off a shiver. The weather was perfect for what he was about to do.

Standing in the middle of the hangar surrounded by six of his most highly trained guards were his two prizes. The woman stood with her feet apart and her head held high, as if daring them to touch her. By all accounts, she'd not come quietly, kicking and biting until she'd nearly ripped the ear off one of his men. Silver tape had been forced over her mouth and dried blood was caked on her chin. Her eyes were crazed like a cornered mother bear. Nathan supposed that was exactly what she was. He was going to enjoy breaking her down.

The boy stood next to her, whimpering and shivering in the cold. A brown stain had blossomed on his chinos in the area of his groin. The boy had tried to run, but two men outside the safe house had snared him and quickly subdued him. His eyes now flickered between his mother and the floor, and Nathan could see paralyzing fear on the boy's face.

Nathan strode to his captives and stopped two feet away from Arina Asimov. Two guards took up spots directly behind him. While Nathan appreciated their professionalism, he didn't expect any trouble.

"Hello, Arina," he said. Despite her obvious rage, the woman's body was quivering, perhaps from the cold or maybe from fear. He admired her form. Tall and athletic, Nathan guessed she was an attractive woman underneath her clothing. He removed a knife from his pocket and held it lightly in his hand. It was an MK-2 fighting knife, with a straight blade and leather handle. This one had a seven-inch Bowie-style blade that had been honed to a razor edge. Nathan had retrieved the knife from the body of a U.S.

Navy vice admiral he'd killed decades ago. He took the tip and prodded the edge of the tape on Arina's mouth. Then he reached up and ripped the tape from her mouth. She cried out in pain.

"You leave her alone!" Nathan heard the boy's voice pipe up.

Nathan laughed and watched as the boy struggled to free himself from the grip of a guard. "Well now, you're a brave one, aren't you. Keep your mouth shut, or I'll have my friend there shut it for you." He turned his attention back to Arina. "Hurts, doesn't it? Try to remember that pain, my dear. Soon we're going to have a little chat. If you don't tell me what I want to know, that pain is going to get much, much worse."

"Fuck you, you coward," Arina said. "I'm not telling you a thing."

Nathan laughed again. He trailed the tip of the knife down her exposed neck, drawing a white line in Arina's skin. A drop of blood appeared where the knife sank in too deeply. She tried to twist away, but two of Nathan's men gripped her arms and held her in place. Nathan caught the tip of the knife on the first button of her blouse, flicked his wrist, and the button flew off, exposing a lacy brassiere. Her chest began to heave with panic.

"Better men than you have tried to resist. Everyone talks in the end, my dear. The only question is how much pain they have to go through before they do." He flicked his wrist again and a second button flew off her blouse. Two more flicks of the knife and the white skin of her stomach was fully exposed. He trailed the knife tip across the pale flesh near the edge of her jeans. Arina stood frozen in place.

"Leave her alone, you big bully!"

Nathan saw the boy struggling again. He turned away

from the woman and squatted down in front of the boy. He saw tears on the boy's cheeks, but also saw defiance. He held the knife up to Alex's face and the boy stopped struggling. "You're about the same age as my son, aren't you?" Nathan said. "Do you think you can stay quiet? Or shall we put a gag on you?"

Alex started to say something and Nathan clamped his hand over the boy's mouth. "Bring me some of that tape," Nathan said. A piece was produced and Nathan slapped it over the boy's mouth. "Apologies, but I want you to see this and I can't have you interrupting."

"Now. Where were we?" Nathan asked, standing and facing the woman again. "Let's see. Ah, yes. You and I have a common interest, don't we?" He raised the knife and wedged it between her skin and the front clasp of her bra. She let out a little scream as the knife dug into her skin, drawing blood. Nathan wrenched the knife and her bra came loose. A drop of the crimson liquid ran down her stomach. With a few more flicks of his knife, Arina's blouse and bra had fallen off in tatters and her front was completely exposed. Nathan paused with the knife pointed directly at her sternum, the tip digging in. The blood was flowing more freely now, dripping to the concrete at their feet.

"We both want to see little Alex live." Nathan pointed at the boy with his head. "When the time comes, we will make a trade. His life for the location of your brother."

Nathan didn't see it coming until it was too late. Arina moved her head back a fraction, then spat a thick wad of phlegm directly between his eyes. A spray of spittle covered his face. It took all of his willpower to refrain from jamming the knife into her chest. Instead, he pulled back and hit her in the jaw with his fist closed around the hilt of the knife. She fell to the cement, out cold before she hit the ground.

Nathan spun on a heel and walked away from the group, using a handkerchief to clean his face. "Strip her down and get her into a chair," he yelled. "Then soften her up a little. Just enough to tame her. When I get back, she'll talk."

FORTY-SEVEN

Prague, Czech Republic

The tiny cafe was deserted. The proprietor was an old friend of Max's father, and Max had tried to give the rotund man a stack of euros for the private use of the restaurant for the evening. The owner had steadfastly refused the cash, then shooed his customers and staff out. After an awkward stream of condolences, the proprietor had removed his stained apron and left Max and his companion to their own devices.

Spencer busied himself in the kitchen while Max shoved tables together and spread out sets of blueprints and security schematics. He poured himself another coffee and lit a cigarette. It was going to be a long night. Sleep was a luxury he couldn't afford. Not while his sister and nephew sat in mortal fear for their lives in some godforsaken prison. As he dragged on the cigarette, he reasoned that they might already be dead. Then he shoved that thought from his mind. Until he knew for sure, he had to stay positive. If he put himself in Abrams' shoes, Arina and Alex were too good a bargaining chip to kill outright. He focused his mind on the task ahead of him.

There was a knock on the door. Through the glass, Max could see a tall woman dressed in jeans and a white leather jacket. Her blonde hair was fixed back in a barrette, and she had a wry grin on her face.

Max opened the door and ushered Julia Meier into the cafe. A cloud of smoke clung to the low ceiling, and Julia stifled a cough. She pecked him on the cheek. "Can I have one of those?" she said.

He fished the pack out of his pocket and offered her one. She cupped her hand around his lighter, then blew smoke at the ceiling.

"It's nice to see you again, Mikhail. But what, may I ask, is so damned urgent?"

Spencer emerged from the kitchen, and Max offered brief introductions, staying as opaque as he could about each of their backgrounds. They shook hands and regarded each other coolly.

Spencer disappeared back into the kitchen and Max offered Julia a chair. "Fortunate for me you chose Prague as your new home."

Julia took another puff on the cigarette, then leaned back in her chair as she blew smoke at the ceiling. "Why is that, Mikhail?"

"Because you're going to help me flush Nathan Abrams out of the bushes."

"Who?" Julia asked.

Max took a few minutes to catch her up on everything that had happened since they'd last talked, leaving out the part about Max's new relationship with the CIA; he still didn't know Julia's true allegiances. When he described how Nathan had kidnapped Arina and Alex, her eyes went wide. Max ended with the statement, "I know I can trust you, Julia. You knew my father better than anyone, and I'm sure you would want to help find his killer."

Spencer emerged from the kitchen with steaming plates of pork and dumplings smothered in a thick gravy. Julia looked at the plate he set in front of her, then wrinkled her nose.

"Hey, when in Rome—" Spencer said, and dug into his food. Max wasn't hungry.

"I'm not in the game any longer," Julia said. "I don't think I'm going to be much help."

"You may be a little rusty, but you're still in the game," Max assured her. "That much was obvious after our time together in Zurich. Besides, Spencer and I will be doing the heavy lifting. You'll be in a support role."

"Nathan Abrams is the man who killed Andrei?" Julia said, referring to Max's father.

"He's the one who pulled the trigger," Max said.

"Abrams has a client that put out the contract on your family?"

"Correct," Max said. "The way to the client is through Abrams. And the way to rescuing my sister and nephew is through Abrams."

Julia examined her nails for a moment, then said, "Ok, I'm in. I'm tired of the museum circuit anyway."

Max took a long drag on his cigarette, then crushed the butt out in a bowl on the table. "You might want to hold your decision until you hear the plan."

———

It was one of those overcast spring nights in Prague where

the air was heavy with moisture, but no rain was in the forecast. Max sat in the passenger seat of a new sprinter van Julia had acquired. Spencer sat in the driver's seat. They were positioned on a hill that gave them a wide view of the prep school grounds where Abrams' son was enrolled. Max checked his watch. Ten minutes until go-time. Nothing to do but wait. Both men were silent, and Max's mind wandered to a moment with his father he'd never forget.

"Mikhail, my boy, that was awfully fine shooting," his father bellowed from across the range. It was Max's twelfth birthday, and his father had presented him with a brand-new Makarov pistol. It was ice cold but sunny outside, a rare occurrence in Belarus that Max relished. For several years, he and his father had been sneaking away on the weekends to this field, several kilometers northwest of Minsk, for shooting practice. Later, Max would find out the house and land belonged to the KGB. It had an outdoor shooting range in the back, and no matter the weather, Max spent his Sunday mornings shooting at targets, rusty cans, wooden stakes, or whatever else his father came up with.

The elder Asimov always had something new to teach him. A new kind of weapon, or a new stance, or a new drill. Some days they'd just practice reloading the Makarov until Max's hands were raw and numb. The drill was to use one hand to eject the magazine and slap in a new magazine using his opposite hand. "Slam it in hard, son, like you mean it, or it might jam," his father would pound into his head. His father always had a theme for the day, whether it was practicing a quick-draw drill until his fingers were bleeding or a discussion of some kind of spycraft theory.

But this day was a little different than most.

"*Come over here, Mikhail,*" *his father yelled.* "*I want to talk to you about something.*" *Max dropped the magazine out of the pistol, then racked the slide a couple times to ensure there was no bullet left in the chamber. He set the gun on the table and trotted over to where his father sat. On that day, his father wore a great coat and was smoking his favorite filter-less Turkish cigarettes. There were two metal lawn chairs set up next to a small table, and his father was leaning back in one, far enough that Max thought the two legs might break under the man's weight.*

"*Sit,*" *his father growled. Max sat obediently.*

"*Ever wonder why we do this every week, rain or shine, hot or cold?*"

"*No, Papa,*" *Max replied. In fact, up until this point, he'd never thought about it, he'd just enjoyed it.*

"*Someday, son, you may need to defend yourself.*" *His father was even more serious than usual. Max sat riveted at the edge of the chair.* "*You may need to defend yourself with deadly force.*" *His father took a pull on the cigarette.* "*Do you know what I do for a living?*"

Max had some vague sense that his father was in law enforcement, but he didn't really know. He shook his head.

"*I'm in charge of keeping the Soviet Union safe from its enemies,*" *his father said.*

Max didn't know what to say, so he kept quiet.

"*Do you know who the Soviet Union's enemies are, son?*"

This Max had studied in school, so he took a shot. "*America and Britain?*"

His father laughed. It was a loud, raucous bellow that reverberated around the farm like an echo. "*Yes, of course. But that's not all. Do you know who else?*"

Max was stumped, sure his father was getting at something, so he stayed quiet.

"EVERYONE!" his father bellowed. "Everyone is an enemy of our great Soviet Union. Even some of our own citizens."

Max was perplexed. Thus far in school, he'd learned that Western countries were evil and would stop at nothing to tear down the great Soviet Union using their nuclear weapons. "I don't understand, Papa," he said.

His father laughed again. "Someday you will, my son. Someday you will." He took a deep drag on the cigarette, then flicked the butt into a pile of snow. "For now, though, I want you to understand something very important."

"Yes, Papa." Max paid strict attention.

"I have many enemies. Enemies that may want to hurt me or, God forbid, hurt our family. Above all else, family is paramount. You cannot trust anyone who is not a member of our family, do you understand?"

"Yes, Papa."

"Repeat that back to me."

"I cannot trust anyone who is not a member of our family."

"Repeat this also," his father said, looking closely at him. "Someday I may be required to use deadly force to defend our family."

Max's throat was dry, but he soldiered on. "Someday I may be required to use deadly force to defend our family," he repeated.

"And if I am, I will do so without hesitation, fear, or remorse."

"And if I am, I will do so without hesitation, fear, or remorse," Max said.

"I will shoot to kill, with aggression, and use every skill and weapon I can muster to defend our family."

"I will shoot to kill, with aggression, and use every skill and weapon I can muster to defend our family."

"Excellent. Now go wash up so your mother doesn't smell the gunpowder on your hands."

Max walked slowly toward the barn and used a hand pump to wash his hands. He let the cold water run until his hands were numb, realizing that his life had just changed in a powerful way.

"One minute," Spencer said, jolting Max from his thoughts.

From that day forward, Max's life was never the same. The lessons became more urgent and more in depth. At the end of most of their sessions, Max's father would make him repeat the mantra he'd told him that day. Now, Max realized that his father hadn't been training him to follow in his footsteps. His father had been training him to protect himself and their family; he'd been training Max for just this occasion. It was a mandate that he'd been bred for.

He took a photo of his nephew from his pocket. The boy's earnest blue eyes stared back at him. Max slipped the photo back into his pocket, resolute in what he had to do.

"Let's go."

FORTY-EIGHT

Prague, Czech Republic

Getting onto the school grounds was the easy part. Thanks to a quick black-bag job by Spencer three nights previous, both Spencer and Max had on uniforms identical to those worn by the school's security guards. The sprinter van was wrapped with a replica of the security firm's logo, and Max hoped the darkness would obscure its shoddy workmanship.

Spencer rolled up to the gate leading to the rear loading dock and honked the horn.

"You sure this is going to work?" Spencer asked quietly.

"No," Max replied from the passenger seat. "Just stick to the plan."

The guard on duty emerged from the hut, looking quizzical.

Max got out of the van, his face stoic. "We're here for a drop-off. You want to take a look?"

For a moment, Max wasn't sure the guard would take

the bait. His hand inched toward the gun in the shoulder holster under his jacket.

After a brief hesitation, the guard nodded. He approached the rear of the van and moved to open the door. The moment he turned his back, Max grabbed him. The guard was big around the chest and shoulders, but he was out of shape and no match for Max. Max wrapped his left forearm around the guard's throat, choking him off, then jabbed a hypodermic needle into his neck and forced the plunger down. He caught the unconscious guard as he fell and dragged him into the guard shack. He released the gate and Spencer drove through.

Without hesitating, Max jumped into the golf cart parked next to the guard shack and jammed the accelerator down. The cart lurched forward. For a moment, he was surprised at the engine's torque, then realized the school's security team must have improved the cart's engine performance. He wrenched the wheel to the left, narrowly missing a bench, and managed to get the cart under control.

Getting the boy out would be the hard part. Ordinarily, Max would have spent weeks planning this operation. He didn't have weeks, so he was going in hot. A shoulder holster nestled under his jacket carried a silenced SIG P226. He had enough magazines in his pockets to shoot his way out if it came to that.

He couldn't have picked better weather for the operation. The night air was heavy with moisture and dense cloud cover hid a crescent moon. Unfortunately, the campus was well lit by rows of streetlights and floods emanating from each building. The boys had picked one of the only spots on campus where the shadows were long enough to hide in while they smoked their cigarettes.

Max knew this from Goshawk's research. As part of

their preparation, she'd hacked into the school's records and found the boy's Achilles heel. Three times, Ethan Abrams had been busted by school security for smoking, a clear violation of school policy. Each time, the boys had snuck out between curfew and lights out, hidden behind a utility building, had their smoke, then been caught as they returned to their dormitory. Review of the school's security film for the past week revealed that the boys had snuck out each night. Max was counting on them repeating their performance tonight.

Timing was critical. Max needed to get to the location before the boys showed. He rounded a corner and made for the rear of the tiny outbuilding where the boys would hide. As he neared the building, he checked his watch. He knew students were required to be in their rooms by nine o'clock. Lights out was at ten. Guards made their rounds past this point at about nine-thirty. It was during the thirty-minute window between nine o'clock and nine-thirty that the boys would take their smoke break. Max's watch read 9:03. He pulled up to the maintenance shed, used a pair of bolt cutters to remove the padlock on the shed's barn-style doors, then hid the golf cart inside. He made his way around the back of the building and crouched among a half-dozen steel drums. Another check of the watch showed 9:07.

By 9:13, Max was starting to get concerned that perhaps the boys had decided against smoking that night. If they did show up, he'd be cutting it close to the guard's arrival. He stood to stretch his legs, then crouched down again. If the boys didn't show, Max would need to depart by 9:23 in order to ensure a safe exfiltration. Another glance showed 9:18. Max couldn't help but get nervous. Everything hinged on this one snatch-and-grab. If they failed, security at the school would be doubled. This was their one chance.

Then he caught a whiff of cigarette smoke, and heard the hushed tones of whispered voices. Instead of coming all the way to the rear of the maintenance shed, the boys had stopped along the side of the building. Max stood and moved to the corner, and removed a heavy leather sap from his pocket. He could tell from the smoke and the voices that the boys were just around the corner. His watch showed 9:20. It was now or never.

He pulled on a balaclava to hide his face, then moved around the corner fast and silent. The boys were standing close together, Abrams' son facing him and the other boy with his back to Max. Max swung the sap with a short, efficient move that struck the first boy across the back of his neck, dropping him like a sack of flour. Ethan was quicker than Max anticipated, and made it two steps before another swing of the sap sent him reeling. Max removed a syringe from his pocket and jammed it into Ethan's neck, pushing the plunger down to expel a sedative. He had reduced the strength of the drug to account for the boy's youth and weight. He secured the arms and legs of Ethan's friend with zip ties and dragged the unconscious boy behind the steel drums.

Then he darted to the front of the shed, pulled open the door, and raced the golf cart around to where he'd left Ethan. With a grunt, Max heaved the dead weight onto the passenger seat, then moved around to the driver's side. He pulled the boy close with his right arm and jammed the pedal down. The cart didn't move. He swore, and checked his watch. It was 9:25.

He jabbed at the pedal a few more times, but the cart didn't budge. Max felt his heart rate elevating. He checked for the key, finding it still in the on position. Then he checked the forward/reverse lever, and found it in neutral. He realized he must have knocked it into that position when he put the boy in the passenger seat. He jammed it into drive, then mashed the pedal down. The cart shot forward. It was 9:28.

Max veered right and kept to a path between the buildings and the back fence. At one point, he thought he saw a golf cart carrying guards heading the opposite way, but he couldn't be sure. He rounded a corner and pulled to a stop next to the guard shack. Spencer came out, moving fast for a man with a limp, and helped Max maneuver the boy into the back of the van. A moment later, they were moving through the gate and out into the street.

As Spencer drove, Max pulled up a section of the van's floor. There was a shallow box welded onto the underside of the van's floor that would pass casual observation of the vehicle's underbody. A piece of foam had been placed in the bottom. Max rolled the boy into the container, then replaced the flooring. In a couple hours, Max would have to re-administer the sedative.

"Any problems?" Spencer asked as he guided the van through quiet city streets, keeping to the speed limit.

"None," Max replied.

————

The man responsible for investigating the missing child, the Chief Investigator of the Prague City Police, would later marvel at the professional manner in which the abduction was carried out. It was clear to him the perpetrators had thoroughly researched the security protecting one of the academy's most important pupils. He realized they must have been intimately aware of the student's schedule and habits. Somehow they had known that the student liked to sneak away from his dorm to smoke cigarettes with a fellow student. It wasn't until the two students turned up missing at the pre-bedtime roll call that another student had come forward with information about where the two boys liked to smoke.

An organized search revealed the second boy, still unconscious, hidden behind a set of 55-gallon steel drums. A soft pack of Marlboro Reds along with a lighter were found on the pavement next to the unconscious boy. His testimony would reveal nothing; one moment he was pulling on a smoke, the next he'd felt a blinding pain. That's all he could remember.

Witnesses would later report seeing a white van with a security logo, but no one remembered details. It wouldn't matter anyway. An hour after the abduction was discovered, the vinyl wraps of the security firm's logo were found under a deserted overpass, along with a set of license plates, all the boy's clothing, and two sets of authentic security guard uniforms. Special alerts were sent to border checkpoints, train stations, and airports. The chief investigator reasoned the boy would be kept within the Czech borders, and that soon they would hear from the abductors with ransom demands.

An hour after the boy's disappearance, the chief investigator watched in amazement as every investigative agency in Eastern Europe descended on his office. Shortly thereafter, a senior man from the Czech Security Information Service took charge of the investigation. It was rumored the Prime Minister himself had telephoned the Chief's Captain. Then, the chief investigator watched in surprise as a helicopter landed on the lawn of the school and four men in suits deplaned and joined the men from the Secret Information Service. Someone told him they were Moscow FSB.

When a shout went up that a white sprinter van had been found abandoned on the southern border of Prague, no one bothered to invite the chief investigator. He watched as the office emptied, then refilled his coffee cup and put his feet up on his desk. Whoever this kid was, his parents held plenty of pull. The case was way above his pay grade.

FORTY-NINE

Highway East of Prague

It's said that Prague is the equal of Paris in terms of beauty. At over 1,000 years old, the city is an eclectic mix of gothic, renaissance, and modern architecture, and hosts some of the most expensive art galleries in Eastern Europe. Despite its growing reputation as an iconic European city, Max scoffed at the notion that anything had a parallel to Paris. To him, Prague was a gritty city struggling to emerge from its recent misfortune of having been behind the Iron Curtain. It might be poised for a renaissance and have earned a reputation among the clubbing set and the beer connoisseurs of the world, but to Max, it would always be a gateway between East and West. A city where Soviet spies could shed their Eastern lives and don Western personas. He'd spent many a long, cold night in a dirty Prague tenement, meeting with his handlers, eating cold stew and drinking acidic vodka. He was happy to be leaving.

He drove the exact speed limit, keeping two hands on

the wheel and the window open a crack to allow fresh air to wash away the stench of fear and adrenaline. Despite the initial success of the mission to capture Abrams' son, Max couldn't shake the underlying sense of anxiety he felt at not knowing the fate of his sister and nephew. The unknown threatened to eat away his sanity.

Next to him, Spencer rode in grim silence, but Max was thankful for his presence. The older operative had a calm, almost Zen-like manner about him that Max found comforting. The silenced SIG, another source of comfort, was wedged between Max's right thigh and the vinyl seat.

On the dashboard in front of him, Max had taped the picture of his nephew. He knew it was a risk. If he had to leave the van in a hurry, he'd lose a precious second grabbing the photo. But he wanted the reminder of his nephew front and center, to keep him focused.

Earlier in the week, Spencer had revealed why Kate wanted him along on the operation. Kate had a team standing by at Ramstein in Germany, ready to move on Abrams' operation as soon as they had a location. The CIA would benefit from the treasure trove of information Abrams would reveal.

Spencer took out his satellite phone, thumbed it on, and let it warm up. After it had acquired a signal, he hit a speed-dial button and waited. When he got an answer, he said, "Operation Pumphouse, phase one, successful. Currently exfiltrating. Next update when we arrive at the farm."

The next test would come at the Czech border with Poland. The van they rode in now was wrapped with the yellow and red markings of a DHL delivery vehicle. They had papers showing them to be DHL employees, with proper authorizations to cross the border with a van full of packages. Their DHL uniforms were real, lifted from a facility outside Prague. Even the van's license plates would hold up under scrutiny. The whole thing could unravel if the border guards inspected any of the fake packages stored in the back, however. Or if they found the hidden compartment containing the sedated twelve-year-old boy.

After three hours of driving, they found themselves winding up a two-lane road outside the Czech town of Harrachov, ten kilometers from the border. Max knew from an assignment many years ago that Harrachov was a tiny hamlet of red-roofed houses designed in the Bavarian style. Normally, Max would have spent days reconnoitering the town and its nearby border crossing. The urgency to rescue his family demanded he rely on his memory. He hoped his haste wasn't foolhardy. The pistol he'd placed next to his thigh went into a concealed carry holster fitted to his waist at the small of his back. The silencer went into his pocket. His standard-issue DHL jacket would keep the gun covered. Spencer did the same. He skirted the town and pointed the van toward the Czech border.

Ten years ago, the border crossing had been manned by two uniformed guards in a multi-directional guard shack. Black and yellow gates would methodically move up and down, permitting vehicles to proceed after papers were examined. Max had chosen this route due to its relative remoteness, figuring that at this late hour, traffic would be sparse.

He also knew that there were no longer routine immigration or customs checks when traveling between any of the twenty-six European countries that were part of the Schengen Agreement. The Czech Republic and Poland were two such countries. With the relatively open borders between European countries, the odds were that they'd sail right through.

As they rounded a corner, Max saw flashing red and blue lights through the trees. He rounded another corner, and saw two border security cars with Czech markings positioned next to the gates leading into Poland. Four men in uniforms holding semi-automatic weapons stood in front of the gate. Max instantly knew they had miscalculated. He felt Spencer shift in his seat and say, "Oh shit."

"Relax," Max said. "Remember, we're legit. The moment they smell fear, we're dead. The truth is what we want it to be." A momentary vision of Arina and Alex huddled in fetal positions in a dank cell entered his mind. Then he put himself into the persona of a DHL employee.

Turning around now would raise an alarm, so Max proceeded as if they were ordinary Polish citizens returning with a shipment of packages for distribution. He kept his speed steady and guided the van to a halt in front of the gate. He rolled down his window and greeted the guard in perfect Polish.

"Dobry wieczor," Max said. He knew a smattering of Czech, but Polish had been imprinted on his brain from an early age. It was the language of Eastern European spies, his father had insisted. Max handed their papers to the guard in the shack. "Extra security tonight?" he asked, keeping his voice light. The guard in the shack ignored his question.

Two of the guards with automatic weapons began circling the van. Max forced himself to relax as he saw one check the underside using a handheld mirror. He watched in the side mirrors as they both rounded the rear of the vehicle. Then he heard and felt pounding, and one of them barked, "Open up the back."

They'd rehearsed this scenario. In a situation of increased security, the goal was to stay in the van. Spencer got up from his seat and walked through the van to the back, hunched over, picking his way through packages. He opened the rear door and pushed it open.

"Exit the van, both of you," Max heard in Polish. The guard in the booth still had their papers, and was typing into a computer. For an instant Max considered gunning it, but then thought better of it. In reality, their chances in a chase were slim. The road into Poland was tree-lined with no crossroads for a long distance, leaving few options to shake pursuers. He got out, leaving the door open.

"Is there a problem?" he asked, suddenly realizing he'd left the photo of Alex taped to the dash.

"Routine checks," said one of the guards at the rear of the van. Max saw Spencer climb down from the back and stand to the side, his hands clasped behind his back. One of the guards entered the van. Max heard him moving around in the rear. He was convinced the guard nearest him could hear his heart thumping in his chest.

The guard at the rear produced a photograph, and Max almost groaned when he caught a glimpse. It was a picture of him, taken from a distance, plucked directly from his KGB file. Lucky for him it was a poor picture taken in profile, many years ago when he wore his hair longer. The guard first shone his light at Spencer's face, then quickly moved away when he saw the obvious dissimilarities. The guard then moved in front of Max and shone the flashlight directly in his eyes, comparing him to the photograph.

The guard was shorter than Max, but stocky and well built. He shone the light in Max's face, then back at the photo, then back at Max's face, then down at the photo again. Max willed himself to stay calm. The picture was twenty years old, and Max's features had hardened and weathered over the years. He stood riveted in place, tensed for action, waiting for the man's verdict.

The guard in the back of the van stepped down, saying something in Czech that Max didn't catch. He saw the guard slam the rear door, then move back toward the front. Then the guard in the shack stopped typing and said, "Ok, looks good." He heard Spencer ask if he could get back in the van. The guard nodded and ushered him forward with his hand.

The guard in front of Max was holding the light steady in Max's face, as if trying to make a determination. Finally, as if swayed by the decisions of the other guards, he lowered the light and said in Polish, "You may go."

Holding his breath, Max got back in the front seat, shut his door, then accepted the papers from the guard in the shack through the open window. The gate rose, and Max nudged the van over the border, into Poland.

"Holy fuck," Spencer finally said, expelling a deep breath.

Max just nodded, his mouth too dry to respond.

FIFTY

Lukow, Poland

Max pulled into the long drive just as the sun was appearing in the eastern sky. All around them sprawled extensive farmland, framed by tree stands and long drive-ways. The fields were rolling with freshly planted corn, sunflowers, and soybeans, and at this hour, Max could see several large tractors making slow progress. The farmhouse itself was decrepit and tilted, its owners doing a poor job of upkeep. Max knew this was because the farmhouse had been an old Belarusian KGB safe house, left to crumble from disuse after the fall of the Soviet Union. Behind the beige wood-framed farmhouse sat a long, low building that served as storage, and another taller structure that used to be a barn. The entire facility was affectionately known among old KGB hands as The Farm. The nearest house was over ten kilometers away.

He and Spencer both exited the van, shrugged off their DHL uniforms, and put on clothes they pulled from a duffle bag they'd left in the barn. After stretching his arms, back, and legs, Max helped Spencer retrieve the boy from the hidden compartment and carry him into the farmhouse. They manhandled him down a set of stairs into the dank basement and dumped him onto a stained mattress in a holding cell. The cage had been in place since the KGB had taken over the farmhouse from the Germans in 1945.

Lukow's claim to fame, Max knew, was its role as a staging location for about 16,000 Jews starting in 1941. About 13,000 of the interned Jews had been transported by train to the Treblinka extermination camp. The rest had been slaughtered in execution pits on the south side of Lukow. Only about 150 Jews from the town survived the holocaust. Rumor had it that the farmhouse had been used by local resistance fighters until the town had been overrun by the Germans in 1941.

Max arranged a few things in the cell. He put a large jug of water on the floor next to a covered container of lunch meats, cheeses, and bread. He made sure the lid was sealed tight so the rats couldn't get to it. Next to the mattress, he placed a large stack of comic books and a hand-held video game. He cut the boy's bonds, arranged a blanket over him, and turned on an electric space heater. When he was satisfied that the boy would be as comfortable as possible given the circumstances, Max closed the cell door and locked it, putting the key in his pocket. He estimated the boy would wake within the hour.

Upstairs, he and Spencer secured the farmhouse. On the top floor, Max arranged four security cameras, each facing a different direction through windows, and routed the closed circuit down to four monitors sitting on the kitchen table. From the kitchen, they'd have almost a 360-degree view of the perimeter. In the upstairs hallway, they placed a Dragunov semi-automatic sniper rifle and several magazines of 7.62x54mm ammunition. The rifle had a nicked and scarred wooden stock and might have been manufactured in the 1980s, but it was the best they could find. Max had put a hundred rounds through the rifle at an outdoor range and declared it satisfactory. They both slung H&K MP5 assault rifles over their shoulders. Lastly, Max covered each entrance to the farmhouse with a thin line of filament secured to the pin of a hand grenade. It was a crude but effective trap.

When Max was comfortable with the security, he left Spencer to prepare some food and went downstairs to check on the boy. Ethan was still dozing from the sedative, his small chest rising and falling under the wool blanket. Max placed a metal folding chair a few feet from the cell and sat down.

The dark basement sprawled off in every direction from the cell's location near the main stairs. The floor was dirt, and looked like it had been stained by grease or maybe blood or other fluids. Trying not to breathe through his nose, Max was assaulted by the stench. It was a moist odor consisting of rotting vegetables, mold, dirt, and something else that smelled like decaying animal flesh. When they'd visited the farm the previous week, they'd scouted the expansive basement and found it empty of human or animal remains. Max thought the stench might be ingrained in the cement walls and the dirt floor.

He went back upstairs. Spencer put a plate of steaming hot breakfast in front of him. Max shoved the hot food into his mouth, thankful for real nourishment.

"I checked in," Spencer said.

"Any word on the phone number?" Max asked between bites. Kate had engaged the NSA to dig up a phone number or an email address for Nathan Abrams. Something Max could use to contact the man to begin the negotiations.

"They're working on it," Spencer said. "Don't worry, they'll get it."

"Clock's ticking," Max said. He ran a piece of bread across his plate, mopping up the last of the eggs. Then he pushed back from the table and went back downstairs. Until now, he'd had the operation to occupy his mind. Now, worry and concern began to bleed back in. All he could do was wait.

———

Eventually, the boy stirred. Then groaned. Max knew he would have an enormous headache from both the head wound and the sedative, and his mouth would be too dry to talk. Finally, the boy sat up and rubbed his eyes, then seemed startled by his surroundings.

"Hello, Ethan," Max said, leaning forward.

As the boy became fully awake, Max could see him go through a cycle of emotions. First, he was horrified, probably by the smell and his surroundings. Then Max saw fear overtake his face. The fear was quickly replaced by anger, which Max thought curious. Ethan pushed the blanket away and looked down at the clothes Max had supplied. They were clean, but not fashionable and were slightly too big, making the boy look a bit like a puppet.

"Drink some water," Max said. "You'll feel better."

The boy glared at Max, then saw the water jug for the first time. He grabbed it and had a hard time raising it to his mouth. Max watched him struggle, and had a small pang of guilt. The boy looked remarkably like his nephew. Finally, the boy managed to slosh some of the water into his mouth.

"There is food, too. I'm sure you're hungry," Max said.

The boy glared at Max again, then looked at the food, not moving.

"Oh, right. You're probably too nauseated to eat," Max said. "Try to get something down. Maybe start with a couple crackers. You'll feel better."

Ethan glanced at the food, then pulled his knees up to his chest and wrapped his arms around them, resting his chin on a knee.

Max moved forward and reached between the bars. He pried the lid off the food container and held up a cracker. "Go ahead. Take it."

The boy regarded him a moment, then reached a hand out and took the cracker. He took a bite, chewed, then ate the rest of it. Max sat back down in the chair and watched as the boy took a handful of crackers and started to eat. He wondered how his nephew would cope with being in this boy's place. He could only hope Alex's captors were half as considerate.

"Do you know who I am?" Max asked.

The boy regarded him for a moment, then said, "Fuck you." He clenched his brow and glared at Max through the bars. Now that the boy had found his bearings, Max sensed he was starting to return to his arrogant, cocksure self. Max saw a defiance in his face that probably stemmed from a life of privilege. He respected the boy for the bravado.

"I have a beef with your father," Max said.

The boy glared at Max and said nothing.

"Do you know what your father does for a living?" Max asked.

"Go fuck yourself," Ethan said.

Max sensed panic starting to creep into the boy's demeanor as he realized where he was.

"Can't really do that," Max said. The reality was that he didn't have much to say to the boy. He didn't want to get into the details of what was going on. If Ethan was ignorant of his father's crimes, Max didn't want to taint the boy's mind. Ethan was simply a pawn. If everything went right, the boy would soon be replaced by his father. Max got up to go, then hesitated. A part of him didn't like the idea of leaving the boy down in this dungeon by himself. He turned back. "What's your favorite subject in school?" he asked.

"Fuck you," Ethan said again. He grabbed the food container and started to hurl it, then realized the cell's bars would prevent it from traveling far. He smashed it down onto the ground instead, scattering the food.

Fine, thought Max. He didn't blame the boy, but also didn't see the point in trying to build a bridge between them. He turned to go.

Max made it two steps up the stairs when he heard the word, "Math," in a small voice.

FIFTY-ONE

Undisclosed Location

"I told you, I don't know."

The woman sitting in front of Nathan was stripped naked and shivering in the cold room. Her chest was covered in dried blood from the cuts he'd made earlier. She sat on a folding chair, which had been placed on top of a large sheet of plastic. Nathan held the Kimber up to her forehead. She'd gone from sniveling in fear to anger to desperation to resignation all in the space of five minutes. Nathan felt no pity. This woman's brother had stolen his son, a crime for which she would pay dearly.

Up to this point, Nathan had not hurt her badly. The knife wounds were superficial, meant to inflict psychological pain. Now, however, Nathan meant to get serious. "Arina Asimov," he said, gently pushing the barrel of the Kimber into her forehead. "You are my ticket to your brother. Tell me where he is, or at least give me a clue, and I'll let Alex go free."

At the sound of Alex's name, Arina wailed, tears streaming down her face, her breast heaving. "He could be anywhere," she managed between sobs. "I can't tell you something I don't know."

Nathan slapped her with the back of his left hand, the smack echoing in the enormous chamber. She began to cry harder. Behind her chair stood two soldiers, legs spread, arms behind their backs. To one of them, Nathan said, "Fetch the boy."

Arina's face contorted with rage and fear. "No!" she said, her voice now husky from anger. "Leave him out of this. He's innocent!"

Nathan swept his hair back and looked at her, disgusted by this woman and her family. The Asimov family had caused him more pain and suffering than he'd experienced in his lifetime, and that was saying something. This time he punched her with a closed fist, connecting with her eye socket. The punch lacked Nathan's full weight behind it, but she still cried out in pain. "No one is innocent when it comes to kidnapping my son," he growled at her.

Around him, Nathan had a small audience. The hangar had been converted to an operations center. Nathan's problem was that even though he had the sister and nephew in his clutches, he had no way of contacting Asimov. He knew the famed assassin would stick his head up eventually, but he hadn't been prepared for Asimov's offensive move. Snatching his son had sent Nathan into a rage. First he'd destroyed a set of monitors by flinging them across the hangar, where they'd burst into pieces on the concrete. Then, the team had watched while he'd tossed chairs and tables until he'd run out of energy. He'd purposefully stayed away from the two captives, knowing he could easily have killed them, thus eliminating any leverage he might possess.

"Sir," came a yell from the corner of the operations room. "Sir!"

Nathan turned toward the voice, angry at the disturbance. "What?" he growled. The speaker was Enzo, one of the newer recruits to his staff.

"The tracking beacon is active again, sir," Enzo shouted, running over to where Nathan stood.

Nathan could hardly believe his ears. For the past eight hours, he'd been teetering between a complete anxiety breakdown and a tumultuous rage that threatened to consume him. Asimov had the audacity to kidnap his only child. His own flesh and blood, his own DNA. If any hair on that boy's head was harmed, Nathan didn't know what he would do. It was possible he'd go on a rampage of violence that might end in his own self-destruction. Nathan was self-aware enough to know he was capable of such a thing. Now, however, there was a new ray of hope.

"Let me see," Nathan demanded, forgetting about the woman. He grabbed the tablet from Enzo's hands.

The screen showed a GPS map. In the center was a green, pulsing dot. How in the world his son's tracking device had suddenly become active was beyond his guess. All he could think was that either it was a trick, or somehow the boy had been hidden in such a way as to not let the tracking device attach to a GPS satellite.

The tablet showed a map of Poland. Nathan zoomed in until he found Warsaw, then swiped until the tiny town of Lukow showed. The blinking green dot was a centimeter to the southeast of Lukow. He did a quick calculation in his head.

"Scramble the choppers," he yelled. "We need to go, now."

Wing knew better than to disobey her boss's orders. She knew this situation called for appeasing rather than fighting him. Wing didn't have children of her own, but she imagined that if she did, a protective instinct would take over, rendering her completely irrational if she were in a similar situation. She put in the order to scramble two choppers with a team of four men each.

All eight soldiers were battle-hardened operatives, each of whom had years ago sworn an allegiance to Nathan. These eight had been handpicked by Nathan to be at the ready, and were on full operational alert. Each man would have on battle armor, night-vision goggles, and be armed with silenced assault rifles and pistols. They were an eight-man wrecking crew that Wing wouldn't wish on her worst enemy.

Someone tugged at Wing's sleeve. Wing looked over to see her number two gesturing wildly at the headset on her head. Tall, dark haired, with strong Latin features, Marisa was the wife of another one of Nathan's operational directors. She was the best communications specialist Wing had, and Wing had pulled strings to ensure the woman was on her team. Wing picked up her own headset and Marisa patched her in.

"I have an urgent call for Nathan Abrams. It's for Nathan Abrams only," came the harried voice. Wing recognized the voice as that of Lieutenant Special Command of the Czech Secret Services. He was on their payroll, and was spearheading the official investigation into Ethan's disappearance.

"Wing here. What is it, Nikola?"

"I've been instructed to speak only with Nathan

himself," Nikola stated. He sounded tense and uncomfortable. "Otherwise, the caller says Nathan will find little bits of his son spread across the Czech countryside."

She turned in time to see Nathan hastening through the hanger on his way toward the door. She called out to him, "Nathan, you're going to want to take this call."

———

A combination of rage and fear sank into Nathan's mind. He strode over and snatched the headset from Wing's hands and jammed it onto his head. "Nathan here," he said. His voice was rough and low. He clenched his fists until his fingernails dug into his palms, drawing blood.

"Mr. Abrams," he heard. "Nikola here, sir. I have a call—"

"Patch it through," Nathan growled.

"Hold, sir." There were a series of clicks, then a voice came through Nathan's headset. The voice sounded metallic and stilted, like it was being fed through voice-disguising software. For a brief moment, Nathan thought it might be his client. That illusion vanished immediately.

"Nathan Abrams?" A chill went up Nathan's spine. It felt like he was talking to a robot. A deadly robot. Despite being off balance from the voice, Nathan steeled himself. This wasn't his first operation, he reminded himself. He was the one to be feared, not the other way around.

"Who the fuck is this?" he said, gritting his teeth. "You'd better—"

The metallic voice cut in, reeling off a series of numbers. "52.128522, 21.057074."

Nathan instantly memorized the series of numbers, realizing they were latitude and longitude coordinates.

"You have four hours to be at that location," the voice continued. "At that time, we will trade Ethan's life for you, my sister, and my nephew. Failure to meet those requirements will ensure the Warsaw police find bits and pieces of Ethan strewn over a large portion of the city."

"How do I know—" Nathan started, but the line had already gone dead. "Fuck!" he said, gripping the headset hard enough that the earpiece snapped off. "Did you trace that call?"

""We attempted," Wing said, "but we lost it. It was a voice-over-IP call and the sender bounced it over at least ten different servers. We couldn't trace it fast enough."

"Fuck," Nathan said again. "Choppers?"

"Mobilizing, sir. What are you thinking?"

"We go to the green dot. If the green dot disappears, or it moves, we'll know and can adjust. Until then, we go to the green dot. That's where Ethan is. The captives stay here." He turned on a heel and strode toward the door and the whine of the helicopters warming up in the night.

FIFTY-TWO

Lukow, Poland

"I have a son about your age," Max said. Ethan had sat back down on the mattress with his back to the cement wall, looking out of the cell. Max sat back down on the aluminum chair. "I mean, he's actually my nephew. But his father is dead, so I'm looking after him. His favorite subject is math, too."

"What happened to his father?" Ethan asked.

"He was killed," Max said. "By a very bad man."

"That's terrible," Ethan said. "What's his name?"

Max thought a minute, staying on his guard. The less information Ethan had about Max and his family, the better. "Marko," he lied.

Ethan scrunched up his face. "Is that Russian?" he asked.

"No, Ukrainian."

"That where you live?"

"No, but he lives in Kiev," Max lied. "Do you like

school?"

"It's ok. Soccer is fun and the other kids are alright. Some of them are rich preppies, which is lame."

"How about the girls?"

Ethan's face lit up. "They're fun. There's this one girl named Elsa. She helps me with English."

Max wondered if Alex was interested in girls. The thought of his nephew made him anxious, and he had to remind himself to stay calm.

"Do you have any uncles or aunts? Brothers or sisters?" Max asked.

"Nope. Just me," Ethan said. "Dad says he broke the mold when they made me." The boy gave a little laugh.

"What about your mother?" Max asked.

"Nope," Ethan said, looking downcast. "She's gone."

"Gone? Gone how? Passed away?"

"No. She left. A few years ago. One day she was there. The next day she was gone."

"I'm sorry," Max said, realizing he actually meant it.

"It's ok. I know where she is. She still sends cards on my birthday."

"Why do you stay with your father and not with your mother?" Max asked.

"Dad won't let me live with her," Ethan said. "He said she's an alcoholic and sleeps around, that she'd be a bad mother to me and that I should stay away from her. But I know that's not true."

"How do you know?"

"I just know. She's my mom. We email all the time. She showed me how to use a secret encrypted account that Dad can't see. I just think she couldn't stand to be around him."

Max nodded his head at that. "What's her name?"

"Dinah."

"That's a pretty name. Where does she live?"

"Vienna. She's a banker," Ethan said.

"You miss her?"

Ethan nodded, looking down. "I hate living with my dad."

"Why is that?" Max asked, leaning forward.

"He's too busy. He's never around. Always on his phone. He comes to my soccer games sometimes, but never watches. Misses most of my parent-teacher meetings. Has no idea how I'm doing in school, much less cares if I'm getting good grades so long as I don't flunk out. If I flunk out, then I become a problem for him. He's all about minimizing his own problems."

"I think your father loves you very much," Max said.

"Well, he has a funny way of showing it," Ethan said. He appeared uncomfortable with the topic. "Why am I here?"

Max was tempted to tell him the truth, but he suspected Ethan wouldn't believe the story. Also, oddly, Max was growing fond of the boy. He was just a child trying to figure out the world, having fun and goofing off. A tinge of guilt started to grow in Max's mind, and he decided to lie.

"Like I said, I have a disagreement with your father. He and I need to talk, and he's avoiding me. So, unfortunately I had to use you as bait. I'm very sorry about it, Ethan. I promise I will not harm you."

The boy glowered again, but Max felt like he'd connected with him at least a little. While Max didn't regret what he'd done, he was going to try to minimize the impact on the boy, and meant what he said about not hurting him.

"Why did you have to put me in these clothes?" Ethan asked, looking down at his shabby attire.

"I needed to make sure there weren't any tracking devices in your clothing," Max said.

Ethan got a funny look on his face, like he'd just eaten a lemon. "The tracking device isn't in my clothes," he said. "It's in my armpit."

Max's blood went cold. "What did you say?"

"The tracking device. It's not in my clothes." He shrugged out of his shirt, then pointed to a spot under his right arm. "It's here, in my armpit."

Max rose to his feet and moved closer to the bars. He saw a two-inch scar in the fleshy muscle just under Ethan's scapula.

"Shit," Max said. He dashed up the stairs and found Spencer in the kitchen fixing a cup of instant coffee. "We have a problem."

———

Nathan sat in the lush leather chair in the back of the Bell AB139 helicopter, his stomach in a ball and his heart pounding in his ears. He'd gone from triumphant to horrified to mildly frightened to panic stricken over the past ten hours. Now he was just plain angry. He knew his anger might be clouding his judgment, so he was trying to calm himself by using a breathing technique he'd learned years ago.

Across from him sat three of his top commandos, men who had worked for him for years. A fourth sat to his right. Each of them knew this was personal. Nathan bought loyalty by paying more for talent than anyone else in this business. He knew there were plenty of places for these men to ply their trade, so he overpaid and then treated them with respect. He knew each would fight for him to the death.

On his lap sat the tracking tablet. The winking green dot hadn't moved since it had appeared.

The ground moved beneath them in a blur, rolling forested hills and farmlands punctuated by the occasional town, grey river, or blue lake. Nathan hated Poland, a land of terrible food, rotgut drink, frigid women, and a landscape ravaged by decades of wars, famine, and drought. He thought Poland was fitting for the impending showdown. He removed the Kimber from his belt. The warm rosewood handle was reassuring to his anger-addled mind.

A voice cut into his headset. "Sir, approaching the point of no return." This was the point, Nathan knew, where he needed to decide whether to proceed to the rendezvous point, or the location of the green dot. He didn't hesitate. "Go to the green dot," he said.

"Aye, sir," the voice responded.

Nathan stroked the barrel of the gun. God help whoever had taken his only son.

———

Max raced back down the stairs, leaving Spencer to make preparations to depart. He reached the basement floor and turned to the cage. Ethan was still standing in the same spot, his shirt partway over his head, looking confused.

"What's happening?" Ethan asked.

"We're getting out of here," Max said. "But first, that tracking device is coming out of your armpit." He unlocked the cell door, then advanced on the boy holding a hypodermic needle.

The boy backed away with saucer-sized eyes. "What are you doing?"

"I'm going to give you a sedative," Max said. "Then I'm going to remove that tracking device. When you wake up, you'll be in a new place."

"Ok, good," the boy said.

Max hesitated. "Good?"

"Yes, I don't want that thing in me. I don't want my father knowing where I am."

He grabbed the boy's arm. "Don't be scared, Ethan. This won't hurt." Max shoved the hypodermic needle into the boy's shoulder muscle, then helped him lay down on the mattress. As he waited for the sedative to take effect, an idea occurred to Max, spurred by Ethan's words. He mulled it over while the boy sank into unconsciousness.

When Ethan was fully out, Max pulled out his knife, briefly held the blade to a flame from his lighter, and, with as much care as possible, shoved the tip into the boy's flesh at the exact spot of the scar. He made an inch-and-a-half-long incision, then held it open with two fingers while he fished around. It took a couple more cuts before he was able to get a finger on the small electronic device, then another sideways cut so he could grab it and yank it out. Max doused the wound in hydrogen peroxide and fixed a large bandage over it. The cut would leave an ugly scar. He slung the boy over his shoulder, shoved the bloody tracking device into his pocket, and went up the stairs.

FIFTY-THREE

Lukow, Poland

"I'm staying here," Max said, breathing hard from hauling the dead weight of the boy up the stairs.

Spencer looked up at him from the bag he was packing. "The hell you are."

"Listen," Max said. "I'm not arguing about this. Abrams is going to show up here, because that's where the transmitter will be. If I go with you, I'm just running. I need a confrontation with him, and this is the best spot. I can see them coming. I've got an arsenal. The house will be booby trapped. Trust me, I'll be fine."

He saw Spencer reach for his satellite phone. "Don't do it," Max said. "She's not here, and if she were, it's not her decision."

"Max, you can't stay. You'll be slaughtered. They'll bring a force of highly trained guys who will overwhelm the house and grounds, and you'll be killed. And that's not good for anyone."

"I have a couple of things going for me," Max said. "He thinks Ethan is here, so he'll tread lightly. And I have a few tricks up my sleeve. Capturing him will be the only leverage I'll have. It's the only way I'll be able to find out where he's hiding Arina and Alex. My decision is final."

Max ignored the rest of Spencer's pleas and carried the boy out to the van, then secured him in the hidden box. Spencer followed, carrying two duffle bags. "You'll need to re-apply the sedative every four hours, minimum," Max reminded him.

Spencer donned the DHL uniform, then stood looking at Max. "This is the wrong plan," he said. "Maybe I should stay here. Or we call Kate and get someone out here to pick up the boy."

"It'll be too late at that point," Max said. "Do you have kids, Spencer?"

"Two. Son and a daughter. Neither one talks to me."

"Why not?"

"I left their mother years ago, when I discovered mixing home life and agent life wasn't working. I always wanted to be in the field. I was married to my work, not to my wife. I've tried to reconnect with the kids, but it never works. They know who I am, but don't call. Common theme in our business."

"Would you want your kids to see you captured, interrogated, and possibly killed? Would you want them to witness that?"

Spencer looked at him for a moment. "This is crazy, Max. All of a sudden you care about the boy?"

"I care that this boy isn't traumatized by what I'm going to do to his father," Max said. "The kid deserves to live a life not knowing about his father's sins."

"Or seeing his new friend killed by his own father."

"That's not going to happen," Max said. "Now if you don't get outta here with the boy, I'm going to put a gun to your head." Max glared at him.

"Fuck, Max. Kate is going to kill me."

"Blame me, Spencer. It's out of your hands." Max drew his SIG for emphasis. "Remember, don't stop until you get to Kiev."

With a sigh, Spencer got behind the wheel and started the van. After he'd backed out of the barn, Max slid the door shut and watched the yellow and red DHL van speed out of the drive. He could see Spencer holding the satellite phone up to his ear as he drove.

———

Back in the house, Max checked the action and the scope on the sniper rifle, then left it on a table in the second-floor hallway. He didn't know from which direction they'd come, so he yanked open four windows, each facing a different way, then rehearsed his route from the table to each window. He drilled the sequence of grabbing the rifle, running to an open window, finding a one-kneed stance, and acquiring a target. With a stance on one knee instead of a prone position, his accuracy and range would be diminished. But speed was more important. After fifteen minutes, he was satisfied he could do the sequence within a few seconds. He left a set of night-vision goggles on the table next to the rifle.

Then he went back downstairs and checked his cameras and the monitor. He could see well in each direction in the daylight. The security cameras had a night-vision feature, but could only see to about fifty meters in the darkness. He tapped on the computer for a few minutes, and set an alarm that would sound when the cameras picked up movement with more frequency than grass or trees blowing in the wind. If a mouse scurried across the camera's field of vision, Max would know.

Next, he went around and rechecked the house's booby traps. At each entrance to the house, he made sure the filament line was at an appropriate height, enough to catch a footstep but not high enough for detection.

Last, he rechecked the action on the assault rifle and the SIG. He strapped on a knife, shrugged on a tactical vest with armor plating, and filled the vest's slots with magazines for the H&K MP5 and the SIG. Then he went into the kitchen and made some tea. The homing device that had been implanted in Ethan's shoulder was resting on the table, dried blood caked around it. Silence enveloped the house as Max sat down in front of the security monitor and waited.

––––––––

The first sign of trouble came two hours later. Max had refilled his tea cup twice, gone to the bathroom twice, and eaten a snack. The alarm came from the laptop, a loud *ding* similar to an email notification. He studied the monitors. It was evening, and the light outside had softened. In one monitor, sunflowers in a distant field waved in the breeze. The other monitors were still.

Then he heard a buzzing sound coming from outside, piercing the stillness like a chainsaw. The sound got gradually louder, then faded, similar to a car approaching and receding into the distance. Then it returned again. Now it sounded like a giant insect hovering around the house, darting in, then retreating. The monitors revealed nothing. Max grabbed the MP5 and raced up the stairs. At the window facing south, he hid behind a doorjamb and peeked out. The buzzing was coming from around the corner of the house. A second later, Max saw the source of the sound.

A quadcopter drone appeared, with four tiny rotors and a small camera hanging down from the center. It hovered about ten feet outside the window like a giant, prehistoric insect. For a moment, Max thought about shooting it, but refrained. He decided not to give the drone any indication of life inside the house. Max went back downstairs, unnerved by the presence of the robotic life form outside. Five minutes later, the sound of the drone disappeared. Max thought he caught a glimpse of it in a monitor flying east. He wondered if that was the direction the attack would come from or if it was a deliberate deception.

He nibbled on some food and contemplated the drone. It showed a level of sophistication that Max had expected. He tried to put himself in Abrams' shoes, imagining what he would have seen through the eye of the drone: a large, ramshackle farmhouse with a partially caved-in roof. Silence, no activity. No troops in defensive positions. Max guessed the drone hadn't gotten a good look into the house – it hadn't ventured close enough, probably due to fear of being shot at or destroyed. Max didn't think Abrams would get much more information than he might from a satellite image. If anything, it would set him on edge, not knowing if the farm was the right location, and not seeing any obvious defensive positions. Not to mention the fact that the drone gave away Abrams' presence in the area. In a less hardened operator, the device may have instilled fear. To Max, however, it was a comfort. He liked knowing the enemy was near.

He yawned, suddenly realizing he'd been up for twenty-four hours straight. He knew he had at least another twenty-four hours before his mind would start to break down. During the early days of his training in the KGB, Max had earned a reputation for having inhuman endurance and the ability to go long periods without sleep. In the forced midnight marches, he was often the one at the front of the pack, urging on the rest of the group. It had been the first signal to KGB leadership that maybe Max was something special.

Max sipped more tea, and waited as the shadows grew longer. At nine p.m., he catnapped for fifteen minutes, his head on the table next to the laptop, and woke as refreshed as if he'd had a full eight hours' sleep. He made some more tea, and waited.

FIFTY-FOUR

Lukow, Poland

The first sign of the attack was not the alarm from the security cameras, but the far-off *whoomp, whoomp, whoomp* of helicopter rotors. Max dashed up the stairs and listened intently at the east-facing window. He thought he could make out two birds. Some quick math told him two choppers would bring between eight and twenty soldiers. The game was on.

He checked his watch. It was four-thirty a.m., the standard time for a raid, meant to take advantage of the natural human circadian biorhythms that would typically shut a body down for rest in the early hours of the morning. Max turned his cap so the brim was facing back, donned the night-vision goggles, and wrapped the sniper rifle's strap around his bicep.

A minute later, he saw two Bell AB139 choppers materialize out of the early morning gloom. Through his night-vision goggles, Max watched as commandos began rappelling down ropes to the field below. Max counted eight. They started moving in formation toward the farmhouse.

He calculated the distance between the farmhouse and the commandos to be about 200 meters. Under normal sniper conditions, that distance would be like shooting fish in a barrel. However, with an elbow braced on one knee and the morning gloom to contend with, 200 meters would not be that easy. Max waited.

The commandos moved with effortless efficiency, likely bred from years of working together. The group split in two, with one group following a tree line toward the southeast corner of the house and the other moving through gently waving sunflowers toward the northeast corner of the house. Max waited.

When he calculated they were about 100 meters away, he acquired the lead commando of the south team in his rifle sight. He breathed in, then out, willing his heart rate to slow. Time seemed to stand still. Then, to Max's surprise, the leader held up a fist and the group stopped. Max found the man's hip flexor in his scope, breathed in, then emptied his lungs and squeezed the trigger.

To maximize accuracy, the gun was not silenced, and the rifle crack reverberated around the fields, startling a flock of birds and causing them to take to the skies. The target went down. Max found the second man in the line, paused to breathe, then pulled the trigger. The second target's thigh exploded. Blood, bone, and flesh radiated outward from a jagged hole the size of a saucer.

It wasn't goodwill that prompted Max to aim for the lower extremities – the commandos were wearing body armor and helmets. He knew from experience that the lower extremities would offer the largest un-armored targets. His choice was simply a matter of improving the odds. He moved the rifle to the third man and took aim.

Just then, small-arms fire began hitting the side of the house around the window where Max was crouched. He knew that the assault rifles in the hands of the commandos were ineffective from 100 meters. They were simply pouring cover fire at the house in an attempt to force Max to back down. He ignored the shots and took aim. Bullets sang through the open window and chunked into the wood siding of the house. He found the third man in the column, then breathed. He pulled the trigger. The bullet went wide as the man stood and moved forward in a crouched run.

Bullets continued to pound into the house's siding. The choppers were maintaining their position. Both groups of commandos were approaching the side of the house. Max figured he had maybe one more shot. This one would be on a moving target, but at closer range. He shifted and found the lead man in the second group. The soldier's legs were pumping as he hustled his team toward the cover of the corner of the house, away from the angle of the sniper. Max squeezed off a shot and caught the man in the left kneecap. The knee disintegrated, severing the man's lower leg from his thigh. Max tossed the rifle and scurried back down the stairs to the kitchen. He'd just evened the odds considerably.

———

Max took the basement stairs two at a time. He had one ace up his sleeve that he'd neglected to tell Spencer about – something he knew about the house from using the facility during KGB training missions long ago. When his feet hit the dirt floor, he turned and dashed for the back of the basement.

From upstairs, he heard an explosion as one of the grenades went off, then he heard the patter of debris falling onto the wooden floor. He guessed the booby trap at the kitchen door to the back patio had just detonated. He hoped it had taken out at least one more soldier.

In the rear of the basement, Max stopped in front of the farm's ancient HVAC unit, a sprawling, octopus-like structure with a massive boiler in the center and air-duct tentacles that disappeared into various sections of the basement ceiling. Max ducked underneath a particularly wide conduit and reached for a lever hidden among the pipes and electrical cords along the back. He found the lever and pulled hard, then heard a screeching sound. To his left, through the gritty green night-vision goggles, he saw an opening in the wall that hadn't been there before. He ducked into the opening and moved along a narrow corridor.

The tunnel had been hewn out of bedrock and dirt, and was lined on the floor with decaying wooden planking. The ceiling was crossed with support beams. A string of lights hung along the wall, but had long corroded from disuse. While he'd been waiting for Ethan to wake up, Max had tested the secret door to ensure it was still in working order.

About two feet in, along the left wall, he found a conduit leading to a small electrical box housing a toggle switch. He flipped the switch and heard a scraping sound behind him. The door in the basement closed.

In 1939, when the farmhouse had been in the hands of the Polish resistance, a team of Jewish fighters had built the escape tunnel. They thought it might come in handy if the house became overrun by the Germans. In 1941, exactly

that had happened, according to testimony from the few
surviving Jews of Lukow. Five members of the Jewish resistance holed up in the basement of the farmhouse and
escaped through the tunnel. As Max stood in the passage,
he could almost feel the fear of the Jews as they ran from
their German pursuers.

Now it would be a waiting game. He knew the
commandos would clear the house and the basement in a
few minutes. Not finding him, he guessed they'd begin a
search of the barn and the grounds. When all had been
searched, he guessed Abrams would show up. When their
guard was down, Max would exit the secret tunnel from the
barn side, and use the element of surprise to kill the
remaining commandos and capture Abrams. He just wished
he could smoke a cigarette while he waited.

The tunnel was cool, dank, and pitch black. Max took
off his night-vision goggles and crouched, straining his ears
to hear anything he could. Unfortunately, he was virtually
blind and deaf in this situation, a scenario he didn't like. He
tried to picture Abrams' face when he found the farmhouse
empty of guards and his son still missing. Then Max
remembered he'd left the blood-encrusted tracking sensor
on the table in the kitchen. Maybe that would confuse
Abrams even more.

He grabbed his night-vision goggles and started moving
through the tunnel again. He had to crouch slightly to avoid
hitting his head on the ancient wooden crossbeams. He
walked maybe thirty meters, then came to a stop at the end
of the tunnel. A rickety wooden ladder was resting against
the dirt wall, ending at a trap door that led into the barn.
Max stopped and listened hard. He couldn't hear a thing.
He was deaf and blind, and the tunnel was the only trick up

his sleeve. If this didn't work, or Abrams somehow stumbled upon the tunnel, Max knew he was done for.

He checked his watch. The luminous dial told him he'd been in the tunnel for ten minutes, more than enough time for them to clear the house. He suspected they were working on clearing the grounds, growing more and more perplexed by the minute. He crouched and waited.

Another five minutes went by. Then Max heard a creak above him. He slipped the night-vision goggles on and decided to wait another five minutes.

The seconds ticked by. Unease crawled under his skin with every passing moment. Something was wrong – he couldn't put his finger on what, exactly. But something. Then, another creak sounded above him. He willed his heart to slow, afraid the pounding would give him away.

Max turned, ready to steal back down the tunnel, when another creak sounded. He froze.

Before he could decide what to do, the trapdoor directly above his head cracked open, and Max heard a sound that filled him with dread.

FIFTY-FIVE

Lukow, Poland

First Max heard hissing, then the trapdoor slammed shut. Something metallic clanked to the ground next to his foot. The hissing came from the metallic object.

Max groped for something to cover his mouth and nose, but his T-shirt was trapped under his tactical vest. He yanked a handkerchief from his pocket and tied it around nose and mouth. A moment later, he felt a burning in his eyes. He fought panic as the teargas filled the narrow passage. His mind flashed back twenty years to his KGB training, when he had been subjected to multiple exposures of teargas, mace, and pepper spray. Despite the training, Max knew he wouldn't be able to hold out forever in such a small, enclosed space.

Max dashed the opposite way in the tunnel, trying to avoid the fumes. His eyes started watering, and despite the cloth over his face, he could feel the familiar searing pain in his mouth and nose.

He heard the door at the far end of the tunnel screech open, followed by more hissing and the sound of two more metal canisters bouncing along the wooden floor of the tunnel. Max stopped short and considered his options. There were two ways out, and both were covered by members of Abrams' team. The gas started to overcome him and he found himself coughing and sputtering.

The pain in his eyes and lungs became so intense that Max's survival instincts took over. He ran forward, toward the basement, groping blindly for the toggle that would open the door and lead him to fresh air. He ripped off the night-vision goggles and dropped them on the ground along with his rifle. All he could think about was exiting the tunnel and getting out of the gas. His hand found the toggle switch and he flipped it, hearing the door grind open. He hurled himself forward, falling into the fresh air of the basement, then tripped and landed face down on the dirt floor, gulping for clean air.

He felt hands grabbing him, jerking him upright, then dragging him along the ground. More hands ripped away his pistol and searched him, pulling off his tactical vest and jerking off his knife scabbard. Then he was half carried, half dragged along the basement floor. He pitched forward and fell face first onto a damp mattress. Max rubbed at his face, trying in vain to remove the chemical agent from his eyes. The pain was unbearable. He couldn't have defended himself if he'd tried.

He heard voices. Then someone issued a command and Max felt hands turn him over. A wall of water hit his face. Thankfully, he rubbed the water into his eyes. Someone told him to open his eyes. He obeyed and another wall of water hit him, dousing his eyes and washing away the chemical. Max rubbed and blinked until he could see again.

"Hello, Mikhail," a voice said.

Max tried to ignore the pain in his eyes and his lungs, and looked up. Standing over him, wearing a suit, an overcoat, and expensive Italian loafers, was a tall man with a silver mane of slicked-back hair. Square jawed, with bronzed and leathery skin, he had the demeanor of someone who had lived in wealth all his life. He also looked royally pissed.

Next to the man stood two tall, square-jawed goons with buzz cuts who could have auditioned for television roles in a military series. One of them pointed a pistol at Max's head. The other was holding a bucket.

"I take it you're Nathan Abrams," Max managed to say.

"Where is my fucking son?" Abrams asked.

"Where are my fucking sister and nephew?" Max asked. He was still sputtering from the water, and his eyes were burning.

Abrams pulled something from the pocket of his overcoat and tossed it at Max. It hit him in the forehead and fell into his lap. It was the transmitter Max had removed from Ethan's shoulder.

"I'll repeat," Abrams said. "Where is my son?"

"Somewhere you'll never find him," Max said. "He said you were a terrible father, and he didn't want to be your son anymore."

Abrams threw a punch that Max didn't see coming. The fist hit him square in the jaw, sending a ringing pain through the after-haze of the teargas.

Abrams stood up and moved away from Max. To one of the commandos, he said, "Remove his clothes and get him into that chair. Looks like we're going to have to do this the fun way." Then Abrams disappeared up the stairs.

———

A few minutes later, Max found himself naked and secured to the metal folding chair. A third commando had joined the other two, then Nathan came back down the stairs. He'd shed the overcoat and suit coat. His shirt sleeves were rolled up and he held a pair of pliers in one hand.

Max watched as Abrams came over and slowly walked around him, surveying the job done by his men. There was no worse feeling than being naked, tied to a chair, with your genitals exposed while an angry man stood in front of you with a pair of pliers. Max read a vibrancy in Abrams' eyes, a fire that told him Abrams was going to enjoy what he was about to do. His heart sank as he searched wildly for a way out of his predicament.

"Mikhail Asimov," Abrams said. "I must say this little soiree of yours just saved me from a lot of trouble."

"Who are you working for, Abrams?" Max asked. "Tell me that now, and I'll go easier on you later."

Instead of laughing, anger lit Abrams' eyes and he back-handed Max across the face. Then, Abrams swung a right-handed fist enclosed around the pliers and struck Max on the jaw, causing his eyes to flash stars. He tasted blood on his tongue.

"You think this is a game?" Abrams was enraged, his silvery hair flying in all directions as he stood over Max in a wide stance. Blood had spattered on his shirt front from Max's mouth. The man looked like he was going to strike Max again, but backed up instead.

"Let me get this straight," he said to Max. "You snatch my son from his school. Then you drive him all the way to the middle of fucking Poland and attempt to trade him for information. You get here, an abandoned KGB safe house, then somehow you find the tracking device. Now he's either hidden somewhere around this farm, or he's long gone." Abrams paced around Max in a tight circle, then leaned close to Max's ear and said, "We can do this the easy way, or the hard way," he said. "You know as well as I do that no man can withstand torture." He clicked the pliers in Max's face. "First, I'm going to start with your fingernails. Then I'll move to your toenails. If that doesn't work, I'll move to your genitals. At some point, you'll tell me."

"You're a fucking cliché," Max said. He could feel blood running down his chin. "Where are my sister and nephew, and who is your client?"

This time, Abrams laughed. "You're demented, Asimov. Now where the fuck is my son?"

Max knew Abrams was right. No one could withstand torture. Max had been through so-called torture training while with the KGB. He'd been subjected to waterboarding, chemicals, teargas, and enough pain to last any one man a lifetime. But in the end, no amount of training could prepare someone for the inevitable triumph of pain over the human mind. He figured he may as well get under Abrams' skin. "Your son told me where the tracking device was so I could remove it. So you could never find him. I set him free, Abrams. Free from the tyranny of your poor attempt at fatherhood."

Rage contorted Abrams' face, and he swung at Max again. Max anticipated this time and ducked, and Abrams' fist caught him on the top of his head. With a grunt, Abrams regained his balance, then moved behind Max. "Grab his hand," Abrams said to the nearest guard. "Time to begin the festivities."

Max felt two vice-like hands grip his palms, then his middle finger was bent back until it snapped. He howled in pain. Then he felt the cold steel of the pliers against the tip of his middle finger. First there was a gentle tug to test the grip. Then Max felt a searing pain in his middle finger as the nail was ripped off. Max howled again, the pain radiating from his hand to his spine, then to his head.

"The location," Abrams said.

Max felt the strong hands single out the ring finger on his left hand. He couldn't seem to will the muscles in his hands to resist.

"Your son is long gone," Max said through gritted teeth. He could taste bile in the back of his mouth. "I let him go. I don't know where he is. I'll go to my grave without telling you, Abrams. You can kill my family, but you'll never get your son back."

Pain flashed again as his ring finger was snapped. Then more searing pain radiated through his body as the nail was ripped off. Max fought the wave of nausea, praying he wouldn't give Abrams the satisfaction of seeing him vomit, and struggled to stay conscious.

Just then, through the haze of the pain, Max heard a thump, like a heavy weight had hit the kitchen floor over their heads.

Abrams whipped around to face the stairs. "What was that?" he growled.

FIFTY-SIX

"Go see what that was," Abrams growled to one of his men. The soldier pulled his pistol from his holster and started moving up the stairs. Abrams came around to Max's front and showed Max the pliers. Held tight in the pliers' pinchers was one of his bloody fingernails. Abrams waved it under Max's nose. "Recognize this?"

Max's attention was focused on the man walking up the stairs. The soldier was in a crouch, pistol held up, his back to the wall. He paused at the top of the stairs, then slowly moved through the doorway and out of sight. The only sound was the soldier's footsteps across the thin kitchen floor. Then silence.

The two commandos remaining in the basement drew their weapons. One stood at the bottom of the stairs, pistol pointed up the stairwell. The second pointed his gun at Max's head. Abrams had frozen, the bloody pliers still in front of Max's face, but his attention on the stairs. Nobody moved.

The seconds ticked by and turned into a minute. Another minute went by. Max could see Abrams getting agitated.

Suddenly, Max felt two bullets spit by his head. The first exploded in the temple of the man pointing his gun at Max; the second found the chest of the commando at the stairs. Both soldiers dropped to the ground. Abrams whipped around, moving his hand to the small of his back. He froze when a thin beam of red light appeared on his chest.

"Drop to the ground, Abrams," a voice called out from the darkness of the far corner of the basement. "Do it now."

Max slumped in relief when he saw him drop to his knees. The pliers dropped from Abrams' hands.

"On the ground, Abrams. Face on the ground."

Abrams complied.

Out of the gloom of the basement appeared a man in black pants wearing a tactical vest, holding an H&K MP5 assault rifle at the ready. He wore night-vision goggles over a backward baseball cap. He walked with a pronounced limp.

The fucking cavalry has arrived, thought Max.

Spencer White shed his night-vision goggles, then turned his cap around to reveal the DHL logo. "Excellence, simply delivered," he said, quoting the DHL tag line.

"There's one more upstairs—" Max started.

"No, there's not," Spencer said.

Spencer grabbed a pair of plastic riot cuffs from his vest and secured Abrams' hands behind him, then removed the pistol from the man's waistband. He moved to each of the commandos and felt for a pulse. Finally, he went behind Max and used a knife to sever the duct tape. Max almost fell out of the chair, his legs weak from the pain. Spencer caught him and held him under the shoulders.

"What the fuck are you doing here?" Max said. "I had this under control."

"Clearly," Spencer said. He lowered Max down onto the mattress and examined his left hand. "This looks bad."

"Grab some clothes off one of those soldiers, will you? You're probably tired of seeing me naked."

Max got dressed with a little help from Spencer, and listened as Spencer told him the story in a hushed whisper, out of earshot from Abrams. He had called Kate. Kate had mobilized a CIA staffer in Warsaw to meet Spencer and trade the van for a rusted-out Skoda. The staffer would drive the boy to Kiev, where he'd be met by a CIA team and debriefed. Then they'd deliver Ethan to his mother in Vienna. Meanwhile, Spencer had doubled back, arriving after the short battle had concluded. He'd taken out the guards upstairs, before using the tunnel to flank Abrams.

"Does everyone know about that fucking tunnel?" Max asked, exasperated.

"I didn't, but saw the trapdoor open in the barn," Spencer said. "Listen, we need to go. The helicopter pilots are still out there, and they may be calling in for reinforcements."

"I think we have a couple minutes," Max said. He eyed the prone figure of Nathan Abrams. "I have some unfinished business to attend to. Help me get him up into this chair."

Between the two of them, they propped Abrams in the metal chair. He glared at Asimov with eyes that blazed hatred. Abrams' white dress shirt was stained with dirt and blood and his hair was mussed, silver strands dangling in his eyes. Spencer handed Max Abrams' gun and then secured the man's ankles to the chair with duct tape.

"My reinforcements will be here shortly," Abrams growled. "I'd run if I were you."

Max ignored him. "Two things I need from you, Abrams. The first is the location of my sister and nephew. The second is the name and whereabouts of your client."

"You'll have to kill me, Asimov. I'll never reveal those things. So you can go fuck yourself. But I'd hurry, before my second team gets here."

"You should know, I was being truthful about your son," Max said. "He did tell me where the tracking device was because he didn't want you to find him."

Anger flashed in Abrams' eyes. "You lie. I treated that boy like a prince."

"Believe what you want," Max said. Then he picked the pliers up off the floor. For the first time, Abrams showed a hint of fear. Max waved the pliers in his face. "Last chance. Where are my sister and nephew?"

Abrams said nothing. Max went around Nathan's back, found the index finger of his right hand, and wrenched it hard until it cracked. Abrams cried out in pain. Then Max shoved the nose of the pliers under the fingernail, gripped hard, and yanked. The basement was filled with Abrams' howls of pain.

"We don't have time for this," Spencer said. "We should put some distance between us and this house."

Max came around to Abrams' front and tossed the ragged fingernail onto Abrams' lap. Nathan was rocking his head back and forth. Saliva ran from the corners of his mouth. He blew spittle from his lips and looked at Max. "That sister of yours is quite a minx, isn't she?" Then he laughed. "You should have—"

Max went behind Abrams and grabbed another one of his fingers. Max wrenched hard, feeling the finger snap. Abrams howled again. Then Max felt for purchase on Abrams' fingernail with the pliers once more.

"Ok, ok. Fuck," Abrams panted. "No more."

Max came around to Abrams' front again. "Where are they," Max demanded.

"Do you know what it's like," Abrams asked, spittle flying from wet lips, "to watch your mother be raped and tortured? Do you, Asimov? Know what it's like? Because I do. I saw it with my own eyes when I was eight, and look what it did to me. Imagine what it's going to do to little Alex—"

In fast succession, fueled by rage, Max broke two more of Abrams' fingers and ripped out another two fingernails. When he stood up and let the bloody nails fall to the dirt floor, he found Abrams had passed out.

"Fill that bucket with water," Max said to Spencer.

Spencer grabbed the bucket and filled it with water from the utility sink. He handed it to Max, who sloshed the entire bucket into Abrams' face. The man came to, sputtering.

"Ok. I'll tell you where they are," Abrams said, panting between words. "But you're going to need an army to get them out. And I'm telling you, I don't know who my client is. That's the—" He howled again as Max pulled another fingernail loose.

"When I run out of fingers, I'm going to start on the toes," Max said. He took no pleasure from the pain he was inflicting on Abrams, even if the man was responsible for his parents' death. He'd been anticipating this moment for weeks; now that it was here, he knew he'd be hearing Abrams' screams in his sleep. Max suddenly felt hollow. His left hand was throbbing. His head was pounding. Still, driven by an almost animal-like need to protect his family, he grabbed another finger.

"I'm being honest," Abrams yelled. "I don't fucking know. He sends for me in a private jet, then blindfolds me and keeps to the shadows when we meet. I don't know who he is."

Max considered this. He supposed it was possible that Abrams was telling the truth. Knowing firsthand how much pain Abrams was in, Max knew it would be difficult to lie. Still, he needed to make sure. He wedged the pliers up under another nail.

Abrams started talking as fast as he could, spilling everything he knew, including the address of his offices and the location of the operational facility two hours southeast of Prague where Arina and Alex were being held. Max breathed a sigh of relief. He saw Spencer turn away and put a satellite phone to his ear.

But despite repeated questioning and threats to break more fingers, Abrams continued to insist that he didn't know who his client was. The only additional thing Max learned was that Abrams had been paid a large sum of money to work with the client's demand for secrecy.

"What does he look like?" Max asked.

"Caucasian. Old, probably in his late eighties or early nineties. Liver spots. White hair. In a wheelchair," Abrams said.

"I assume you traced the electronic payments?" Max had asked.

"We tried, but got nowhere. Afterwards we were threatened not to continue our inquiries. Whatever enemy you made," Nathan said, "they're very powerful people. Their reach extends into the upper echelons of institutions and corporations. They are more powerful than governments and work outside the law. Whoever they are, they wield more power than you can imagine. You can kill me, but they'll keep coming after you until you're dead."

Max squatted in front of Abrams, rubbing his injured left hand. Abrams' wet and bloody shirt clung to his chest like a shroud. His hair was a tangle and one of his Italian loafers had come off, revealing a bare foot. Max almost felt sorry for him. With the information Max and Spencer had learned, the CIA and FBI would be able to work with the Czech authorities to shut Abrams' operation down for good.

His original intent had been to kill Abrams in retribution for his parents' death. Certainly, Max felt justified in his mind. How many other families had Nathan and his team of operatives destroyed? What irreparable damage had he done to Arina and Alex? It would be simple: Just use Abrams' own pistol and put a bullet into the man's head. The world would be rid of one more bad guy.

Max pulled the Kimber from his waistband. Max could hear Spencer talking rapidly into the mouthpiece, providing location and operational information. Spencer turned and watched as Max put the gun up to Nathan's face.

"Go ahead," Abrams said. "Kill me. Save my client the trouble. Save me from the pain of incarceration and interrogation. Save me from the shame of having my son see me like this."

Max pulled on the trigger, testing the tension. He saw Abrams go rigid. Then he heard the beep as Spencer hung up the satellite phone.

"Don't do it," Spencer said. "We need everything in his brain. Don't give him the satisfaction, Max."

"Do it!" Abrams yelled, spittle flying. "Do it for what I did to your sister! Do it for what I—"

Max felt rage well up inside him, and he tightened his finger on the trigger. Then he felt a hand on his shoulder.

"You don't know what he did to your sister, Max. He's just taunting you. He wants you to kill him. Don't give him the satisfaction."

Max froze and watched in slow motion as Spencer slowly pushed the pistol down and away from Abrams face.

"Let's go," Spencer said. "The FBI field team from Warsaw is on their way." Max turned and walked up the stairs, shoving the pistol into the waistband of his trousers.

FIFTY-SEVEN

Lukow, Poland

Max had made it halfway up the stairs with Spencer ahead of him when he heard Abrams call out.

"Your father was dirty, Asimov! You can try to pretend otherwise, but your father was the most corrupt man in the KGB!"

Max paused on the stairs.

Spencer grabbed his arm and tried to pull him up the rest of the way. "Ignore him, Max. He's just trying to get under your skin. Come on, we need to go."

Max brushed Spencer's hand aside and retreated back down the stairs. Abrams' eyes were wide and bloodshot. Drool and mucus had dribbled down his chin.

"What did you say?" Max said, pushing his face down close to Abrams'. Max heard Spencer groan behind him.

"I said your father was dirty," Abrams said, a smirk on his face. It was the kind of look that said he knew something Max didn't.

"What do you know about my father?" Max said. He grabbed Abrams by his shirt with his good hand and shook him hard enough to make the metal chair clatter. "What do you know?"

Abrams just smiled, letting his head loll back and his eyes roll up toward the ceiling, as if he knew he'd found Max's weakness.

Max hit him, out of anger and frustration and weeks of confusion and fear. He unloaded on the man he viewed as the source of his family's distress. He hit Abrams' face with the closed fist of his good hand. Then he started swinging with short, compact punches, each one landing on Abrams' face and neck. Blood sprayed onto Max's shirt and face as Abrams' mouth caved in and teeth flew out. Then Max felt himself grabbed from behind and wrestled backward. Spencer had him in a half nelson. Max calmed.

"Ok, ok, let go," Max said.

"You going to calm the fuck down?" Spencer asked.

"Yes. Fuck. Let me go." Spencer let his grip loosen and Max pulled away. He looked at Abrams. The man was a mess. Blood dripped down his chin and onto his shirt. A front tooth hung from his mouth by a thread. Max wiped his hand on his own shirt and bent down to Abrams.

Abrams tried to spit blood at Max, but couldn't seem to muster enough energy. After he'd cleared the fluid from his mouth, Abrams started talking.

"He was a common criminal, a thug. Just part of Russia's organized crime. A boss. Extortion, gambling, smuggling, prostitution, the whole thing. How do you think he made so much money? You're so naive, Asimov."

Max staggered back a step. Was this true? It couldn't be. His father was a patriot. He'd hated the new criminal elite that had infested Russian and Belarusian society. Then doubt clouded Max's thoughts. Other than the training, he hadn't spent much time with his father. How well had he really known Andrei Asimov?

Spencer grabbed his arm. "Come on, Max. Don't listen to him. He's telling you lies. Let's get out of here. Now. Before people start showing up, investigating the gun battle. Let's go."

Max shoved him aside. He grabbed Nathan again with his good hand. "That's bullshit," Max said. "What do you know? Tell me, goddamn it, or so help me God I'll cut off your balls and shove them down your throat!"

Abrams just cackled with laughter. He seemed to have lost his mind from the pain and the stress.

"I was going to let you live," Max said. "Now I've changed my mind." He pulled the Kimber from his waistband and put it up to Abrams' forehead. "Tell me what you know about my father. Details. I want details."

Abrams just looked at him with cloudy eyes.

"Talk, Abrams. I need to know why my family is being targeted for elimination."

Finally, Abrams opened his mouth enough to talk. His words came out slurred from his shattered mouth. "You think I care whether I live or die, Asimov? You've taken the one thing from me I care about. Without my son in my life, I'm nothing. Go ahead. Kill me. I don't care."

"Don't make me do it, Abrams. What did my father do? What was his crime that turned the world against him?"

Abrams laughed a wet, sputtering laugh that was accompanied by grotesque blood bubbles at the corner of his mouth. "You mean you don't know?"

Max's anger started to well up again, and he pushed the pistol barrel harder into Abrams' forehead, threatening to tip the captive over in his chair.

"Fuck you, Asimov," Abrams said. "I'm a dead man either way. Kill me now. If you don't, my client will."

"You'll be under lock and key, Abrams. No one will be able to get to you there."

Abrams laughed again. "You're a fool, Asimov," he said. "These people can get to anyone, anywhere, anytime. You let me live, they'll kill me. You kill me, they'll just hire someone else to find you. You're the walking dead, Asimov. Just like me. It's only a matter of time."

Max pulled the Kimber's trigger. The force of the 9mm hollow-point jerked Abrams over backward in his chair. He was dead before he hit the ground.

"Now we can go," Max said.

FIFTY-EIGHT

Minsk, Belarus

The street where his childhood home used to be was dark and silent, its inhabitants asleep in their luxurious beds. All the cars were securely stowed in garages behind wrought iron fences. A light rain fell and a cloudy mist hung in the air. Max guided the stolen Audi sedan down the street at a slow pace, the wipers moving steadily on the windshield. He was taking one last trip down memory lane, and seeing the street for the last time through a kaleidoscope of rain-drops on the windshield.

At his parents' home, the yellow police tape had been taken down, the flood lights had been removed, and the emergency vehicles and press vans were long gone. He nosed the car into the drive and through the open gate, killed the lights, and drove the quarter-mile circular drive slowly. He took the Kimber from the passenger seat and shoved it into his waistband as he stepped into the rain. He held a large flashlight in his bandaged hand.

While Max and Spencer had been on the road south toward the Ukrainian border, Kate called to inform them she had completed a raid on Abrams' airfield compound. The operation had resulted in the rescue of Arina and Alex, and had yielded intel about Abrams' activities. Now, as Max walked through the wet grass, he took comfort that Arina and Alex were heading to an undisclosed and safe location in the US.

The crater looked foreboding in the darkness. Scorched and scarred pieces of wood and cement, wet from the rain, glistened in the beam of the flashlight. The hole in the ground was filled with unidentifiable debris. With resignation, Max realized all of his family's pictures, heirlooms, and keepsakes were gone, the military medals his father and his grandfather had earned among them. The antique furniture his mother had loved was destroyed. Pictures from his and Arina's childhood, nothing but ashes. It all seemed like such a waste. Max flashed the light around the interior of the crater, but saw nothing recognizable.

Three weeks ago, Max wouldn't have cared about his family heirlooms. It was such an easy thing to forget about. He'd just assumed his parents would live forever. Thoughts about family had rarely entered his mind. Now, he had the weight of his family's legacy squarely on his shoulders.

He walked in a slow circle around the hole toward the barn. He wasn't quite sure what he was doing. He wanted one last look before he disappeared into his new life. It might be the last time he'd ever see his childhood home.

When he reached the barn, he yanked the tall door open, then stepped in. This time, instead of making for the locked door to his father's study, he strolled around the main floor of the barn. All the normal things were still there – horse feed, tackle, mucking shovels, and all manner of work clothes, boots, and gloves. He rummaged for a minute and found a riding crop. He swished it in the air, then set it down. The stalls were all empty. He found a desk in the far corner that seemed to have served as the barn's center of operations. It was made from thick butcher block and stood on two saw horses. A rickety wooden chair stood in front of the desk at an angle. The table held several pens, a pile of notebooks, a horseshoe paperweight, and some other knickknacks. A picture hung on the wall over the desk in a corroded metal frame. The frame's glass was dusty and caked with grime. Inside was a small photo, perhaps six inches by four. Max took it off the wall and used his jacket sleeve to wipe away the grime. It was of his mother and father, his sister, and himself when Max was twelve. He remembered the exact moment the picture had been taken. They were all standing next to the barn, which had been under construction at the time. Everyone was smiling, perhaps in anticipation of the family fun that would be had here. It felt so long ago.

Max put the picture in his pocket. A little polish would clean the frame up. At least he'd have one keepsake from the family compound.

He left the barn, and pulled the door closed behind him. As he walked back to his car, he wondered again who had ransacked the office. Then he wondered where the ownership papers were to the house and the land. Resigning himself to the realities of his new life, he got into the Audi and drove off. He didn't look back.

———

Max pushed the buzzer. Through the door, he could hear the chime of the bell. He waited a moment, then pushed the buzzer again. Getting no response, he looked at his watch. It showed 6:54 a.m. He knew Anatoly was an early riser. He turned and walked to the garage and cupped his hands to look through the grimy windows. The shiny Mercedes sat unbothered among a jumble of yard implements.

He knew Anatoly hadn't left the house during the night, because Max had been sitting in the driver's seat of the Audi down the block, watching. Either Anatoly hadn't been in the house, or he wasn't answering. Or maybe he couldn't answer.

Max leaned on the buzzer again, looking through the kitchen door window for any sign of movement. He could see the same mess of dirty dishes, empty food boxes, and bottles of vodka that he'd seen the last time he'd been there. There was no movement inside.

Max pulled the Kimber from his waistband and used the butt to break a windowpane in the kitchen door. He reached his hand in and unlocked the door from the inside, then pulled the door open and stepped in. He looked for the alarm console, and found it hanging from the wall by two wires. One wire had been cut.

His concern growing, Max pushed through the kitchen and into the living room. That's when the smell hit him. He glanced around the room and saw nothing but the same piles of pizza boxes, beer cans, and dirty clothes. The stench grew worse as he neared the stairs. He covered his nose with his T-shirt and bounded up the stairs two at a time, then rushed toward Anatoly's bedroom.

The smell was seeping in through the thin material of his T-shirt, and he had to quell his gag reflex. Max could now see why. Anatoly's body lay on the bed, naked except for a pair of stained, white undershorts. In the morning light from the window, Max could see Anatoly's body had turned a dull olive green, and had started to bloat from the gasses produced by the decomposing organs. Max knew the body would turn green, and the eyes would bulge out and the tongue would typically swell and protrude after about two days of decomposition. The only problem was, Max couldn't see Anatoly's eyes and tongue because the front of his face had been blown off, leaving a gaping, bloody hole. The offending shotgun lay across Anatoly's chest.

Max yanked the window up to get some fresh air into the room, then examined the space around the bed. A half-empty bottle of vodka sat on the nightstand, surrounded by a dozen stubbed-out cigarette butts. Breathing through his mouth, Max rummaged under the pillows, trying to avoid the blood and gore. Not finding what he was looking for, he looked under the bed. Anatoly's Makarov, the one he always seemed to sleep with, was missing.

Max examined the shotgun. It was a double-barrel, over-under, break-action, IZh-27. It was made in Russia, and one of the more popular models in the Soviet Union. Using his shirt-sleeve, he turned the gun over and searched for the serial number. As he expected, it had been filed off.

Another quick search revealed no note, but he wasn't surprised. Max left the room without a backward glance.

————

As he exited the kitchen onto the rear stoop, Max almost ran into the diminutive figure of a man in a neat suit. Max recoiled, reaching for the Kimber in his waistband, then relaxed as he recognized the figure of Victor Dedov, Director of the Belarusian FSB. Oddly, Dedov was traveling without his usual contingent of guards.

"Hello, Victor," Max said. Dedov looked as surprised to see him as Max was to see Dedov.

"What are you doing here, Asimov?"

"He's dead, Victor. Someone blew his head in with a shotgun."

The surprise on Dedov's face looked genuine. Then Dedov slumped, an uncharacteristic reaction from the stoic leader. He put one foot on the stoop and shoved his hands into his pockets. "They finally got him, I guess."

"Who is they?" Max asked.

Dedov let out a deep breath. "Might as well tell you. Anatoly was working for us as an undercover operative, funneling information to Abrams' team. He was a double agent, in deep. Your father had been running the operation. We knew we had a leak, and Anatoly was trying to build enough trust with Abrams to learn who the leak was."

"So why would Anatoly have me set up at the butcher shop?"

"He had no choice," Dedov replied. "He figured he was being watched, and knew if Abrams found out about your midnight visits, he'd be compromised. He did what he had to do to preserve his cover."

"Why were you running an operation against Nathan Abrams?" Max asked, feeling like he was on the cusp of finally understanding.

Dedov looked at him. "I'm sorry, Mikhail. But that's classified. I wish I could tell you, but it's way above your grade."

Max was too tired to get angry. Instead, he contemplated the gravity of what Dedov had just told him. If it was true, it meant Anatoly had been one of the good guys after all. Somehow that made Max feel a little better.

FIFTY-NINE

His choice was a small, agile Honda motorcycle that looked just like any of the thousands already on Prague's roadways. Max wore his standard leather motorcycle jacket, leather motorcycle pants, and a black helmet with a smoke-colored visor. He kept the bike at a moderate speed, and followed three car lengths behind the black BMW, keeping a city bus between himself and the sedan. Traffic was heavy, and Max was confident she hadn't picked up the tail.

He'd found her at a restaurant she seemed to frequent in the art district of Old Town. From a distance, Max had watched her lunch with two men and another woman, and briefly wondered if she was on a date. He found himself hoping she was. The day was warm, and Julia wore a bright red and yellow sundress, a floppy hat, and large round sunglasses. She looked like a movie star traveling incognito. When she finally had her car brought around, Max had scrambled to his bike and managed not to lose her as she pulled into the street.

Now, he made a right turn, then another, following at a safe distance. Then the BMW turned into an alleyway and disappeared. Max gunned the throttle to catch up, then turned into the alleyway. Just then, he saw a flash of tail-lights and heard the crunch of metal on metal. He flew over the handlebars, hitting the back trunk and window of the sedan, causing the safety glass to crack. He fell to the ground with a jarring thump, heaving and struggling for breath.

A second later, Julia was standing over him holding a pistol aimed at his chest. He flipped up the visor of his helmet, and she groaned.

"Dammit, Max. I swear to God I'm going to end up killing you one of these days."

———

They found a shaded cafe with a sparsely populated patio. Julia ordered white wine, and Max ordered a beer. After the pregnant waitress had delivered the drinks, Max said, "I'll pay for the damage to your car."

Julia snorted. "I don't care. I'm thinking about switching to an SUV anyway. I need room to carry my art. I've started painting, you know. Something I've always wanted to do. Next time you visit, you should just ring the doorbell like an ordinary human. I can show you my studio."

They both laughed and sipped their drinks. Max felt oddly comfortable with this older woman about whom he knew so little. She was one of the last connections to his father, and he found that he enjoyed the silent pauses in their conversations. She'd been a huge help in their operation against Nathan Abrams, and that experience had brought them a little closer.

"He's dead, Julia," Max said finally.

"I figured," she said. "Although I have to admit I would have appreciated better communication. I've been wondering."

"I'm sorry," Max said. "It got tough there for a while." He held up his bandaged left hand.

She nodded. "I'm used to it, Max. In this business, you get used to waiting for loved ones."

That comment lingered in the air for a moment, and Max wondered if she meant anything by it. It was an intimate comment to make to someone you'd just met three weeks prior. They sipped their drinks through more silence, then Max gave her the details. By the time he reached the part about Nathan's proclamation about his father, their first round had disappeared and a second round was on the table. When he finished the tale, Julia looked off into the distance, a habit Max was still getting used to. He'd already learned to give her some room, hoping she'd eventually reveal her thoughts.

Finally, she said, "I find it hard to believe your father was involved in organized crime, Max. Of course, he and I had grown apart in the last few years, so anything is possible. But it's just not in your father's blood. If anything, it was the opposite. I'd think the Russian Mafia would be a key suspect for Nathan's client."

Max nodded his head. The same thing had occurred to him. He looked closely at Julia. The news of Nathan's death didn't seem to have affected her. Her eyes still looked sad, the crow's feet around them more pronounced. She glanced up and saw Max looking at her. She smiled. "You're wondering why I haven't told you details about my relationship with your father."

Max smiled back. "You can read minds, too?"

"Some of the wounds run deep, Max. It was the best part of my life, but also the worst, if that makes sense."

Max nodded.

"You're just like him when he was your age, you know that? You look and act the same. You have the same steely confidence and purpose. Even your voice and your eyes are exactly like his were when I fell in love with him. It's unsettling, frankly."

Max nodded again, saying nothing. He was trying to be patient.

"He was a natural teacher, you know that?" she said finally.

"I was the recipient of a lot of those teachings."

Now it was her turn to nod. "So was I. He taught me everything I know." She sipped her wine. "So, what now?"

"Alex and Arina go into hiding, while I keep looking," Max said. "I won't rest—"

"Your father wouldn't have, either," Julia interrupted.

"Maybe someday you'll tell me about him?" Max asked.

She nodded. "I just need some time, Max. Go get your family settled, then come back and we'll have a real talk."

They both stood and hugged. When Julia pulled away, Max saw tears in her eyes, and something else. Something that looked like pride. It was then that he knew for sure – the thing that had been lurking in the back of his mind from the time he'd seen the photograph in the basement of the butcher shop. The thing that his mother had called him home to tell him.

He kissed her cheek and left her sitting in the cafe, her face turned up to the sun.

Maybe in time, he thought, they'd be able to come to terms with their past and grow closer. Eventually old wounds would heal, and he'd be able to forge a relationship with this mother he'd never known. In time, he thought. In time.

SIXTY

Ramstein AFB, Germany

"Where the fuck have you been?"

"Good to see you too, Kate," Max said. He dropped his leather jacket on the couch, walked to the kitchenette, and poured himself a cup of coffee. He sat on a low couch that formed an L with the couch occupied by Kate. The room was small, beige, and institutional.

Despite the ridiculous cabin noise in the C-130 transport into Ramstein, Max had managed to sleep most of the way. He still felt drained, his muscles ached, his hand throbbed. He was sure he could sleep for a week.

Kate wore her standard uniform of a pantsuit with a white blouse. The same clunky watch hung from her left wrist. Her curly hair was pulled back and held with a barrette. The cut on her neck was healing nicely. She peered at him through tortoise-shell glasses. She looked fresh as a daisy, even though Max knew she'd taken a civilian red-eye from Kennedy to meet him.

"How's your hand? When we're done here, we'll have one of the base doctors take a look at it."

"It's fine," Max said. The bandages were dirty and scuffed from his travels, but his wounds were healing well.

"Seriously. Where have you been?"

Max filled her in on the visit to his family estate, then to Anatoly's. He left out the trip to Prague.

"That's not much for disappearing for five days," Kate said.

"I had some personal business to attend to," Max said. He stared at her, daring her to ask more.

Kate regarded him for a moment. Max figured she was trying to decide how much to push him. Finally, she seemed to let it go.

"You didn't have to kill him," she said, changing the topic.

"Yes, I did," Max said. "He was right. He was already dead. Might as well have been me."

"He could have divulged tons of useful information," she said. "By the time we raided his headquarters, everything was gone. The entire place had been scrubbed. Not a computer, hard drive, or file was left."

"Fuck," Max said. "How'd that happen?"

Kate looked uncomfortable for the first time. "We're not sure. The only explanation I can find is the mole – the same one who gave up our locations in Minsk. But now that he's dead, we may never know. If you're going to work for us, you're going to have to learn to put the greater good ahead of your own agenda."

Max looked at her.

"Don't worry, Max. Only me, the director of the CIA, and the president know where Alex and Arina are. We're using the Secret Service for security until we figure out the mole, on POTUS's directive."

Max contemplated that while he removed a pack of cigarettes from his pocket. "I wasn't on your clock," he said, "I was on mine. When I'm on your clock, we'll run things your way."

"Can't smoke in here," Kate said as she got up from the couch and moved toward the coffee maker. "Do you at least feel better now?"

Max thought about the question as he lit the cigarette. He inhaled deeply, then blew a cloud of smoke toward the ceiling. "It's not about feeling better," he said. "It's about justice. It's about truth. It's about survival. And it's about finding them before they find us."

Kate glared at him as she wrenched open a window. "What do you make of Anatoly's death?"

Max took another drag. "Not sure, other than at least I know the KGB didn't kill my parents. If you put what Abrams said alongside what Dedov told me, this thing is much bigger than the KGB."

Kate looked skeptical. "I'd think if there were a syndicate of men that powerful, they'd be on our radar screen, Max."

Max shrugged. "Maybe. I'm just telling you what I've been told. What if they're not on your radar screen? You guys don't know everything, or you'd have headed off 9-11."

"That's a low blow—" her voice trailed off.

Max put out the cigarette in the dregs of his coffee, rose from the couch, and got himself a new cup of the thin brown liquid. He reminded himself to pick a new home in the States where they had great coffee. He'd heard both Seattle and San Francisco had some of the best coffee in the world.

"How's Ethan?" Max asked as he plopped back down.

"Reunited with his mother. Turns out she runs a bank in Vienna. The Austrian government agreed to grant him asylum after she produced his birth certificate."

"That's great," Max said.

"That was a reckless thing you did, Max. If Spencer hadn't had the foresight to return, you may not be alive right now."

"But it worked out for Ethan," Max said. "He can now go his entire life not knowing about his father's background."

"Is that a good thing?" Kate asked.

"I don't know," Max said. "You can only make the best decision you can make at the time, knowing what you know. Maybe his mother will tell him one day. Maybe not. That's up to her now."

They sat in silence for a few moments and sipped their coffees.

"We sent a team to your place in Paris," Kate said finally. "We cleaned out all your stuff. It's in a shipping container here at Ramstein."

"Was there still surveillance?" Max asked.

"No, Max. That was us. Although I'm disappointed that you made us."

Max nodded his head. "And the club?"

Kate shrugged. "What do you want to do with it?"

Max thought for a moment. He was going to miss that place. But perhaps he'd be able to start a similar venue somewhere in the States. Or maybe he'd start a rock-and-roll club like he'd seen in Austin, Texas, many years ago, during his one and only trip to America. "Let's sell it to Della for a euro."

Kate nodded as if she approved. "We'll take care of it."

He sipped his coffee. "So, now what?"

"Tomorrow we head to the States." She tossed a bundle of documents at him. Max caught them in his injured hand. "Your new documents," she said. "Of course, when you're on an operation with us, you'll be on false papers." She seemed to find some humor in that.

"The life we choose," Max said. He set his coffee down and removed a blue passport with a gold embossed seal from the packet. The cover had been nicked and scarred and dirtied, like it belonged to a seasoned traveler. He flipped it open, and saw dozens of stamps from around the world, then flipped to the front and saw his picture. The name read *Max Sienkiewicz.*

He looked up at Kate. "Sienkiewicz? I don't think so."

She laughed, and said, "You got any better ideas?"

Max thought for a moment. "How about Austin? Max Austin. That has a nice ring to it."

Kate rolled her eyes at him as he tossed back the packet of papers.

———

The caravan of black Suburbans rolled past a large white-fenced paddock, and Max could see three horses galloping in a wide circle. On one of them, he saw a small towheaded boy, bouncing in rhythm with the horse like a seasoned pro. Standing alongside the white fence, he could see the broad-shouldered figure of his sister. Upon hearing the vehicles on the gravel drive, she turned and watched the procession.

The driveway led to a large circular drive in front of a sprawling ranch-style house with a broad front porch. On the porch, Max saw two paramilitary types, both wielding semi-automatic rifles and wearing body armor. "Most of the security around here is hidden," Kate said from the seat beside him. "It's all state of the art. We own all the land around the ranch for ten miles in each direction. We know if anything moves. A fucking field mouse sticks its head up from the ground and we know. This is foreign dignitary and elite civilian-level security, Max. Just short of what the President of the United States gets when he stays here."

The enormity of what Kate was doing for him suddenly hit him. He turned to thank her, but she had already slid out of the vehicle. Max jumped down and was immediately set upon by a ten-year-old boy.

"Uncle Max! Uncle Max!" Alex yelled, and Max caught him with his good hand. He hugged the boy hard and, despite the foreign surroundings, finally felt like he was home. Arina joined them and they hugged until Alex pulled them apart. The boy grabbed Max's hand and pulled him toward the house. "Come on, Uncle Max. You have to see this place. It's fancy!"

Inside the house, Alex and Arina showed him around the sprawling mansion, then led him upstairs and showed him his bedroom. Arina pulled Alex away so Max could get cleaned up. He found a closet full of clothes and a bathroom full of men's toiletries. He removed the bandage applied by the efficient doctor at Ramstein, then stood under scalding water as long as he could stand to. He shaved and dressed in a pair of work pants and a new black T-shirt that had the tags still on. As he hung up his leather jacket, he felt the picture frame he'd kept in the inner pocket. He pulled it out, then used the wet corner of a towel to remove the rest of the dirt and grime. Finally satisfied, he set the photo on the bedside table, next to a fresh flower Arina had left for him. Maybe it was fatigue from the past few weeks, or maybe it was his injured hand. Perhaps it was simply kismet or Asimov family luck. Whatever the reason, Max inadvertently bumped the picture and sent it tumbling to the wood floor. The glass front shattered and the picture separated from the frame's back.

Cursing, Max bent down to pick up the pieces of the broken frame. Then, he paused. The thick cardboard of the picture frame's backing lay upright among the shards of glass. He saw something taped to the backing. He picked it up and looked closer. An indentation had been carved into the thick cardboard, so a tiny item could be inset into the cardboard without showing through the backing. Set into the indentation was a micro memory card, the kind that might fit into a smartphone. A piece of tape secured the memory card to the cardboard. Max removed the tape and pried the memory card out with his fingernail.

Whatever Max was holding, he realized, was what the people searching his father's office must have been looking for. He slid the card into the available slot in his Blackphone. A second later, the screen was filled with gibberish, and Max realized the contents of the card were encrypted. Perhaps Goshawk could get past the encryption.

He removed the card from his phone, then hid the tiny chip in the pocket of his leather jacket. He cleaned up the glass shards and leaned the photo of his family up against the nightstand lamp. He'd ask Kate to have someone get a new piece of glass for the frame.

When that was done, he went downstairs, found some bourbon in the cupboard, and joined the group talking in the living room. He sat down next to Arina and across from Kate, sinking into the deep leather couch. He sipped the pungent liquid and grimaced, then willed himself to choke it down. If he was going to be an American, he was going to have to learn to drink like one.

———

Max sat at the kitchen table working on his third bourbon and listening to Kate talk on the phone. Arina walked into the kitchen, holding Alex's hand. She had been silent much of the time since Max had arrived, exhibiting symptoms of classic post-traumatic stress. Her face was healing, but her black eye was still dark and puffy. Max knew it would take much longer for the non-physical wounds to heal. He smiled at her, but she didn't smile back. Instead, she coaxed Alex toward him.

"Alex has something he wants to give you," Arina said.

Alex approached Max with something in an outstretched hand. Looking down, Max saw a purple rabbit's foot with a tiny chain, the kind one might use as a key chain.

"This is for good luck," Alex said. "So you won't get hurt and can find the bad guys." The boy smiled up at him.

Max took the rabbit's foot, gathered the boy in his arms, and hugged him for a long time.

EPILOGUE

Undisclosed Location

The velour hood was yanked off her head and Wing Octavia stood blinking her eyes against the dim light. Before she regained focus, she picked up the scent of must and moss and earth. Her skin felt clammy with moisture. Somewhere in the distance, she heard water dripping. As her eyesight returned, she made out hundreds of pinpoints of light flickering in a faint draft. She shivered in her silk blouse and light suit jacket.

Her eyes cleared and she saw the source of the light. Hundreds of lit tapers were set in candle holders along the edge of the room. They were the room's only illumination. Her eyes began to pick out shapes along the walls, hidden in the shadows created by the candles. In front of her and above, the cave extended into darkness.

A gritty rolling noise echoed in the chamber, somewhere behind her. She heard a faint whirring, like a small drill. The crunching and whirring noises grew louder. She turned.

"Do not move," a voice commanded. She resumed her position and tried to make out the rest of the room. As she realized what she was seeing, she sucked in her breath. Lining the walls, extending into the darkness, from the floor to far overhead, were thousands of wine bottles. In front of her was a scarred wooden table that held a dozen wine glasses of all shapes and sizes. A silver spittoon was at one corner of the table and a pitcher of water sat at another.

The whirring noise stopped somewhere behind her. "An impressive display, don't you think, Ms. Octavia?"

The voice was high-pitched, but strong, and echoed off the chamber walls.

"Yes," she said. "Like nothing I've seen before."

The whirring and crunching started again and an old man in a wheelchair materialized next to her. He turned to face her, keeping a few feet of distance between them. "Welcome to the Old World, Ms. Octavia. Over one-and-a-half million bottles of wine. The second-largest collection in the world."

Wing regarded the old man. His cheeks were sunken and his arms and legs were folded around him like a skeleton. Her first thought was that he hadn't had a full meal in months. Age spots covered the top of his head and strings of white hair fell to his collar. Red, wet lips stretched around yellow teeth when he talked. It was as if he were some grotesque puppet operated by someone in the base of the chair. Despite the man's physical appearance, fire blazed behind obsidian pupils. She realized he was a young soul encased in an old and decrepit body.

"The largest known collection is over two million bottles," he said. "A winery in Moldova with the somewhat romantic name of Milestii Mici. Of course, our collection is private. We have no use for world records, although we are on pace to surpass Milestii Mici in about six months' time."

"It's impressive," Wing said. "Why am I here?"

"Ah, just like Mr. Abrams. Straight to the point. A regular chip off the old block." He emitted a sharp cackle at some joke known only to him.

At the mention of Nathan's name, a rush of emotion welled in her. Tears wet her eyes and she fought to keep herself in check. Later, she'd have time to grieve. But now, this old man had snatched her from the streets of Budapest, blindfolded her, and flown her several hours in a private jet. She needed to keep her wits about her.

"Come. Join me," he said. He waved a thin arm at the table. "Let me offer you a taste of luxury. Have you ever tried a bottle of wine worth 14,000 euros?" From somewhere in the shadows, a young man appeared in a tight-fitting black suit with a fashionably thin tie. He produced a bottle and deftly pried out the cork, then emptied the contents into a decanter.

"We decant the wine in order to infuse it with oxygen," the old man said. "The oxygen opens up the flavors." The man with the black suit put a large, round wine glass containing a tiny amount of burgundy liquid in the old man's hand. He swirled it, then sipped.

Wing stepped forward to the table. Behind her, she heard a footstep on the dirt floor. She assumed one false move would result in her immediate incapacitation.

"Richebourg Grand Cru," he said, the appreciation evident on his face. "1985." The man with the thin tie handed Wing a glass with a small portion of blood-red liquid. She hesitated.

"Go on, my dear. If I wanted you dead, I certainly

wouldn't poison a perfectly good bottle of wine to do it." He laughed again, his thin body shaking in his suit. She sipped, letting the liquid settle over her tongue and into the back of her mouth. She couldn't help but smile. It was the smoothest, most velvety liquid she'd ever tasted.

"Ah, I see you enjoy it. I'm glad," the man in the wheelchair said. The server filled their glasses and receded into the shadows. "Now that we've shared some of the best plonk on the planet, let us get down to business."

"By all means," Wing said, taking another sip.

"You and I share a common enemy, Ms. Octavia. Do we not?"

"You tell me, Mr.—" she said, then paused. "We seem to be at a disadvantage. You know my name. I do not know yours."

The old man's wet lips stretched over his large yellow teeth in a wide smile. "And it shall remain that way, Ms. Octavia. Believe me, it's safer for you. See, Mr. Abrams and I had a contract. A contract which he was unable to fulfill. Our mutual enemy, one Mikhail Asimov, did me a favor. You see, Abrams' penalty for failure to fulfill his end of the bargain was death. Asimov simply did for me what I would have had to do myself."

It was all Wing could do to keep her composure. Nathan Abrams had been like a father to her. In the weeks since his death, she'd fought to keep it together in front of the staff, overseeing their exfiltration out of Prague to their new compound in Budapest. She'd worked hard to retain clients that threatened to leave. She'd fought tooth and nail to keep the team together and to elude the pursuit of the CIA. She'd worked too hard to give herself time to grieve. And now here was this man, this grotesque old man, speaking so cavalierly about

Nathan. She forced herself to replace her grief with simmering anger.

"I see I hit a nerve," the old man said. "Forgive me, I forget my manners. I know Mr. Abrams was, for all intents and purposes, your foster father. See, I know everything about your background, Ms. Octavia."

A chill went up her spine. Her glass stayed in her hand.

"I know that you've taken over Mr. Abrams' company," he continued. "I know the staff there trust you and will follow you. I know that you have skills that Nathan did not, and I predict, given the right clients and support, that you will grow that company into a true force to be reckoned with. See, I know a great many things." He paused to sip his wine, letting the liquid roll around in his mouth before swallowing. Wing could see the overly large Adams apple bouncing as he swallowed.

"I also know something that you would like to know." He paused for effect. "I know where your true father is."

Wing's knees almost buckled. By some miracle, she hung on. Orphaned at birth, Wing had never known her parents and figured by now they must be dead. She'd buried that part of her life. Now it threatened to come up again, something she wasn't prepared to deal with.

"Our deal is simple, Ms. Octavia," he continued. "Kill Mikhail Asimov. Kill his sister and nephew. In exchange, I will pay you an enormous sum of money and tell you where your father is. Believe me, he could use your help. Fail me and I will draw you a map to the spot where his dead body is buried."

The old man fingered the chair's controls and started away, then paused as he rolled up next to her. He reached out with a cold, clammy hand and gripped her wrist with a strength she didn't think possible. "My associate here, Mr.

Mueller, has a contract you'll need to sign. Do not fail me, my dear. Your father's future depends on it."

Then he fingered the controls again and disappeared behind her. She could hear the faint crunching and whirring of the wheelchair as it moved away. Suddenly, Wing's knees did give way, and the wine glass fell to the ground and shattered. As she fell toward the dank floor of the cave, she felt herself being caught and carried off into the darkness.

THE END

IF YOU LIKED THIS BOOK ...

... I would appreciate it if you would leave a review. An honest review means a lot. The constructive reviews help me write better stories, and the positive reviews help others find the books, which ultimately means I can write more stories.

It only takes a few minutes, but it means everything. Thank you in advance.

-Jack

AUTHOR'S NOTE

This is a work of fiction. Any resemblance to persons living or dead, or actual events, is either coincidental or is being used for fictive and storytelling purposes. No elements of this story are inspired by true events; all aspects of the story are imaginative events inspired by conjecture.

This story was inspired by a novel I wrote last year that remains unpublished. After my editor went through that story, she and I decided that I'd begun the story of Max Austin too late in the trajectory of his character's arc. So, this novel starts when Max's story really begins, and shows his struggles as he attempts to uncover bits of his father's past in order to save his own life and the lives of his sister and nephew.

One of the more complicated aspects of this story is the history of the KGB. As most know, the KGB (which stands for *Komitet gosudarstvennoy bezopasnosti*, translated into English as *Committee for State Security*) was responsible for both internal and external security of the Soviet Union from its inception in 1954 to its dissolution in 1991. The KGB earned its reputation through extensive espionage activities on both its own citizens and foreigners. Split into multiple departments, or Directorates, the KGB performed foreign espionage, counterintelligence, internal political control, military intelligence, security, censorship, economic espionage, surveillance, cryptology, communications intelligence, and many other activities. Its history is of one of extensive brutality against its own citizens and pervasive repression of basic civil rights. The KGB also operated many Republican affiliations in other Soviet Bloc countries, including Belarus, where much of this story takes place.

When the Soviet Union collapsed in 1991, the KGB was dissolved, and the functions of the agency were thrust into a tumultuous period where multiple agencies were created, then disbanded. Ultimately, the Federal Security Service of the Russian Federation (aka FSB) emerged and persevered as the main replacement agency for the KGB. The FSB has purportedly picked up where the KGB left off, performing many of the same brutal repressive activities against Russia's citizens. To make things more complicated, some of the Republican affiliations of the former KGB have kept the old name. Belarus is one of the countries that still operates a KGB.

For the purposes of this fictional tale, I've tried to simplify the history of these two agencies. The key players are the KGB in Moscow pre-1991, the FSB in Moscow post-1991, and the KGB in Belarus.

I hope you enjoy the story. Drop me a line if you have feedback or just want to say hi.

Jack Arbor
June 2016
Aspen, Colorado

ACKNOWLEDGMENTS

Writing a novel takes a village, and this one is no different. First off, I'd like to thank my number-one fan, who just happens to be my wife, Jill Canning. Without her support, I'd still be talking about writing a novel instead of actually having written and published one. Second, I'd like to thank my amazing editor, Jen Blood, whose acute wit is only surpassed by the deftness of her red pen.

No independently published author is successful without their Beta Reading Team. I'd like to thank all of them, in particular Eric Rutz, Kristin Werner, my mother Gay Birchard, Holly Smyth, Susan Chastain, and Connie Cronenwett. It's quite a thing to commit to reading a novel, and I'm grateful for their willingness to plod through a story full of typos, missing commas, inaccuracies, and improperly hyphenated words before taking the time to email me feedback.

No section of acknowledgements would be complete without thanking my father, John Lilley. From day one, he admonished me to follow my heart. Forty-some years later, I finally did.

Last, but definitely not least, I'd like to thank the independent publishing community for blazing a trail and being so giving to the group of hardworking writers who follow behind. Specifically, I'd like to thank Joanna Penn, whose amazingly consistent podcasts kept me company on long commutes up and down I-70, JA Konrath and Russell Blake for their truths, Mark Dawson for showing us how it's done, and Bob Dugoni for his selfless acts of giving. If karma is any measure, these folks deserve all their success.

Before I sign off, I'd like to thank the public library in Basalt, Colorado, and its wonderful staff for putting up with me every weekend. They never saw the food I had hidden under my hat.

If you like free books and want to join my Advance Reading Team, please email me at jack@jackarbor.com. I'm always looking for more readers to join the team.

JOIN MY MAILING LIST

If you'd like to get updates on new releases as well as notifications of deals and discounts, please join my email list.

I only email when I have something meaningful to say and I never send spam. You can unsubscribe at any time.

Subscribe at www.jackarbor.com

ABOUT THE AUTHOR

A digital technologist by day, Jack writes fast-paced adventure thrillers at night with much love and support from his amazing wife Jill. Jack and Jill live outside Aspen, Colorado, where they enjoy trail running through the natural beauty of the Rocky Mountains. Jack also likes to drink bourbon and listen to jazz, usually at the same time. They both miss the pizza on the East Coast.

You can get free books as well as pre-release specials and sign up for Jack's mailing list at www.jackarbor.com.

Connect with Jack online:
(e) jack@jackarbor.com
(t) twitter.com/jackarbor
(i) instagram.com/jackarbor/
(f) facebook.com/jackarborauthor
(w) www.jackarbor.com

ALSO BY JACK ARBOR

The Pursuit, The Russian Assassin Series, Book Two

Former KGB assassin Max Austin is on the run, fighting to keep his family alive while pursuing his parents' killers. As he battles foes both visible and hidden, he uncovers a conspiracy with roots in the darkest cellars of Soviet history. Determined to survive, Max hatches a plan to even the odds by partnering with his mortal enemy. Even as his adversary becomes his confidant, Max is left wondering who he can trust, if anyone...

If you like dynamic, high-voltage, page-turning thrills, you'll love the second installment of The Russian Assassin series starring Jack Arbor's desperate hero, ex-KGB assassin-for-hire, Max Austin.

Cat & Mouse, A Max Austin Novella

Max, a former KGB assassin, is living a comfortable life in Paris. When not plying his trade, he passes his time managing a jazz club in the City of Light. To make ends meet, he freelances by offering his services to help rid the earth of the world's worst criminals.

Max is enjoying his ritual post-job vodka when he meets a stunning woman; a haunting visage of his former fiancé. Suddenly, he finds himself the target of an assassination plot in his beloved city of Paris. Fighting for his life, Max must overcome his own demons to stay alive.

CHAPTER ONE FROM THE PURSUIT

BOOK TWO OF THE RUSSIAN ASSASSIN SERIES

Dubrovnik, Croatia

The Russian colonel's head wavered in the rifle scope as Max adjusted his sitting position. He switched from the scope to a wider-angle view through a Bushnell spotting lens. The target was sitting in a frothing hot tub, a melon-chested girl on each arm, sipping from a champagne flute. His mostly bald pate glistened with sweat, and reflections of multi-colored lights from the yacht's disco ball glinted from his head. Two bodyguards stood at attention several paces behind, their eyes roving restlessly over the undulating party.

Hoots and shouts and clips of music from the boat came through the open window. Three hot tubs were full of obese old men surrounded by hired girls. Partygoers carried bottles of Cristal in their fists. It was approaching midnight, and the festivities were in full swing.

Despite the cool breeze coming through the window, a bead of sweat dripped down Max's forehead. While he waited, he absently fingered the rabbit's foot he kept in his pocket, a token of safety given to him by his ten-year-old nephew.

Using a sniper rifle required that the assassin know exactly where the target would be ahead of time. That knowledge was usually hard to come by. Today, though, he knew. Max's handler at the CIA had a source in the colonel's organization – a Ukrainian sympathizer who had supplied minute details about the target's schedule. Despite the intel, this was a rush job, and Max hated rush jobs. He prided himself on a spotless record and preferred to spend months researching a target's habits. Killing a man was an intimate act, one not to be hurried. Still, Max's new boss at the CIA wanted to take advantage of the opportunity, so here he was, perched in a decaying tenement, about to end the life of a man whose sin was profiting from supplying weapons to the pro-Russian rebels in Eastern Ukraine.

His target was about the length of two football pitches away. At this distance, using the Leupold scope and a M2010 ESR rifle, Max's assignment was relatively easy, even with the long silencer attached to the barrel. The rifle was chambered for a .300 Winchester Magnum, a bullet proven to produce more long-range effectiveness with less weight than other .30 cartridges. It was probably overkill for this job, but that was how Max operated – he always stacked the deck in his favor. As he waited, he admired the workmanship of the matte-black, American-made rifle. Most of the gear he'd used in the KGB had been decades old and poorly maintained. Restlessly, his hand checked the SIG P226 at his side and the fighting knife strapped to his leg.

Max felt no remorse or conflict about killing a former colleague. He knew the FSB had played a role in his parents' death and he'd recently sold his soul to the CIA in exchange for the protection of his family. He owed the FSB nothing.

He moved his eye back to the spotting lens and watched the colonel tip his head back to laugh at something one of the girls had said. An oversized gold diver's watch glittered on the man's wrist. In contrast to the colonel's obese underlings, Konstantin Koskov was built like a rugby player – short and stocky, chest and arms rippling with muscle. He spent as much time working out as he did chasing girls and counting his money.

Max checked his own watch. Two minutes. He moved into firing position. The rifle's bipod legs rested on a wooden kitchen table pushed up to the window. Next to the rifle, a Nikon digital camera fitted with a long-range lens sat on a pocket-sized tripod. A cord ran from the camera's shutter to a foot pedal on the floor. A wireless data card in the camera would automatically transfer the photos to his smartphone. In his pocket was the remote control to a small block of C-4 he'd attached to the underside of the kitchen table. When the job was done, he'd activate the bomb and destroy the evidence. He reacquired the target in the scope. The man's head came through the view finder in magnified clarity.

Max reached into his pocket and fingered the lucky rabbit's foot again. He believed in making his own luck, but the little token reminded him why he was doing this job. He checked his watch again. One minute. He moved the chair back from the table, taking care not to make any noise, and took a wide stance. The flag on the pole visible through the window lay limp, but the spring air held significant moisture. Max went over his firing solution one last time, made a tiny adjustment, then re-acquired the target. The colonel was pawing at the girl next to him, who was trying to wiggle away.

As the second hand on Max's watch jolted to the 12 mark, a loud explosion sounded a block away. The table rattled slightly. Glass bottles chattered above the stove. Max watched through the scope as Koskov looked up, startled by the diversion Max had planted hours before.

Max ensured the scope's crosshairs were a shade above the colonel's temple, breathed out, and let his heartbeat slow. Using the pad of his index finger, he pulled straight back on the trigger, simultaneously pressing down on the camera pedal with his foot. The muted *thump* from the bullet passing through the silencer and the whir of the camera's servo motor were drowned out by the pounding music on the yacht. The target's head disappeared from the view through the scope.

Max switched to the spotting lens and watched Koskov's body slip into the roiling hot tub, the top portion of his head ragged and bloody. The two girls appeared frozen, their minds not yet registering what their eyes had just seen. The chest and neck of one of the girls was covered in a dark, silky liquid. Then, in unison, the girls started screaming. The bodyguards reacted more quickly, drawing weapons as they scanned the area. Their training made them act, but Max could see the incredulity in their eyes even from this distance. Max pulled the rifle back from the window and left it on the table.

Suddenly, he heard a creak in the floorboards behind him. To most, the sound would be imperceptible. To Max's tightly honed senses, it was like a rifle shot in a still forest. Instinct took over and he ducked and rolled away from the table, coming up on both feet, the SIG in his hand.

Made in United States
North Haven, CT
05 July 2022

20947901R00221